the
truth
about my
Success

the
truth
about my
Success

Dyan Sheldon

CANDLEWICK PRESS

First U.S. edition 2015

Library of Congress Catalog Card Number 2014945721
ISBN 978-0-7636-7272-0

15 16 17 18 19 20 BVG 10 9 8 7 6 5 4 3 2 1

Printed in Berryville, VA, U.S.A.

This book was typeset in Berkeley Oldstyle.

Candlewick Press
99 Dover Street
Somerville, Massachusetts 02144

visit us at www.candlewick.com

For the two Carolines, R and S

Another day, another drama

It's a beautiful spring morning in Southern California.

High in the hills of Hollywood, with a heart-stopping view of the tireless sprawl of Los Angeles, sits a large, elegant white building with pillars and turrets and leaded-glass windows that would make most monarchs feel right at home. This house (for reasons that will never be obvious) is called Paradise Lodge. But although the day outside is bright and cloudless, inside a storm is raging.

There are two people at the center of this storm: the girl sitting at the table, screaming, who was born Susan Rosemary Minnick but is now known as Paloma Rose; and the woman standing beside her, stoically, whose name is Josefina Primavera Trudenco but who around here is called Maria. Neither of them thinks she is anywhere near Paradise.

"I can't eat this slop!" Paloma's voice is shrill as a siren, her pretty face distorted by rage. "It's, like, disgusting! It's total garbage! I don't know why I can't ever have anything *I* want. Is that so freakin' much to ask? Just *once* to have what *I* want?"

You might wonder how someone can be so emotional over a disappointing breakfast. The reason is that Paloma is a princess. Not the kind descended from European royalty, but the kind who stars in what until recently was one of the most popular television shows of all time. Today Paloma is a princess in a very bad mood. Which lately is about as rare an event as freezing temperatures in Siberia. Paloma's bad moods are caused by the fact that she is very unhappy. It may seem strange that a girl who has so much — celebrity, money, looks, adoring fans — can be unhappy, but having everything is no more a guarantee of happiness than beauty is a guarantee of love.

Paloma pushes her plate away with so much force that a slice of toast shoots onto the table. "I mean, like, look at it! Just look at it! It's so gross I could barf. It's like two revolting yellow eyes staring up at me."

Because Paloma is usually pleasant and polite only when someone's pointing a camera or a microphone at her, the housekeeper knows better than to remind ·Paloma that she asked for fried eggs. Maria has worked for the Minnicks for four very long years (a record for the Minnicks, who usually go through help the way other people go through socks) and is still here because she says so little that the Minnicks are under the impression that she doesn't speak much English. Now Maria puts the toast back on the plate and says, "Scrambled? Boiled? Omelet?"

"Boiled. And only one." The person who says these words is not Paloma, but her mother. Leone Minnick snaps into the room on her Louboutins like a soldier on parade. Always impeccably and immaculately put together, Leone can walk through a rainstorm without getting wet. This morning she is wearing a seriously understated dark suit set off by several pieces of gold jewelry, and looks as if she might be on her way to address a meeting of investment bankers. Nevertheless, from her pinched expression, it seems likely that Leone doesn't think she's anywhere near Paradise, either.

Things haven't been going well this year. Ratings for Paloma's TV show, *Angel in the House,* are dropping steadily; the network is threatening to cancel after the upcoming season; and the sponsors are very unhappy — which in this world is not unlike God being very unhappy in the world of the Old Testament. Leone blames Paloma for all these problems. Paloma is pissing everyone off even more than usual. Arguing. Complaining. Acting out. She brought the set to more than one standstill during the last season. That could be forgiven, but what can't be forgiven is the bad publicity and notoriety Paloma attracted over the winter. Drunken incidents. Suggestive photographs. Compulsively bad behavior. Most of this her agent and her publicist have dismissed as gossip and rumor, but the hostile interviews and on-air temper tantrums couldn't be made to go away without supernatural help. Since her meltdown on the most popular late-night talk show — when she threw the contents of the water pitcher over the host — Paloma has been banned from such appearances. Which has done nothing, of course, to improve ratings, win over the network, or gladden the hearts of the sponsors.

"You know you shouldn't have fried food, Paloma," says Leone. "Think of your skin." She puts her handbag on the counter with a thump. "And your hips. You're supposed to be thirteen, not thirty." Thirteen being the age of Paloma's character, Faith Cross.

Think of your freakin' skin, mimics Paloma. Paloma blames her mother for her unhappiness. Paloma is sick of looking like she's thirteen. She's almost seventeen, which is practically an adult. She doesn't want to be treated like a child anymore. *Think of your freakin' hips.* And, before

Maria can step away, Paloma reaches up, grabs one of the eggs from the plate, and hurls it across the breakfast nook, hitting the wall. She wipes her hand on the tablecloth.

"Paloma, please . . ." Leone, searching through her bag for something, still doesn't look at her daughter—or at the mess made by the egg. She won't give Paloma the satisfaction. "I'm in no mood for one of your childish displays of histrionics right now. I have errands to run before lunch, and I don't want to be late."

"God forbid you're late for lunch," snarls Paloma. "I mean, the whole freakin' world would just drop dead and roll over with its feet in the air if you were late for lunch. I mean, oh, my freakin' Lord, can you imagine the chaos and destruction if Leone Minnick was ten minutes late for her martini and bowl of lettuce?"

"Language, Paloma." The more heated Paloma gets, the calmer and more reasonable Leone becomes. "You do still have an image to maintain." If barely. "You can't go around talking like a guttersnipe." She sighs. "And it happens to be a business lunch." Besides being Paloma's mother, Leone is also her personal manager. This not only is a handsomely paid job, but also means that Leone considers just about everything she does—from having a manicure to mailing a letter—to be business. "Although, for all I know, you do live on the street now. If I'm not mistaken you didn't come home until dawn. Which is not going to be tolerated, Paloma. I told you that." Leone *has* told her that, but Paloma, apparently, hasn't been listening. If anything, her escapes and escapades have increased since "the problem" was resolved. "You are not allowed out by yourself. Not after what happened last winter. How many times do we have to have this argument?"

What happened last winter was that Paloma was secretly seeing Seth Drachman, the head scriptwriter on *Angel in the House*. Until, Paloma believes, Leone found out, made him break up with her, had him fired, and ruined Paloma's life. Which means that the answer to the how-many-times-do-we-have-to-have-this-argument question is: until penguins are skating up Sunset Boulevard.

"What're you going to do?" taunts Paloma. "Chain me to my bed?"

Chaining Paloma to her bed is just about the only thing Leone hasn't tried yet. She took away Paloma's car keys; Paloma, who's never been seen to so much as microwave a cup of coffee, somehow managed to hot-wire the car. Next, Leone had the car disabled; Paloma started calling cabs and sneaking out of the house. Leone locked her in her room; Paloma climbed out the window. Leone had it nailed shut; Paloma set fire to her wastebasket—and then she broke the window. Leone's next move was to hire a full-time bodyguard to drive Paloma everywhere she went and pad after her like a loyal dog. Paloma then developed a spy's ability to give Vassily, her bodyguard, the slip, leaving him wandering through elegant shops where a man built like a bear has no business being on his own and is eventually asked if he needs any help. Vassily quit.

"If that's what it takes to keep you in this house, then that's what I'll do." At least if Paloma's chained up, she won't be able to burn the house down.

"That'll look great on the front page of the papers won't it?" Paloma squares off her hands as if she's holding up a sign. "'MOTHER CHAINS TEEN STAR IN ROOM.'" If smiles could kill, Leone would already be a lifeless body on the floor. "I can't wait to see the pictures of you being tried for child abuse."

Leone sighs and decides to try reason instead of threats, since her daughter is obviously so much better at them than she is. "All right, Paloma. Let's forget about your tight schedule. And let's forget your millions of fans who look up to you and want to be like you. And let's forget about the fact that Ash drove all the way out here this morning for your training session and you were passed out like a drunk. But let's not forget your career. Aside from the fact that you're going to end up looking ten years older inside of a month if you keep running around like this—drinking and God knows what—filming for the new season starts soon, and you have to be ready for it. Because you know what'll happen if you're not? I'll tell you what, Little Miss—"

"Shut up!" Paloma isn't quite up to standing, so she leans forward, pressing her hands against the edge of the table. "Just shut your stupid mouth!"

But as anyone who has spent more than two minutes with her mother could tell her—and as Paloma very well knows—shutting up never appears on Leone's list of personal options. "Because if you think you're going to continue playing a thirteen-year-old angel when you look like an old hag, you better think again." Leone finally finds her keys and snaps the bag shut. "You know they're talking about canceling the series. And you seem to be determined to give them a reason."

Paloma, of course, doesn't believe her mother. She thinks she's just trying to scare her. Well, good luck with that.

Paloma screams, "What's wrong with you? Are you deaf? Shut the hell up! I don't care! I couldn't care less about losing the series if I was dead. Everybody knows it's crap since you got rid of Se —"

"I did not —"

"Yes you did! You had him fired. Everybody knows that!" shrieks Paloma. "And I'd rather live on the street than in this dump. I'd rather live anywhere but here with you and all your lies and all your freakin' rules."

Leone neatly steps over the part about lies. "There have to be some rules," she says evenly, apparently unaware that she does, in fact, have enough rules to run the government, including all branches of the armed services. Since Paloma's first commercial, when she was still Susan and wearing diapers, Leone has told Paloma what to eat, what to wear, what to say, and what to do and with whom to do it and when. "It's for your own good. Everything I do, I do for you. I've dedicated my life to you."

"Pig crap! Everything you do, you do for *you*!" Paloma, of course, is speaking out of incandescent rage, and doesn't yet really understand how close to the truth she is. But if you own the goose that lays solid-gold eggs, you certainly don't let it wander out in the road.

"That isn't true, darling. Ask anyone. I —"

Paloma clamps her hands over her ears. "Pig diarrhea!" she shouts. "Pig diarrhea just pouring from your mouth!"

Leone glances at her watch and sighs. "Language, Paloma."

Since Maria has taken the uneaten breakfast away and is cleaning the egg from the wall and the floor, Paloma throws the saltshaker this time. It sails past her mother and over the housekeeper's head. Neither Leone nor Maria looks as it crashes to the floor.

"And that's another thing," says Leone. "We can't have any more of this behavior, either."

"Blah, blah, blah, blah," chants Paloma. "And anyway, you're the only person I throw things at."

This isn't quite true, but it's true enough to cause her mother another sigh. "I meant your mouth, sweetheart. People are getting really fed up with you and your rudeness."

"Well, isn't that too freakin' bad? Oh, look, Mommy, look! You're making me cry!"

"I suggest you spend the rest of the day studying your lines. Rehearsals start soon. You want to be ready."

"No, I don't."

Leone hooks her bag over her arm. "We'll finish this conversation when I get back." And she steps around the kneeling figure of the housekeeper and marches down the hall.

Followed by the pepper shaker.

* * *

While the mother and personal manager of the teen star Paloma Rose has her lunch, Jack Silk, the agent of the teen star Paloma Rose, sits in his vintage Jaguar, talking on the phone to Maria Trudenco. Or, more accurately, listening in a there-really-isn't-anything-else-to-do way to the housekeeper's tale of recent events at Paradise Lodge. The staying out all night. The tantrum. The screaming. The egg.

Jack is only half listening, his mind on other things. The static clog of traffic like a blood clot in an artery. How late he'll be for his meeting. What he's wearing to the party he'll be going to tonight. The egg, however, catches his attention. Only Paloma would throw a fried egg. He bets she wiped her hands on the table. "I'm not really sure why you're telling me all this," says Jack.

And whom else would she tell?

"Because I am worried about Miss Paloma," says Maria. "I think that maybe she is going crazy."

Jack chuckles. Soothingly. "She's a prima donna. She always acts like she's going crazy."

Although he can't see her, Maria shakes her head. "No, she is worse. And now she is going out again." There is no doubt in Maria's mind who will be blamed for this. "Mrs. Minnick said she has to stay in the house, but she isn't."

Of course she isn't. Jack closes his eyes. "And where exactly is Mrs. Minnick?"

"She went to lunch."

Of course she did. Flying eggs aren't going to keep Leone Minnick from one of her see-and-be-seen lunches.

"You hear that music?" demands Maria. In the background Jack can hear very unattractive music playing, very loudly. "That music means she is going out, and she only just came home. There are clothes all over her room."

Jack yawns. He's pretty sure that there are always clothes all over Paloma's room. "She has nowhere to go, Maria. She has no friends." Not now that he's put the fear of God—or at least the fear of failure—into Drachman. "What's she going to do, go shopping?"

"She has friends," says Maria. "She meets them on the Internet."

"Yeah, but you don't go out with those friends. You e-mail them. Or tweet them. Or send them a message on Facebook." Thousands of friends, not one of whom you'd recognize if she were sitting next to you on a plane.

Maria repeats that Paloma is getting ready to leave the house. "She has friends," Maria insists. "She has real friends."

"She's just saying that to wind you up," says Jack. "You know what a drama queen she is. She's just pretending she's meeting someone."

Jack Silk should know Paloma better than that, if

anyone should. He's been her agent for most of her life. He's watched her grow from a baby you'd want to bounce on your knee to a brat you'd like to push into the pool. She's a girl who believes in getting her own way as firmly as Louis XIV of France believed in the divine right of kings; nothing Leone can say or do — much less anything Maria can say or do — is going to keep her at Paradise Lodge if she doesn't want to be there.

"No." Maria is shaking her head again, but all Jack sees, of course, is the sun glinting off the polished bumper of his car. "She is meeting someone. I don't know who. And I don't know where. But she is going. And Mrs. Minnick said —"

"Maria." Most of Jack's patience has been exhausted by sitting on the road instead of moving over it. "Maria, I'm very sorry, but I'm on my way to a meeting. An important meeting. And even if I weren't, I've been stuck in traffic for the last twenty minutes. Hear the horns?" He turns the mouthpiece of his headset so she can hear the horns. "I don't know what you expect me to do."

"Maybe if you talk to her . . ."

"Talk to her? Maria, I'm Paloma's agent, not her mother."

"But that is why you should talk to her," says Maria. "She won't listen to her mother. If Mrs. Minnick says go left, Miss Paloma will go right. Miss Paloma listens to you."

"Well, what about Mr. Minnick?" In theory, if nothing else, as well as being Paloma's father and business manager, Arthur Minnick is supposed to be a responsible adult. "Where's he at? Why can't he stop Paloma?"

"He went to dinner," says Maria.

She means last night, of course. Arthur Minnick is pretty much an absentee husband and parent even though he lives with his wife and child.

"Well, what about Vassily? Isn't he supposed to keep tabs on her?" Protect Paloma; protect the rest of humanity from Paloma.

"Mr. Vassilovitch quit after Mrs. Minnick yelled at him for losing Miss Paloma again," Maria informs Jack. "He said he's a soldier, not a babysitter."

And I am? But that isn't what Jack says. What Jack says is, "Look, Maria, I think maybe you're overreacting here." It's the Latin temperament: more emotion than logic, thought Jack. "Paloma's car doesn't work, right? The Minnicks' cars are with the Minnicks. The limo's programmed so it won't let Paloma drive. And she sure as hell isn't going to walk to town. Which means she has to take a cab. So all you have to do is wait by the front door and send the cab away when it comes."

"He's here." Maria's voice is sharp with urgency. "He's here."

14

"Who's here? The cab?"

"No, not the cab. A man."

"A man? What man? Maria, what man?"

"A young man. I don't know. I never see him before. He has a beard."

"A beard?" At least it's not Drachman. But it could be someone else from the show. He thinks there may have been beards in the cast at some time.

"And a ponytail."

Ponytails are the kind of thing that appears among the crew. Ponytails. Earrings. Tattoos. Good God, now she's dating workmen.

"And a ring in his nose like a bull."

"A what?"

But Maria is no longer talking to him.

"Miss Paloma!" yells Maria. "Miss Paloma, you must stay here. Your mother —"

Paloma bellows back, telling Maria what she can do with Leone Minnick in words clear enough to crash through any language barrier.

"But Mr. Silk, he is on the phone. Mr. Silk, he wants to talk to you," calls Maria.

Paloma comes close enough to tell Jack what he can do with his talk.

"So long, suckers," shouts Paloma. "See ya later!"

Too late, perhaps, Jack realizes that, just maybe, he should have taken the housekeeper's concern more seriously. Should have paid more attention. He suspects that there are things he hasn't been told. Possibly a lot of things. He knows how rude and unlikable Paloma Rose can be—it's not a secret, it's a legend—but he's never known her to throw things before. He knows the car is disabled, but he was told Paloma wasn't allowed to drive because of the speeding and the time she smashed through a fence and ended up on somebody's lawn. And, of course, there were the pictures and a couple of other unfortunate incidents and, most unfortunate of all, Seth Drachman. But he thought all that was behind them. Paloma had seen the error of her ways and had straightened out. Isn't that what Leone said? Now he wonders why he believed her. Leone Minnick didn't get where she is today by always telling the truth. Certain words of Maria's echo in his ears. *Losing Miss Paloma again . . . Staying out all night . . . She has friends. . . . real friends . . . crazy . . . worse . . . If Mrs. Minnick says go left, Miss Paloma will go right. . . .*

"For God's sake, do something!" orders Jack. "Stop her!"

"Mr. Silk," says Maria, "I am the housekeeper, not one of your football tacklers."

16

Jack hasn't been having a good couple of years, and it doesn't look as if things are going to get better any time soon. He leans his head on the steering wheel. Why doesn't God just have him run over by some crazed, disgruntled actor while he's crossing the street one day and send him straight to Hell? Why play with him like this?

A new volley of honking sounds behind him. Traffic has finally started to move.

His phone goes dead.

Bad moods here and bad moods there—bad moods happen everywhere

Like many of us, El Paraíso started out life with high hopes. A simple, two-story complex, it was never intended to define luxury, but it did offer efficient, modern apartments with good views, parking, and a swimming pool at reasonable rents to people who also had high hopes. It once shone with newness, and everything had worked. The tiles surrounding the pool had been squash-blossom yellow, and the water had been clear and blue as a tropical lagoon. But that, of course, was a long time ago. These days El Paraíso is cheerless and run-down, and what does work doesn't work well. Where they aren't missing, the tiles surrounding the pool are broken, and the only thing that fills it are weeds. A wire screen stretches over the top to stop garbage, rodents, birds, and drunks from falling in. The views are only good if you like strip malls and traffic. You park at your own risk. The first time

Oona Ginness saw it her immediate thought was, *If this is Paradise, I really don't want to go to Hell.* She had to carry Harriet into the apartment because Harriet, who is sensitive to atmosphere, didn't like it, either. After moving in, Oona's father wouldn't get out of bed for two days.

But now, on a day as bright and full of promise as El Paraíso is dilapidated and defeated, Oona whistles and Harriet wags her tail as they cross the ruined pool area, both of them looking completely at home. Which, of course, they are. El Paraíso may not be much, but it is a home. For their bodies if not for their hearts. It's a lot better than sleeping in the truck. As Oona herself would say, if you can't change something then you have to learn to live with it. That's her motto. You do the best you can.

Mrs. Figueroa is waiting for her, peering through the curtain of her living room window. Mrs. Figueroa is always on guard. She starts talking even before she opens her door. "I'm so sorry to ask you. I know it's not really the super's job." And Oona, of course, is not really the super. "I know it's Saturday and you have to get to work, but I really can't do it myself. Not with my arthritis." The wonder is not that Mrs. Figueroa can't change a lightbulb, but that she manages to do anything — dress or eat or shop or turn on a faucet or sweep the floor — with her crimped and crippled hands and her dissolving bones.

Mrs. Figueroa, however, is a warrior, even if she doesn't look like one (no muscles, no weapons, and a fondness for bright red lipstick). She may never have heard of Emiliano Zapata, but Mrs. Figueroa would agree with his opinion that it is better to die on your feet than to live on your knees. She's not going to let the pain defeat her. She and Oona have a lot in common.

"It's OK, Mrs. F. It's no trouble." Oona doesn't like everyone who lives in the apartments, but she likes Mrs. Figueroa. "I would've been here sooner, but I had to sweep the stairs and get the cans out, and Mr. Janus locked himself out again, and then I promised Andy in number six I'd walk his dog because he sprained his ankle."

"There's always something," says Mrs. Figueroa. "Your father not feeling well today?"

"No," says Oona. Although he rarely leaves the property, sometimes her father can get through a whole week — maybe even two — before he has one of his "setbacks." And sometimes he can't. "He had a bad night." It's either a bad night, a bad morning, or a bad afternoon. (Though, to be accurate, this current bad night happened two days ago.) If he cuts back on his medication it can be a bad week. There hasn't been a good year since Oona was twelve.

Mrs. Figueroa nods. "Life is a hell of a thing." This, of course, is merely a statement of fact. You don't live at El Paraíso because you want to. You live there because luck deserted you, Fate dealt you a lousy hand, and then things got even worse. The people there don't judge; they sympathize. They all know what it's like. "You're a good girl to help him out like you do."

As if Oona has a choice.

"He's my dad," she says. She's all he's got. And vice versa. Except, of course, for Harriet.

The burned-out bulb is in the bathroom. While Oona changes it, and then does a few other small things that Mrs. Figueroa can't do because of her hip, her knees, and her hands, Mrs. Figueroa chatters on and feeds Harriet dog biscuits.

When Oona's done, she refuses the tip Mrs. Figueroa tries to put in her hand. She often does Mrs. Figueroa's shopping when she's not well enough to get out with her walker; she knows how much money Mrs. Figueroa has.

When Oona and Harriet get back to their apartment, Oona's father is exactly where they left him two hours ago. Which is on the sofa in front of the TV. The plate and cup from the breakfast she made him is still on the coffee table. He is still in his pajamas. He might still be

21

watching the same show, for all she knows. The expression on his face is also exactly the same as it was when Oona left. If Abbot Ginness were a piece of property and not a person, he would be a vacant lot. But he turns as soon as he hears the door shut behind her.

"There you are," says Abbot. "What took you so long? I was getting worried." He may not do much, but he can manage worry.

"I had a couple of odd jobs to do. Mrs. Figueroa . . . and Andy. Remember, somebody shoved him off the bus?"

"Right. Right. I should've realized." Abbot nods. "It's just that I was texting and you didn't answer."

"Sorry, Dad. I left my phone here." She makes it sound as if it were an accident, but in fact Oona always leaves her phone at home unless she's at work or at school—somewhere that keeps her away most of the day and that Abbot knows he can call only in a real emergency. Otherwise he'd be texting constantly to make sure she's all right.

"You should try never to forget it." This is something Abbot says at least once a day. "I know you were only outside, but things can happen, Oona. You know that. People get killed just taking a shower."

"You want me to bring my phone into the shower with me?" teases Oona.

Once upon a time, that would have made him laugh,

but he doesn't laugh now. "Of course not, honey. I'd hear you if you fell."

Unlike Mrs. Figueroa, Abbot Ginness is not a warrior. He lives firmly on his knees, though he wasn't always like this. He used to go to work and ride in cars and walk up streets and run down stairs and take showers and laugh and sing and have dreams and never think about what disaster was huddled around the corner waiting to jump him. Until his wife, Lorna, got sick with a cancer. She was only in her early thirties. The doctors got rid of that cancer, but then she got another. And then another. And another after that. That was when he stopped praying.

The bills mounted. Abbot was trying to work and look after Lorna and look after Oona, but he couldn't keep up. Lorna's death didn't make anything easier. He had debts he could pay only if he were a criminal or a gambler on a serious winning streak. He was too depressed to go to work most days, and when he did go he just messed up. The job went, then the house went. He and Oona and Harriet wound up living in his truck. And now here he is, so defeated he thinks the world is trying to destroy him; so terrified of all the bad things that could happen that he can barely leave the house. And so worried about losing his daughter that he'd be happy if Oona never had to step outside their front door.

"Anyway," says Oona, "I did all the Saturday chores, so unless somebody locks themselves out or knocks out the power there shouldn't be anything you have to do. I'll bring the cans in when I get home."

His eyes are back on the screen. "Thanks, honey. That's great."

"You not going to get dressed today?"

"No. No, not today. I think I'll just stay in today. Stay here."

When he's OK, she tries to get him to at least step outside because she read that sunshine is good for depression. But when he's like this it's better to keep him inside. The sun may shine the blues away, but it also shines on the liquor store down the road. The last thing he needs is a drink. Even one beer will make him cry.

"Right. You take it easy. I'll make a sandwich for your lunch and leave it in the fridge."

"You don't have to do that," says Abbot. "I can fix myself something."

But he probably won't.

Oona makes him a sandwich and leaves out a bag of potato chips and a can of soup. Then she changes her clothes and puts Harriet in her backpack. She always takes Harriet to work with her. Brightman, the manager, lets Harriet stay in his office, and all the staff take turns walking her during their breaks. If Oona left Harriet at home she'd never get walked, and she'd be lonely with only Abbot and daytime television for company.

When she's ready Oona goes back to the living room and gives Abbot a hug. "OK, Dad, I'll see you later."

He looks up at her. "You're going already?"

"'Fraid so. It's Saturday, Dad. My shift starts at eleven."

"I wish you didn't have to go," says Abbot. "As soon as I get back on my feet—"

"As soon as you do, I'll quit the job," Oona quickly agrees. This is something else Abbot says fairly frequently. "But for now I need it." Weekends during school; at least five shifts a week in the summer. She saves every penny she can for college. Oona has plans.

Behind Abbot's head, twin sisters who were separated at birth and have just been reunited in front of the entire nation after fifty years are crying. Abbot looks as if he may cry, too.

"I just wish—"

"I really have to get going, Dad. The bus—"

"I know, it's a long ride. But you'll be careful, won't you?"

"You just rest," urges Oona. "I'll be home before you know it."

"No you won't," says Abbot.

Age does nothing to improve the day

Jack has called an emergency meeting of the Dependents of Paloma Rose. Which means him and Leone, since Arthur, apparently, is still at last night's dinner. A heart-to-heart with Leone gives Jack Silk no more pleasure than having a tooth pulled, but he has no choice. He may have lost sight of the ball for a while, but now that his eyes are locked on it he can see the clawed foot of Disaster trying to kick it out of his way.

They meet at Ferlinghetti's late in the afternoon. Ferlinghetti's is designed to look like a beatnik coffeehouse in the 1950s. The chairs and tables are all mismatched, the walls are covered in yellowed newspapers and old book jackets, the floorboards are scrubbed but worn. The lighting's so low that the room is dark and shadowy, and though smoking is, of course, no longer allowed, it feels as though clouds of smoke are drifting past the tables.

Leone sits down as if she expects the chair to collapse. "I don't know why we had to come here," she complains. "I feel like somebody's going to start reading some depressing poem about foot fungus in a minute." Leone likes cutting-edge modern—and astronomically expensive. Places where the customers who aren't celebrities are only there to see the ones who are. "Why couldn't we go to Funky Monkey or Z? They have coffee."

"I like it here," says Jack. "It's quiet. A good place to talk." He's passed Ferlinghetti's a couple of times, but he's never been in here before, either. Which is why he chose it. If they went somewhere Leone wanted to go, she'd run into at least a dozen people she knows, and then the only conversation they'd have would be hello and good-bye.

"It makes me itch," says Leone.

"You can take a shower when you get home." Jack hands her one of the menus stuck between the sugar bowl and the salt and pepper shakers. It's stained. "Let's just get the ordering over with so we can discuss the matter at hand."

Leone is as enthusiastic about discussing the matter at hand as she is about being in Ferlinghetti's, and starts prattling on with talk so small it's like a dust cloud, obscuring everything. By the time the waitress comes over, neither of them has more than glanced at the menu.

"What do you recommend?" Jack isn't hungry, but he doesn't want this to be a quick-cup-of-coffee-and-go meeting.

The young girl with the order pad is dressed more like a pallbearer than a waitress, but she has a nice smile. "Well . . ." Her eyes move from Jack's face to his suit, to the gold rings on his fingers and the clear polish on his nails. Leone might be fooled, but the waitress knows he's never been there before. She leans toward him conspiratorially. "You're pretty safe with the *On the Road* all-day breakfast. The home fries are epic."

"*On the Road* it is." He shuts his menu, still looking at the waitress. There's something about her. . . . He almost feels that he knows her. No, that's not it. He feels as if he *should*. Maybe it's just that she seems like a good kid. Pleasant. Uncomplicated. Unlikely to sling an egg your way. *Simpática,* as Maria Trudenco would say. And she does have a nice smile. "How's the coffee?"

"It's really good."

"Right. Then I'll have a large *americano.* Soy milk, no sugar."

The girl turns her smile on Leone. "And for you?"

She might as well have stuck out her tongue. Giving the impression that she is here only because her companion has a gun on her, Leone shoves the menu away with the very tip of a fingernail. "Just a double espresso. And make sure the cup's clean."

"Yes, ma'am," says the waitress. Though that isn't what she mutters under her breath.

Their order comes, the waitress goes, and Jack says, "Right. So now, if it's not too much trouble, Leone, how bad is it? What exactly is going on?"

Leone stirs the tiny spoon around and around in the tiny cup. "I would've said something, but I didn't want to worry you, Jack. I know you have enough on your plate."

"You're all heart." It wasn't the extraordinary talent and beauty of the infant Susan Minnick that made Jack take her on as a client. It was the extraordinary determination and single-mindedness of her mother. Leone was going to make her daughter a star or kill them both in the attempt. She has about as much heart as a machete. "So how bad is it?"

Leone switches on a smile. "Not that bad."

"I'll repeat my question, shall I? What's going on?"

"Oh, you know . . ."

"If I did, Leone, I wouldn't be asking."

She finally stops stirring. Very carefully, Leone places her spoon on her saucer. "Well, she has been acting up a little lately." Staying out until all hours. Disappearing for whole days. More photos turning up on the Internet.

Nothing really scandalous, just slightly provocative in underwear and bikinis. "No worse than your average magazine ad," promises Leone. She doesn't mention the one of Paloma on the Mad Tea Party ride at Disneyland, wearing mouse ears and swinging her T-shirt over her head.

Leone does leave out one or two other minor things—the fact that she had to cancel Paloma's credit cards because she kept maxing them out, and the money that's gone missing from Leone's bag since she stopped those cards, and Paloma coming home so drunk that she either passed out or threw up before she could get to her room—but otherwise she does a reasonable if reluctant job of catching Jack up on the life and times of Paloma Rose, including the final weeks of shooting the last season when she stormed off the set at least once a day (which he'll eventually hear about anyway), and the new, non-mother-approved clothes she sneaks out in (which sooner or later he's bound to see).

"So that's it," she says when she's given her version of this morning's scene with the egg. "Now you know the whole pathetic truth." And she laughs in that way she has that always reminds Jack Silk of funeral bells: *Bring out your dead. . . .*

"This is the beginning of the end." Jack closes his eyes, but when he opens them Leone is still sitting across from him with her smile like a replica watch, and the specter of Paloma is behind her, wearing very little and sulking. "You know that, right, Leone? The beginning of the end. The glory days are just about over."

The whole pathetic truth is, of course, even worse than Jack feared. Matter-of-fact as Leone's account has been, he can read between the lines. Hollywood can be very forgiving, but its forgiveness is in direct proportion to how much you're worth. Unless you're seen as a tragic genius, of course. Paloma's value isn't limitless. There are thousands of girls who are just as pretty and just as good at memorizing their lines and delivering them who would be only too happy to take her place. The business and people's memories being what they are, Paloma could be forgotten in a month. And as for genius, the only claim she has to genius is the genius of pissing everybody off. Nonetheless, she's creating a mountain of offenses for which she'll need to be forgiven. Not only has Paloma alienated everyone connected with *Angel in the House*—cast and crew, cleaners, makeup, security, and the passing visitor—but during the break between seasons she's been disappearing with such skill and such frequency that it's a wonder she hasn't been asked to join a Vegas magic act. He doesn't even want to think about the pictures on the Internet. Or where she goes when she stays out all night. Or with whom. What if she gets pregnant? What if she runs away with some guy who makes Seth Drachman look like Prince Charming?

"Oh, come on, Jack," coaxes Leone. "Don't be such a gloom goon. Look at the stuff other actors do. This is nothing. I mean, let's be real here. It's not like she's been arrested or anything."

"Not yet. Thanks to me." It was Jack who kept the lid on things when Paloma drove into that fence.

Leone doesn't like to think about the fence, and so she doesn't. "And she only throws things at me."

"Stop trying to cheer me up." One day you're throwing a fried egg at your mother, and the next you're throwing your phone at the maid. "It's not going to work."

"I'm only saying—"

"What about the drinking?" asks Jack. "How bad is the drinking?"

Leone shrugs. "Not that bad."

"Not that bad," Jack repeats. "I'll take that as a not-that-good. She's following in her father's wobbly footsteps. She gets totally blitzed and vomits in the hall." He taps his fork against the table. "Smoking?"

"I don't know, Jack. She uses mouthwash."

"And what about drugs?"

"She's only sixteen."

"Drew Barrymore. Tatum O'Neal." Jack can feel his blood pressure rising. He's going to get palpitations, for sure. And the tic. The tic will be coming back. He'll be living on the street with palpitations and his eye blinking like a hazard light. "You want me to keep going? Bring the list up to date?"

"I don't think so." Leone shakes her head. "No, I don't think she's into drugs. She's just being a spoiled brat."

Spoiled brat is putting it mildly, if you ask Jack Silk. She's as spoiled as a Chinese emperor. It amazes him that Paloma isn't dizzy all the time, considering how she thinks the entire world revolves around her.

"At least that's not putting a strain on her acting talent," says Jack.

Leone taps the spoon against her empty espresso cup. "It's not that big a deal, Jack. It's just a phase."

Just a phase. Jack sighs. In the last five years he's had three clients who phased themselves into oblivion. He can't afford to lose another one. Jack Silk was a very big deal yesterday; tomorrow he may be no deal at all.

"Leone, have you replaced your brains with Styrofoam? Don't you get it? The ratings are down. The sponsors are backing out the door. The network may not renew. Paloma doesn't have the luxury of having a phase. By the time it's over she'll be a has-been."

"Oh, Jack, I think—"

"That's the problem, Leone. You don't think. If you'd told me what was going on, at least I could have done some damage control. I am Paloma's agent, Leone. I do have a right to know."

"I just figured she was acting out because of what happened with what's-his-name."

"Drachman."

"Yeah. Him. I figured she'd get over it."

"That's worked well, hasn't it?"

Leone is trying to catch the waitress's eye. "What do you have to do to get another coffee around here? Beat a bongo?" Any second and she'll be snapping her fingers.

Jack gives the girl a nod, indicating Leone's empty cup. She gives him her nice smile. And Jack realizes that he isn't the only one Leone's annoying. The waitress has been deliberately ignoring Leone because of the crack about the clean cup. He smiles back.

"You still haven't answered my question. Why didn't you tell me?"

Taptaptap goes Leone's spoon. "I told you. I didn't want to worry you."

Jack resists the urge to slap the spoon out of her hand.

"Naturally, I appreciate your concern for me and my mental anguish, Leone, but now that I do know what's going on, I'm very worried. If I were any more worried I'd probably have a stroke right on the spot."

"You see?" says Leone. "I knew you'd be like this."

"Well, I'm glad I'm not disappointing you."

"It's because you're not a mother, Jack. If you were a mother you'd know this really isn't a big deal. I told you, it's a phase. All teenage girls go through it. It's so they can separate."

God help them, Leone's been watching daytime TV again. "Leone," says Jack, "this is not an average teenage girl living in the suburbs we're talking about here. This is our meal ticket. Yours and mine. We can't afford to have a train wreck. Are you listening to me? Watch my lips, Leone. The ratings are down. The sponsors are nervous. The network's debating another season. If you'd told me sooner, we could have done something about it before it's too late. But now I don't know if we can."

"I've tried to keep her in the house—"

"But she doesn't stay in the house, does she? What we could have done was send her to one of those brat camps. Make her come to her senses. But that takes a couple of months, and we don't have a couple of months. The new season's about to start."

"She's just acting out, Jack. I can control her. Trust me."

Trust Leone. Not even as far as he could throw her.

"Really? You can control her? And that's why as soon as you left the house she ran off with some guy with a ring in his nose?"

Leone is spared the effort of coming up with an excuse for today's escapade by the arrival of the waitress with her coffee.

The girl puts the cup down in front of Leone without a word, but says to Jack, "You didn't like the *On the Road*?" It's hardly been touched.

"No, it's not that," says Jack. "The fries really are epic." He was too busy watching his life go down the toilet to eat. "It's just that . . . I guess I'm not all that hungry."

"I know what you mean." Her eyes dart from him to Leone and back again. "You want me to wrap it up for you?"

He should take it. If Paloma loses the show he'll wish he had it. "Yeah, thank you. That'd be great."

Leone groans. "Oh, for God's sake, Jack. Now you're taking doggie bags?"

But Jack is watching the waitress and doesn't hear her. "Leone," he says. "That girl. Does she remind you of anyone?"

"Morticia Addams."

"No, seriously. Someone you know pretty well. Look at her, Leone. Look closely." Leone looks. "Picture her with blond hair. Shorter. Shorter blond hair." Leone frowns, getting as close as she can to looking thoughtful. "And with a little wave," Jack goes on. "Picture her with wavy, short, blond hair. And no glasses."

"That girl's nose is bigger," says Leone at last. Forgetting, perhaps, that Paloma's nose was once bigger, too. "And her eyes are brown."

"OK, her nose is a little bit bigger and her eyes are brown. So she's not her identical twin separated at birth. But it's still pretty uncanny. She's practically her double."

"She's shorter," says Leone.

She's also a hell of a lot more likable, thinks Jack.

In an out-of-the-way weekend cottage that has yet to be opened for the summer, a group of teenagers is having a party. Technically, what they're having is a beach party, since the beach could be seen only yards away through the living-room window if anyone wanted to open the shutters. Their backpacks, coolers, buckets of fried chicken and potato salad, and bags of chips cover the coffee table and a great deal of the floor. The cottage is decorated in a style called midcentury modernism, but what it looks like now is midcentury war zone. Things have been spilled on the carpets and chairs, furniture broken, lamps knocked over, pictures taken from the walls and replaced by graffiti. It looks as if someone once tried to build a fire on the footstool. The room is filled with smoke, which comes not from the footstool but from the joints being passed around.

The cottage belongs to a man named Barry Taub, who isn't here (and who wouldn't be very happy if he were). No one at the party knows Mr. Taub; they picked his cottage because it was the easiest to break into. Among the uninvited guests, sitting in a corner of one of the sofas, in shorts that wouldn't cover a small pumpkin and a red halter top (a color her mother has always told her does her no favors), is Paloma Rose, teen idol and icon. In one hand Paloma holds a chicken leg so greasy it might as well be made of oil; in the other she holds a can of beer.

Paloma is feeling pretty happy. Paloma rarely does anything without a script. If it isn't the script given to her by the director of *Angel in the House,* it's the script given to her by the director of her life, Leone Minnick. But here she is, just like a regular teenager, hanging out with her friends. Laughing. Dancing. Fooling around. This is more like it. It makes her feel real; feel empowered. And it's exciting. Paloma has gone to several Hollywood pool parties (with her mother), but the only beach party she's ever attended was in an episode of *Angel in the House* (season 3, episode 2)—the one where Faith Cross saves the stranded whale. She has also never eaten chicken from a cardboard bucket before. Never touched a joint. Never before been involved in breaking and entering. It's certainly a lot more exciting than a makeup call or being yelled at for blowing your lines. Just the sight of the fried chicken and beer would make Leone pale beneath her yearlong tan and start muttering about Paloma's skin and hips and image—never mind the breaking and entering part. Or the joint. Forget the joint; Leone would never notice it. She'd have gone into shock when she saw what Paloma is wearing.

Paloma tosses the chicken bone onto the pile on the floor. This is living.

Maria was right, of course. Paloma's new friends are not from the Internet. She met them by chance when she was giving her bodyguard the slip one afternoon and they helped her get away. At this exact moment, they remind her of a group of characters that appeared in an old episode of *Angel in the House*—though anyone who isn't Paloma might have trouble seeing the similarity. In the show these characters were members of a biker gang whose rough, often scarred, exteriors hid hearts of gold, and it was up to Faith Cross (Paloma) to make them—and everyone else—realize that. In real life, Paloma's new friends aren't a gang, and only two of them ride bikes—and those are Vespas. The others drive cars. It's too soon to tell of what metal their hearts are made, but, as well as the ponytail there are several piercings and tattoos among them, so, to Paloma, they look like they might someday own Harleys and secretly do good deeds. They seem to have the drink and drugs and illegal-entry parts covered.

Paloma prefers Diet Coke to beer, but there isn't anything to mix with the Diet Coke and her mother doesn't disapprove of Diet Coke on its own, so she sips her beer, pretending to enjoy it. Just as she pretends to understand what the others are talking and joking about.

"Hey, Suze," calls Micah. It is Micah, the group's lock picker, who recently rescued her from Paradise Lodge—her hero. "You wanna toss me another brew?"

They don't know who she is. These kids are not the target audience of *Angel in the House*—they're too old and too hip; they carry around guitar cases and artist's portfolios, not Faith Cross pencil cases and lunch boxes—so she told them her father's a producer. They think that's cool. It means she gets to go to big-deal parties and hang out with celebrities and attend premieres. At least three of them want to be filmmakers. Indie films, of course, not Hollywood crap.

Paloma opens the cooler. "There's none left," she reports.

Micah turns to the boy sprawled beside the other cooler. "Sammy? You got another can in there?"

Sammy shakes his head. "Cupboard's bare, dude."

"I guess we better make another run." Micah turns back to Paloma. "Suze? You got some more dough?"

The one thing they do know about Paloma that is true is that she's rich. When they went to Disneyland, it was Paloma who paid. When they went bowling, it was she who paid. When they hung out all night watching movies, it was Paloma who bought the pizzas and soda and beer. Just as it was Paloma who filled the coolers today and picked up the tab for the buckets of salad and chicken.

"No. We spent it all." Once she's gone through her pathetic allowance (hardly enough to keep a fish in shoes), Paloma has to rely on what she can steal from her parents (which, since they both work for her, isn't really stealing; it's more like taking it back).

"What about that old magic plastic?"

"I told you. My mom cut them in half." That would be after the Disneyland bill. The picture some creep put on Facebook of her sitting in a giant teacup waving her T-shirt in the air didn't help.

Micah makes a rude remark about Paloma's mother—whom he has never met and never will meet—but his is a philosophical nature, and he bounces right back from this disappointment. "Right," he says. "Then it's plan B, ain't it?" There are more ways to get into a house than through the front door. "Come on, Sammy. Come on, Suze." He shakes his head as Paloma reaches for her cover-up. "No, leave it. Come as you are. Leave your bag here."

Plan B is simple enough. They will drive to the convenience store up the road. Micah will wait out of sight in the car with the engine running while Paloma and Sammy go into the store. Sammy will go first; Paloma will follow a minute or two later, giving Sammy time to pick up something—a candy bar, a bag of pretzels, something small—and be paying for it with the exact change when Paloma bursts through the door, breathless and faintly hysterical. Sammy will stroll past her as she rushes up to the counter wailing that someone stole all her things while she was walking on the beach and that she needs to use a phone to call her mother to pick her up. Micah says she should act helpless, like a maiden in distress. If she can, she should cry. While the clerk is calming Paloma, Sammy, seeming to be leaving, will dart back and grab some beer and make a run for the car. Nine times out of ten, the clerk will chase after Sammy, and Paloma will be able to slip out and meet everyone back at the beach. If he doesn't spot Sammy, Paloma will have to pretend to call her mother. No sweat. "You think you can do that?" asks Micah. Paloma says she thinks she can.

There is only one thing wrong with plan B, and that is that this isn't one of the nine out of ten times; it's the tenth. Plan B doesn't work. Instead of running after Sammy, shouting, "Stop, thief! Stop!" the clerk grabs hold of Paloma and calls the police. "It's Julio down at the Mini Market," he says. "I've got one of those kids."

Paloma is still trying to convince the clerk that he's making a really gigantically enormous mistake, that she has nothing to do with whatever just happened, when Officers Clemente and Leung arrive.

"Well, look who it is," says Officer Leung, the proud father of a nine-year-old girl who is not only addicted to television but also the owner of a Faith Cross pencil case, a Faith Cross backpack, and the series T-shirt. "It's that angel from the TV show."

Jack Silk has an idea

Jack Silk is not happy. Right at this exact moment in time he should be getting ready to go to the kind of party that makes the Golden Age of Hollywood look like it was nothing more than cheap tin. He should be looking forward to an enjoyable — maybe even profitable — evening, with everyone telling him how good it is to see him and asking who made his suit. But is he? No, he is not. Like a progressive, incurable disease, this day just keeps getting worse and worse. All that drama this morning. Then the meeting with Leone this afternoon, which threw the dark cloud of Paloma Rose running amok directly over his comfortable life. And now this: America's favorite angel takes a few more steps toward getting a criminal record. He drives through the hive of photographers, reporters, and oglers outside the gate, honking his horn and looking as though he'd be willing to run them over if they don't get out of his way. And he would if he weren't afraid of damaging his car.

Leone is in the living room, pacing in front of a sofa.

"Beer!" she wails when she sees Jack. "They think she was trying to steal a six-pack of beer! How could they think something like that?"

Jack takes a chair across from where Leone is trying to wear a track in the carpet, but sits on the edge, as if he may get back on his feet at any second. "She had been drinking, you know," he says. "Beer, as a matter of fact."

Leone waves her hands in the air; her bracelets clink and clank. "But that doesn't mean she was trying to steal it."

"No. I know a lot of people who like beer who've never stolen a can in their lives." Jack sighs. "But it does mean she drinks it."

Leone collapses onto the couch. "Oh, Jack, it was hideous, just hideous." Tears start to fall. He can't help but think that they've been waiting for him. "A police car! My daughter came home in a police car! I've never been so humiliated in my life. Thank God they didn't arrest her. I mean, can you imagine? Thank God the policemen recognized her." One of them even got her autograph for his daughter. "And naturally, she denied everything." Leone sniffles. "But of course it's not like they could prove she was with those boys. You talked to your contact on the force, right? They can't prove she was with them."

He's always admired the way Leone can cry without ruining her makeup. It's obvious where Paloma gets her acting talent. "Maybe not, but it doesn't look good. Those boys aren't exactly great criminal minds. They've been doing the same scam up and down the coast. They hit that store twice already. Just not with Paloma."

"It could still just be a coincidence that she was in there at the same time," insists Leone. "And even if they catch them, it'll just be her word against theirs. I mean, who are they going to believe? Petty thieves or Faith Cross?"

Jack knows whom he'd believe. "Maybe. But it's still not all good news, you know."

"Well, yes, I do know that, Jack. Why do you think I'm so upset?"

Motherly love, what else? thinks Jack, but says nothing.

"It's all over the Internet already," Leone goes on. "Even the video from the store of her half-dressed . . ." Leone shudders involuntarily, thinking about all those little girls with their Faith Cross backpacks and their Faith Cross angel wings. And all their parents, watching their children's idol wearing next to nothing and a pair of sunglasses and trying to hold up a grocery store on You-Tube. She can almost hear the cash registers of America go silent as a tomb.

"Don't think the sponsors haven't heard about it already, either. You can imagine how pleased they are," says Jack. The sponsors are the kind of Christians who think Jesus was too liberal. "That should help us get the renewal."

"But you explained it to them, right? And you can do something about the video, can't you?" Leone clasps her hands, almost as if she's beseeching him. "You know people. You can do something."

"Leone, listen to me." Jack leans toward her. "The video isn't the biggest problem."

"What do you mean?"

"I mean there's more to this than the beer. It seems there's also the small matter of breaking and entering. And criminal damage. One of the beach houses along the shore. It seems they've been using it as a hangout for a while. Someone spotted the car."

Leone has stopped crying. "So you mean they did find them?"

Jack shakes his head. "No. They're not quite as stupid as they seem. By the time the cops got their tip, the kids were gone."

"But they can't think Paloma—"

"Why not?" asks Jack. "She was somewhere drinking beer. You know, since she's underage."

Leone frowns, thinking. "So you mean they might want to talk to her."

"Question her," corrects Jack. "Yeah, they might want to do that." He looks around the room as if he's just realized they're the only ones in it. "Where's Arthur? He's her business manager. We have to do some damage control. Pronto."

"Arty's not here."

"*Still?* Did he go to dinner or to a Hindu wedding?"

"He went out again."

"Right." Jack tells himself not to panic. Then he tells Leone. "There's no need to panic yet," he says. "We can manage this. We just have to make sure we're all on the same page. Where's Paloma? We have to make her understand what's at stake here."

"She's in her room. I locked her in."

"Well, unlock her," orders Jack. "Get her out here now."

While Leone goes click-clacking across the living room and down the hall, Jack composes what he'll say to Paloma. He doesn't want to attack her or make her feel bad; that won't get him any farther than a bicycle would get him in a blizzard. But he does have to make it clear to her in no uncertain terms that she has to stop messing around. She has to pull up her socks or her leggings or whatever it is they're wearing these days and get with the program. She wouldn't like it in jail. She wouldn't even like living in a house with only two bathrooms. She's not stupid — at least he doesn't think she's stupid; sometimes it's a little hard to tell. She'll see reason. She'll understand. After all, she has as much to lose as the rest of them do.

Leone returns, her mouth like a lemon that's been squeezed dry. "She's not there."

"What?"

"She's not there. She's gone."

Jack misses a breath. So now would probably be the right time to start to panic. "What do you mean, she's not there? Where is she? How could she get away? I thought you locked her in."

"She's an angel, remember?" Leone throws herself back on the sofa. "She probably flew."

"This is all your fault," says Jack. "If you'd told me what was going on I could've stopped it before it went this far. But oh, no, you couldn't do that. Because you're her mother. You could handle it." The little brat is probably out robbing a bank this time. "Well done, Leone. They're going to make you Hollywood Mom of the Ye—" He breaks off suddenly, his mind pedaling backward. He had a thought. He had a thought that gave him an idea.

Or would give him an idea if he could remember what it was.

Leone sits up a little straighter. "You're not having a heart attack, are you, Jack?"

"Brat," says Jack. That's the word. Brat. "We have to send her to brat camp. Right away. Just in case they do have second thoughts about questioning her." Preventive rehabilitation. "Of course, we have to find her first."

"But we can't send her away." Given so many choices of things to be upset about, Leone is suddenly reasonable and calm. "What about the show? She can't break her contract. And she can't be in brat camp *and* do the show. She can't be in two places at once."

Two places at once . . .

Jack stares past her, unseeing. Jack is thinking. If a herd of unicorns stampeded across the terrace he wouldn't notice. And if he were a machine and not a Hollywood agent, you would hear wheels turning and pistons pumping and a motor humming. You might even hear the ringing of a bell.

"Well, can she?" Leone persists. "I know I failed science, but —"

He holds up one hand. "Quiet, Leone. I think I have an idea."

Leone's smile would turn blue litmus paper pink. "What? You're going to clone her?"

"Something like that."

She laughs. "Something *like* cloning?"

Jack nods. "That's right. Something like cloning." He puts on his final-offer expression. "You remember that girl?"

"Girl? What gir—" Leone breaks off as she finally catches up with him. Now the silence is on her side of the room. It is an awed silence. "You can't be thinking what I think you're thinking. Can you?"

Jack nods. "I do believe I can."

"You mean that girl in the coffeehouse? You mean you think that we can switch her for Paloma—"

"Exactly."

"But it's impossible. People will know the difference."

"Will they?" Jack shrugs. *What makes you think that?*

"Of course they will. Why wouldn't they? She's shorter, for one thing."

"Not by much. She can wear lifts. Higher heels."

"But that girl probably lives in a trailer. How is she going to impersonate Paloma Rose?"

Jack makes the face of someone trying hard not to laugh himself silly. "What? You think somebody's going to miss Paloma's scintillating conversation? The only time she talks to anyone is to yell at them or to give them an order."

"What about Maria?"

"What about her? I can handle Maria. She's not going to say anything. She likes this job. And I don't think she's in any hurry to go back to Mexico."

"But what about everybody else?"

"Everybody who? Vassily's gone. The trainer and the drama coach — that crew — they can all be gone, too. Start again with new people who never met Paloma."

"And the girl? If she sells her story?"

"Leone, please. I don't work with anyone without a contract and a confidentiality agreement. Not even my dentist."

"But the show . . . What if this girl can't act?"

Jack silently thanks his mother for teaching him patience. "Leone, with all due respect, we're talking about Paloma Rose in *Angel in the House* here. Not Dame Judi Dench in *Macbeth*."

"But there's so much she'll have to learn." Leone shudders delicately. "She doesn't even stand properly."

"That's where you come in, my dear." Jack gives her his very best smile. *Just take hold of this apple, Eve.* "You'll be like Henry Higgins in *My Fair Lady*."

"I'll be more like the miracle worker if I pull this off," mutters Leone. But the look she gives him is more calculating than doubtful. "You really think it'll work?"

"If anyone can do it, you can." There are a lot of things Jack Silk doesn't like about Leone Minnick, but her lack of scruples isn't one of them. He knows better than anyone that Paloma Rose's career didn't happen through luck, accident, or chance — and certainly not through talent. It happened because Leone Minnick wanted it to happen and made very sure that it did. Just as she now wants to keep the evil wolf of failure from the Minnicks' ten-million-dollar door. "And in any event, it has to work," he adds. "We're at the very bottom of the option barrel here."

Leone gets to her feet and starts pacing again, her brain already engaged. "We can get colored contacts. We can get some nobody to do the basic cut and dye, and then I'll maintain it myself — we don't want any bigmouthed celebrity beautician selling his story to the press. . . ."

Jack's smile deepens. Eve has just taken her first bite. Crunch.

It's been a normal Sunday for Oona. If it were a child's report card it would read *Could do better,* but it's been OK. Because her father still isn't ready to get out of his pajamas and leave the house, she got up early to sweep the courtyard and the stairs, to fish the week's debris off the netting over the pool, and to replace the lightbulbs that had burned out or been stolen in the walkways. Harriet helped her, of course, trotting behind Oona, pulling the garbage bag, and squeezing under shrubs to bring out a can or a plastic bottle. Once they'd done that, and checked on Mrs. Figueroa, Oona straightened up the apartment, did some errands for her dad, and fixed his lunch. After that, she and Harriet took their usual three buses to Ferlinghetti's. Where she has served coffee and tea and food with ridiculous names all afternoon and, now and then, looked out the window as a nice car went by, wondering about the girl driving—where she was going and whether or not when she got home she'd have to try and talk her father into changing his pajamas since it's been four days and he's starting to smell.

By the end of Oona's shift, her feet ache from so much walking, her jaw hurts from so much smiling, and if she closes her eyes she sees a thick white mug floating in the air and a disembodied voice saying, "So does that come with fries?" Oona believes that, someday, she'll look back at this time in her life and, if she doesn't laugh, she will at least smile. Oona has plans. She's going to do really well in school so she gets a scholarship to go to college, and then she's going to veterinary school, and then, after she's got her practice going and paid off Abbot's debts, she's going to buy a house outside the city and her dad's going to build a big kennel behind the house because he was an ace carpenter before he lost his job and gave up, and she's going to be the best vet in California and he's going to be his old self again and everything's going to be all right. Her mother will still be dead, of course, but aside from that things will be as close to back the way they once were as possible.

With that thought in her head—that someday everything's going to be all right again—Oona clocks out of her shift, puts Harriet and the daily doggy bag donated to her by Brightman into her backpack, says her good-byes, and walks out of the restaurant and into the almost-visible air.

It isn't until the door of the Jaguar suddenly opens in front of her that Oona even sees it.

"Excuse me, Ms. Ginness?" A man leans over the passenger seat. "I need to talk to you. I wonder if I might have a few minutes of your time?"

"How do you know my name?" If she didn't recognize him from yesterday, she wouldn't stop. She'd just keep walking, and if he came after her she'd tell him to leave her alone or she'd call the cops. If he touched her, she'd set her dog on him. Harriet may have (mainly) the body of a Jack Russell, but she has the spirit of a Rottweiler. But of course Oona does recognize him. He was in Ferlinghetti's yesterday with a woman who acted as if she was some big movie star doing a photo shoot at an inner-city McDonald's. He paid for two espressos, an americano, and the all-day breakfast that he didn't eat with a platinum credit card.

"You remember me from yesterday," he says, ignoring her question. "My name's—"

"Jack Silk." Brightman and the other waitress, both of them actors, knew who he was right away. Mega-major-deal, wrote-the-spiel agent, said Brightman. Used to be the biggest shark in the water. Hobs with all the nobs. The waitress figured his car must have broken down. Either that or he was lost. "You're an agent."

This is going to be easier than he thought.

"Oh, so you know who I am." There are times when Jack has the smile you'd expect to see on an angel plucking at a harp as he floats by on a cloud lined with silver, and this is one of them. "So if we could just talk for a couple of min—"

"I don't want to be an actor."

Or maybe it's going to be harder than he thought.

"That's not why I want to talk to you. I have a very inter—"

"Whatever. I don't care what it is." She never should have stopped. That's always the first mistake. "It doesn't matter, I have to go. I have to get home. Like, now."

"Well, hop in," says Jack. "I'll give you a ride. We can talk on the way."

"You have to be nuts." Jack Silk's heart is not the kind to go around leaping for joy, but it does do a little skip. The girl's perfect. She has the same why-don't-you-eat-that-toadstool-and-die expression that endears Paloma to so many people. "You think I'm going to get in your car?" she says. "I don't know you."

"But you know who I am." He opens the glove compartment and reaches inside. "Look, here are my driver's license and my passport. You can hold them out the window while we drive. You—"

"What's going on here? Is this guy bothering you, Oona? Are you OK?"

Oona looks over. It's Brightman. He isn't actually holding a knife, but he somehow looks as if he is. "It's that guy from yesterday. That agent. He wants me to get in his car."

Jack Silk's heart may not be much for leaping, but it has no trouble sinking like a satellite in quicksand. "Look," he says, "it's not like she's making it sound. I appreciate your—I think it's great that you want to protect Ms. Ginness, but all I want to do is talk to her. That's all I want to do."

Brightman jerks his head toward Ferlinghetti's. "Then why don't you talk inside?"

"I have to go home," says Oona. "My dad—"

"I'm sure Mr. Silk will pay for you to take a cab," says Brightman. "That way you won't be late."

"What a good idea," says Jack.

With nothing and everything in common, Paloma Rose and Oona Ginness consider their situations and come to the same decision

Oona thinks it's a crazy idea. Jack Silk's the agent of some TV star who, he says, looks just like Oona. Give or take an inch or two and a couple of other unimportant details. He and this girl's parents want Oona to impersonate her. To live in her house, sleep in her bed, wear her clothes, and act in her weekly show.

They came up with this off-at-least-a-thousand-walls idea because the TV star is overworked, exhausted, hounded by that pack of hyenas known as the press, and possibly on the verge of a breakdown. It's been all systems go for the last few years, with hardly an afternoon to call her own. As if that isn't enough, she broke up with her boyfriend toward the end of last year and took it very hard. "The poor kid," murmurs Jack Silk, "she doesn't know if she's coming or going. She needs a rest." Only yesterday the poor kid was in tears, begging them to let her get away for a few weeks. Just to be able to sit on a beach and do nothing for a while. But a new season is about to begin, and if she steps away now it could jeopardize her entire career. Jack Silk says this is because the politics of Hollywood makes the intrigues and conspiracies of the old royal courts of Europe look like a bunch of four-year-olds playing musical chairs.

Which is why he and the Minnicks want Oona to pretend to be Paloma Rose. To protect her when she's at her most fragile and vulnerable. Paloma Rose wants her to do it, too. Paloma Rose sobbed with joy when they told her their idea. And they'll pay Oona, of course. They'll pay her a lot. But the money doesn't make the idea any less crazy. And that's what Oona tells him.

"You have to be nuts," she says. "That's the craziest idea I've ever heard." This, possibly, isn't strictly true. Before he got the super's job at El Paraíso, her father wanted them to move to Mexico — even though they had no money, knew no one south of the border, were about to have the truck repossessed, and he wouldn't even be able to watch TV since the only things he can say in Spanish are *gracias, buenos días, vino,* and *cerveza.* If that wasn't a crazier idea than Jack Silk's, it definitely ties it for first place. "It won't even work, either," Oona adds.

"It's not crazy," insists Jack Silk. "It's just a little unusual."

Oona silently stirs her coffee. You have to wonder what this man's idea of "sane" is.

"And it *will* work," he further insists. "I know it will."

"Well, I think you're wrong. We're not in a movie, you know," says Oona. "That kind of dumb idea only works in movies."

Jack lifts his cup with both hands, as if he's about to offer her a magic potion. "I'm not saying it'll be easy. But it'll work. I'm certain of that. It just requires some effort."

No prize for guessing who's supposed to make that effort.

"Mmmm . . . well . . . maybe . . ." Oona automatically takes the tone she uses with her father; noncommittal, humoring him. "But I don't even know who this Paula person is."

"Paloma," Jack corrects her. "Paloma Rose. She's very famous."

"Not to me, she isn't," says Oona.

Jack sips his coffee as if counting each drop. "I take it you don't watch much television."

"I don't really watch any." Oona figures Abbot watches enough for both of them. Besides, even in the summer she's studying or reading. She really needs that scholarship. "I have better things to do than that."

Of course she does. In a nation where the average person thinks TV is as important as air, he's found the one girl who has better things to do. "I'm glad to hear it," says Jack. "That's very commendable. But people who don't have better things to do know who Paloma Rose is." He takes another measured sip. "And love her." Which distinguishes them from the people who know Paloma personally.

"But if they love her so much, they're not going to believe that I'm her, are they?" counters Oona. If there were a thousand dogs that looked exactly like Harriet, even down to the black dot on her right paw and the bend in her left ear, Oona would be able to pick her out from the others without a second of hesitation.

"It's not as if they live with her or actually spend time with her," explains Jack, patience and reasonableness made flesh and blood. Assuming patience and reasonableness would wear a hand-tailored suit and gold jewelry and a hand-painted tie that cost as much as two months' rent at El Paraíso. "They know her as the character she plays and from stuff they read about her. And that's how they'll see you." A smile skates across his face. "Once we've done a little cosmetic work."

He can't mean surgery, can he?

"No, of course not," Jack assures her. "Nothing drastic. Just a little makeup. Contacts. That kind of thing."

But Oona isn't as easy to convince as Leone.

"And what happens when I open my mouth?" she wants to know. "Are you saying we sound the same, too?"

Which makes it fortunate that Jack Silk is a man who has an answer for everything. That, after all, is part of his job as well as his nature.

"It's not a problem. Mrs. Minnick happens to be an excellent voice coach. She trained as an actor and singer herself when she was young."

If this impresses Oona, she hides it well. "OK, so let's say she's this genius voice coach. What about the other people in this show? They —"

"I appreciate that you don't know how our business works," says Jack. "Naturally you think that her coworkers will notice the difference."

It's pretty interesting how ridiculous he makes that sound.

"Well, yeah," says Oona. "I bet you Brightman and everybody here would notice if somebody was pretending to be me."

"You can't compare *this*"— he waves his hand as if Ferlinghetti's is more of a coffee spill than a coffee house—"with television." Jack gives the impression that he might laugh at the absurdity of that idea if he weren't such a gentleman. "What you have to understand is that it's very intense and professional on set. It's not like a school play. There's very little fraternizing." Not with Paloma, at any rate. He silently returns his cup to its saucer. "Paloma—and everyone else in the cast and crew, of course—comes in, does her job, and goes home. It's not a social occasion. It's very difficult and demanding. Which is why we have the problem we have."

"But what about her friends?" asks Oona. "Her friends will notice."

"No problem." Jack beams. "She doesn't have any friends."

Like many people—and despite overwhelming evidence to the contrary—Jack Silk thinks that money and status are an indication of intelligence. Which explains why he thought it would be easy, especially with his charm and sophistication and talk as smooth as polished glass, to persuade a girl who works as a waitress and rides on buses to do what he wants. It won't be the last time Jack turns out to be wrong.

"Well, I'm really sorry that your famous star is so tired, Mr. Silk—"

"Please. Call me Jack."

Oona pushes her cup away. "But I can't do it. Jack."

He has found the one teenager who doesn't watch television — and the one teenager who doesn't want to be a celebrity. What were the odds?

"Don't be hasty," says Jack. "I know it's a lot to take in. You need a little time. But think about it. You'll be living the dream. Mansion in the hills . . . expensive clothes . . . Anything you want, you get. . . ."

"Yeah, it sounds great, but there's no way. You'll have to find somebody else."

As if. As if he can just walk along Hollywood Boulevard and take his pick of Paloma Rose look-alikes.

"If you're worried that it's too demanding, I told you, you'll have support and training. There's enough time to get you into physical and mental shape before —"

"It's not that. I can't leave home, that's all."

"Is it that dog?" When they came back into Ferlinghetti's, he discovered that she had the funniest-looking dog he's ever seen in her backpack. It's not even a crossbreed; it's a hodgepodge. As if God had a bag of spare dog parts and just stuck His hand in and put them together without looking. It might even have some mutant wolf in it. "You can bring the dog. The Minnicks love animals. Absolutely crazy about them."

"It's not just Harriet." Oona is now pushing back her

chair. "If you want to know, it's mainly my dad. I can't leave my dad."

Jack stands up, possibly to tackle her before she can escape. "And why is that?" His smile is neither satanic nor angelic now, but the smile of the one person in the world whom you can trust 200 percent.

Though not to Oona Ginness, it seems.

"It's none of your business." Oona goes to get Harriet while Jack pays the bill.

In the universe run by Jack Silk, everything is his business. Or should be. He can even tell you Paloma's bra size and when she usually gets her period.

As soon as they're outside, waiting for the cab, he picks up the conversation where Oona left it. "Obviously, I respect your privacy." He is still patient; still reasonable; still the one person a young girl can trust in a species that invented dishonesty, betrayal, and corruption. "And if you don't want to answer my next question, then, of course, just tell me to get lost. But your answer would help me to know if there's something—anything—I can do to change your mind."

According to the proverb, she who hesitates is lost. Oona hesitates.

"OK." She sighs. "Ask me your question."

"Is it that your father's very straitlaced, is that what it is? Are you afraid he won't approve?"

Oona shakes her head. Maybe she should just catch the bus and not hang around. "No, it's not that."

Aristotle thought that nature abhors a vacuum, but Jack Silk knows that it's people who don't like empty space. If there is one thing he's learned in his years of negotiating deals, it is when to say nothing and let the other person fill in the silence. He stares out at the street as if he knows she has more to tell him.

It's Abbot who tells everyone about his problems, not Oona. She doesn't like to talk about them. She has enough trouble trying to live with them. But it's been a long day in a long week, and she's tired. And he doesn't press her. And there's still no cab in sight. And maybe she wouldn't mind being somebody else—at least for a while. Suddenly Oona hears herself telling Jack Silk about her mother getting sick, and then getting worse. She tells him about the bills piling up like bodies in a war. How her dad tried to work and look after her mom. How he lost his wife. And then his job. And then the house. How they had to live in the truck because there was nowhere else to go. How Abbot's old boss got him the super job at El Paraíso. Even how Abbot's pretty much given up.

Jack Silk says nothing the whole time she talks. His expression is neutral. He makes no clucks of sympathy. He just listens.

"So, you see, I can't leave him by himself," Oona finishes. "He needs me."

"But this could solve a lot of your problems," counters Jack. "As I said, you'll be well paid. Enough to get rid of those debts. Get your dad back on track. Get you some money for college."

"It's not just him needing me. He worries about me all the time. He hates to let me out of his sight." If he left the house more, he'd be following her everywhere she goes. "He's called the cops so many times when he thought something happened to me that they call him Abbot."

"I don't think that's a problem. You can talk to him every day. You can Skype him. It'll be just like you're in the room with him. And it's not going to be that long. Two or three weeks. Four tops."

"I can't." Oona's hand goes up as a cab comes into view. "He'll fall apart without me."

Jack thinks, but doesn't say, that it sounds to him as if her father doesn't have far to fall. "We can work something out." He speaks quickly, wanting to get everything said before she slams the taxi door in his face.

"You sleep on it." He hands her his card. "Let me know tomorrow. But trust me. We can make this work. For everybody."

Oona says she'll think it over; she doesn't mean it. She doesn't even look back as the cab pulls into traffic, and so doesn't see Jack Silk standing on the sidewalk, watching her disappear — ready to smile and wave, though he is neither smiling nor waving at the moment.

Nonetheless, it is Jack and his offer that Oona thinks about all the way home. Not about any of the details or possibilities; not about what it would be like to have nothing to do but learn a few lines and have people wait on her all day. Just about the fact that the offer exists. Like a tiny light on a very, very dark and stormy night. Even though it's crazy. And she can't do it. No way, José. Like, who would believe Oona Ginness was some big TV star with millions of fans? What a joke. And how could she leave her dad?

Who is exactly where he was when she left him this morning. Of course.

"Hey, Dad," she calls as she shuts the door behind her and Harriet. "How was your day?"

He looks around. "Hi, honey. I was just about to call the station. You're so late."

"I got held up at work."

"You should've texted me," says Abbot. "Just so I'd know."

Oona makes Abbot a cup of the tea that soothes his nerves, and feeds Harriet, and takes a shower. She washes the dishes that were left in the sink, and makes supper, and eats in the living room with Abbot, Harriet's chin resting on her foot. At ten she takes Harriet for her last walk of the day.

When she comes back Abbot is laughing at something on the TV. Oona stands there for a few minutes, just staring at the side of his head. Once upon a time, Abbot Ginness was a normal dad who went to work and helped her with her homework and took her camping. In those days he was always teaching her stuff, like how to fix a leaking faucet or put up a shelf. In those days he never watched TV, but he laughed a lot. And that's when it hits her just how ridiculous her plans are. She's not going anywhere. She's never going to look back on now and smile, because she's never going to get out of it. If she can't leave him for a few weeks to go to the other side of the city, how is she going to leave him to go to college? To go to vet school? How will she ever be able to look after the sick animals of California when she has to look after him? Abbot Ginness. Not so much a couch potato as a human shipwreck.

You'll be living the dream, Jack Silk told her. Or she could continue to live the nightmare.

She goes into her room and takes Jack Silk's card from her desk and her phone out of her pocket. "Hello?" she says when he answers. "It's Oona. Oona Ginness. I guess you have a deal."

Paloma is about to leave her room. She's been in her room since last night, sulking and — ironically, since she's spent the last several months escaping from it — refusing to come out. Poor Paloma. What with one thing and another, she's had a day or two that really should have belonged to someone else. Someone terminally ordinary. Someone who only comes near the word *special* when she goes shopping.

Who would ever have imagined that anyone would try to arrest *her*? And not only did that stupid clerk try to have her arrested, he didn't even know who she was at first. A clerk in a deli, and he didn't recognize her. *Give her a break.* And his name's Julio, so he's Latino. Which means he's part of her target audience. The producers and writers of *Angel in the House* make a special point of including Spanish-speaking characters in the stories. So instead of grabbing her and screaming for the police, he should have screamed, "It's Faith Cross!" and begged for her autograph. But oh, no. He wouldn't even let her explain. She tried again and again, but he refused to listen. He was so obsessed with "getting those boys" that he didn't even really look at her. "You can't treat me like this," she kept saying. But he treated her like that anyway. "You'll be sorry when you find out who I am," she threatened. But he wasn't. All he cared about was his stupid beer. You'd think the world was going to end because he was out a few bucks. What a loser.

At least that one cop, Officer What's-His-Name—the one with the gut and the ear hair—at least he was nice. He recognized her right away and was really excited to meet her. Luckily for Paloma, he was one of those people who confuse the actor with the part, and he totally believed she was innocent. Angels don't steal. And they absolutely don't steal alcoholic beverages. But the other one—the one with the chipped tooth and the double chin—wasn't convinced. If it was up to him, he would've taken her in like she was a runaway shoplifter. Being led into a police station in handcuffs is not a good look for a popular TV star. Being driven home in the back of a cop car is bad enough. For the first time in a long time, Paloma was actually glad to get home. Better than glad. She couldn't have been happier if she'd been adrift on the ocean in a rubber raft for two weeks and suddenly been rescued (*Angel in the House,* season 3, episode 4).

She and Leone flung themselves into each other's arms. It was a touching and emotional scene. It is, of course, one that Paloma has played any number of times—though not with her mother—but it has to be said that she has never done it better. It's a pity no one was filming them.

Unfortunately, happy endings don't last long if they're not part of a TV show. After the policemen left, Leone's tears dried faster than a drop of water on a hot iron, and her good mood went with them. Officer What's-His-Name with the fuzzy ears might believe that Paloma was innocent, but her own mother didn't. "Beer!" she shrieked. "My daughter was stealing beer! And you reek of it! Like some common street urchin!" Paloma wasn't completely sure what the word *urchin* meant, but she could tell it wasn't good. She retaliated by calling her mother a selfish, money-grabbing bitch, words with which they are both familiar. During the fairly hysterical fight that followed, Paloma broke a three-thousand-dollar vase by throwing it at her mother, Leone knocked Paloma to the floor, and Maria had to pull them apart. Leone locked Paloma in her room, screaming, "You're not coming out till I say you can! This time you've really gone too far!" Within the hour, Paloma was in a cab heading back to Venice, where Micah and the others had fled after she was caught.

Going back to her new friends didn't make Paloma

any happier. They all thought it was hilarious that she was almost arrested. Micah said it was her own fault. She was supposed to act sexy and flirt to distract the clerk, not concoct a long-winded, complicated story like something out of a soap opera. Which was when Paloma forgot that these weren't people she yelled at, and she yelled at him. For not telling her that they'd used the scam before about a hundred times. For being stupid enough to use it again in a store they'd already hit.

"What do you care, Suze?" Micah sneered. "Your parents probably bleed hundred-dollar bills when you cut them. They can buy you out of anything."

Only a few hours earlier, Paloma had been mad because she was being treated like everyone else. Now, in one of those classic examples of how inconsistent human behavior can be, she was mad because Micah thought she wasn't like everyone else, that it didn't matter what she went through. So she came home again, and has been in her room ever since.

But now she's been summoned. Not by Leone — she wouldn't come out for Leone if she offered Paloma her own country — and not by Arthur, who seeks her out only when he wants something, but by Jack Silk. Unlike her closest relatives, Jack Silk has always been sympathetic and kind to Paloma. He is, she believes, the only person in the world who understands her at all. If he wants to talk to her, it won't be because he has another five hundred rules she's supposed to follow like she's still a little girl, or because he can't find his keys or needs a loan. It'll be because he has something important to say.

Jack stands up as she enters the room. "Paloma, my dear, please have a seat." He gestures to the chair across from his.

Her mother is on the sofa, looking as comfortable as someone waiting for the results of an X-ray and expecting bad news. She doesn't stand up and greet Paloma warmly, but she smiles in her straight-from-the-fridge way. Paloma doesn't smile back. *Eat gravel, you old witch.* Either Arthur wasn't invited to this meeting, or he has something more important to do.

Jack, instead of attacking Paloma like some people did, is full of sympathy. "I hope you've recovered from your ordeal." His voice is like a lullaby. "What a terrible thing to have happen to you. Imagine anyone thinking *you*—you of all people—would be involved in petty theft with lowlife scum like that. I can't tell you how shocked I was. The police commissioner has already heard about this."

Paloma directs a laser-sharp glare at her mother, then turns her crumpling face back to him. "It was terrible,

Jack. Really terrible." Her lower lip trembles. "The way they treated me . . ." She doesn't so much sit down as collapse into the armchair. "It wasn't even human." Several large, perfectly formed tears slide down her cheek. "I didn't know what to do. I felt so — so awesomely alone. I thought they were going to put me in jail." A sob lets loose a few more tears. "Nobody even wanted to listen to me." Her head is bowed; her shoulders shake. "They acted like I was some homeless person or something."

That would be a homeless person who wasn't arrested but instead was asked for her autograph.

This is also a scene that Paloma has played before, but although he is no stranger to it, Jack Silk says, "Don't upset yourself, darling, it's all over now." He sits down, mindful of the crease in his trousers. "There won't be anything in the press, and the studio knows nothing about the incident." His smile is so warm that Paloma, carefully wiping the tears from her eyes, believes he's actually patted her hand. "And I'll see what I can do about the YouTube clip. With a little luck, no one will believe that's really you. So we can all put it behind us and move on as if the whole dreadful misunderstanding never happened."

"Thank you," says Paloma — which might surprise the many people in Los Angeles who think those are two words of which Paloma Rose has never heard. She glances at her mother again. "So, is that it? Is that what you wanted to talk to me about?"

"No . . . no . . . not quite. I — we"—Jack gestures to Leone—"we have something important we need to discuss. Together."

Paloma automatically hugs herself. "About me?"

"Not entirely." Jack leans slightly forward, serious and earnest. But also kind. So very, very kind. "I'm afraid that Audrey's been in a rather serious automobile accident."

"Audrey?" Audrey Hepplewhite plays Paloma's mother in *Angel in the House,* but it takes Paloma a second to identify her. She never thinks of her as Audrey. She thinks of her as Lard Ass or, on good days, the Hepple. Though not now, of course. "Oh, poor Audrey. That's awful. Is she OK?"

Jack sighs. Heavy is the heart that bears bad news. "The doctors are hopeful that she'll make a full recovery, but right now she's in a coma, and it's still pretty touch and go."

"Oh, gosh . . . Poor Audrey . . ." Real distress suddenly makes an appearance on Paloma's face. She isn't acting anymore. As little as she likes Audrey Hepplewhite — who's almost as much of a control freak as Leone — her character is central to most of the plots. "Then the show —"

"Is going to miss a season," finishes Jack. He makes an empty-handed, what-can-you-do-against-the-forces-of-Fate gesture.

You may remember that only yesterday Paloma said that she didn't care if she was replaced as Faith Cross, so you might think this news wouldn't exactly ruin her week. But you'd be wrong. Yet another classic example of how inconsistent human behavior can be.

"But can't they just kill her off?" Though quite a few people consider Paloma to be dimmer than a one-watt bulb, she is more than capable of quick and logical thinking when she needs to be. "Couldn't she have a car crash on the show?"

"I'm afraid not," says Jack. "It's too late to write her out, especially with—" He was about to say "especially with Seth gone," but thinks better of mentioning Seth Drachman, sensing that that road probably leads directly to hell. "Especially because she's such a popular character. And, of course, everyone does hope that she'll recover."

"Well so do I," Paloma lies. "But what about me? What am I supposed to do while she's getting better?"

"That's the other thing we want to talk to you about," says Jack.

And he explains how worried he and her parents are

about her. How guilty they feel. How their hearts have been wrenched with anxiety by what happened with the police. She's been working too hard; they've expected too much of her. Recent events have shown them how much Paloma needs a break. Needs a change of scene; a change of people. Needs a rest. Needs to have a good time. She's a teenager, not a robot. "We haven't been paying attention," says Jack. "You work so hard that you have no friends. No real time to relax and be a kid. When do you have any fun?"

This is not a hard question to answer. Paloma never has any fun. She never has a good time. That was all she wanted, hanging out with Micah and his friends. And what happened? She almost went to jail. How totally, epically unfair is that? Everything Jack says is so true — so exactly how Paloma feels — that her face sags with self-pity. Her mouth wobbles as if it's made of jelly. "That's right," she murmurs. "I don't ever have a good time. I'm practically a slave."

Jack Silk might think that he's never heard of any slave who lived in a mansion in Hollywood, but what he says is, "Exactly, darling. We couldn't agree with you more. We've been inexcusably insensitive. We forgot that you're not a machine, you're a lovely young woman who needs to enjoy herself. That's why we think you should take this opportunity to do something for yourself. To have a real vacation. A vacation with peers."

Paloma frowns. "You mean like on a beach?"

"No, sweetheart." Jack chuckles. "Not piers like on the sea. Peers like kids of your own age and background."

It sounds just a little too good to be true. "I don't know . . ." Paloma's wondering what the catch is. "What about *her*?" She looks over at her mother, the seeping, pus-filled blister on the foot of her life.

"This is just for *you*," Jack assures her. "Nobody but you. You'll be completely on your own, free as a bird. Your mom stays here."

Jack Silk, who, he says, couldn't care more about Paloma if she were his own flesh and blood, has found a wonderful dude ranch that caters to special teenagers. Girls and boys who can't just hang out at the mall or go to the school dance like everybody else. It's completely private. No reporters. No paparazzi. No fans. Just kids like her who need a little space.

Paloma still isn't sure. Her mother is obviously for this plan, which automatically makes Paloma against it. "I don't know if I want to go to a ranch." She squinches up her nose as though she can smell the horses and cattle. "A ranch doesn't really sound like a whole lot of fun, Jack. Aren't they dusty and far away from everything?"

Leone jumps in to say that it isn't as if Paloma's going to be attacked by wild horses, but gets no further than "It's not like —" before Jack silences her with a look.

"This isn't that kind of ranch," says Jack. "It has everything you can imagine or want." His smile falls on Paloma like a prairie sun. "To tell you the truth, it's more like a luxury liner than a ranch. You know, sweetheart, those massive cruise ships that are the size of a small city? Only, of course, it doesn't move. And it's not on water. But some of those boats have to be seen to be believed."

And he begins to describe not the ranch but the yacht belonging to a billionaire of his acquaintance. Movie theaters. Bowling alley. Gym. Hot tubs. Squash and tennis courts. Pools. Boutique. Salon. Dance club. Helicopter pad. It's a yacht Jack may never visit again if his luck doesn't turn itself around very quickly.

Paloma, still trying to decide how she feels about this vacation, doesn't realize that Jack is talking about a superyacht currently docked in Dubai, but thinks he's describing the dude ranch. Not a horse or a cow is mentioned. Now what she smells are gourmet meals and the exotic herbal mixtures used in the spa and the beauty salons. By the time Jack has finished, Paloma is so excited you'd think she's been dreaming of this vacation for most of her life.

Until a less happy thought occurs to her.

"But I can't go somewhere like that." Paloma glares at her mother. "*She* cut up all my credit cards."

"We're getting you a new one with a high limit," promises Jack. "It's already been ordered."

Paloma flings herself from her chair to give him a hug.

"I swear to God, Jack," Leone says later as she walks him to his car, "you could sell a pot of boiling water to a lobster." She laughs. "And get it to jump in."

It's nine-thirty. There is still one lobster without a pot in Jack Silk's scheme, but he isn't worried. It's another interesting point of human behavior that we base our judgments of others on ourselves. Jack Silk loves money. Because he loves money, he believes that there is no one who wouldn't do anything for it. Oona says she can't leave her father? Father, schmather, is what Jack thinks. People have killed their fathers for less than he's offered Oona. And he seems to be right.

He has just turned in to his own driveway when his phone starts to play the "Triumphal March" from *Aida*.

"Hello?" Her voice is like a jab. "It's Oona. Oona Ginness. I guess you have a deal."

Jack Silk smiles into the night.

Splash!

Moving in with the Minnicks

Jack Silk is not a man to leave anything to chance, or to anyone else—not even God—and so he has organized everything. With the smoothness of oil flowing over glass, he convinced Abbot Ginness that it is in his best interest, as well as Oona's, to go along with Jack's audacious plan. "The world's a harsh place, and it's hard to get a break," said Jack, with his instinct for voicing other people's feelings. "When we have a chance to help each other, we should take it." He seemed to look around not just the apartment but the entire complex of *El Paraíso* and read Abbot's whole unhappy history without moving his eyes from Abbot's face. "That's a great kid you have, Mr. Ginness. She deserves better. Much, much better. You owe her this."

And what loving father would argue with that? Certainly not Abbot. It isn't Oona that he doesn't care about.

"But I'll worry about her being so far away," he admitted. "She's all I have."

Jack said that there's nothing to worry about. He bought Abbot a laptop so he can talk to and see Oona every day. "Besides which, I'll look after her like she's my own," promised Jack. "I'll protect her with my own life. You have my word." He had his lawyer draw up a contract guaranteeing payment from him and confidentiality from the Ginnesses. "I'm afraid it's pretty ironclad," said Jack as he watched Abbot and Oona sign the agreement. "You know what these legal beagles are like." He's arranged for Maria to visit Abbot every two days to keep an eye on things and do anything he needs done, so that, said Jack, Abbot will hardly know that Oona's gone.

Jack drives Paloma to the airport himself. He even does her the favor of taking her house keys from her so she doesn't have to worry about losing them the way she often does; she doesn't need them, he'll be picking her up when she comes back, of course. Jack Silk stands waving and smiling as Paloma goes through the gate. *Bon voyage, sweetheart. Have a great time!*

That very same morning, as Paloma's plane noses into the clouds, Oona leaves El Paraíso for Paradise Lodge in the cab provided by Jack Silk. Abbot followed her around while she packed. *Don't forget your parka. Don't forget your vitamins. Make sure you drink plenty of water.* "I hope these people are good drivers," Abbot fretted. "I don't care what fancy cars they have, that's not going to save you if they drive like kamikazes on a mission."

Mrs. Figueroa, who thinks that Oona is going to visit an aunt in Minneapolis, gave her an elaborately engraved silver locket that once belonged to Mr. Figueroa's mother for good luck. "So you come back safe," whispered Mrs. Figueroa.

Abbot, who knows that Oona is only going across town and will talk to him at least twice a day, cried. "You text me as soon as you get there," he ordered. "So I know you got there all right."

"I love you, Dad," said Oona. Abbot said he loves her, too.

It's a reluctant afternoon, muggy and close. The cab carrying Oona and Harriet slowly climbs the canyon and eventually turns onto a lushly tree-lined road. On the plain below, the light is blurred and the air almost gray, but at the top all is vivid and clear. When they finally come to the Minnicks' driveway there is a splatter of camera-toting men standing around or leaning against their cars. "Somebody pretty famous must live here," says the cabbie.

"Not really," says Oona. "I think they must have the wrong address."

Once they stop in front of Paradise Lodge, Oona sits in the cab for a few minutes, Harriet on her lap and her backpack beside her, just looking at her new home. It's a house from a movie or a magazine. She tightens her hold on Harriet and concentrates on breathing normally. Up until now she's tried very hard not to think about today. She has kept her thoughts focused on a few weeks from now—when it's all over and she and Abbot have some money and things finally change for the better. But now, sitting here in the back of the cab, a miniature castle looming in front of her and a posse of paparazzi behind her, all Oona can think of is what happens next. She gives Harriet a hug. So the Minnicks live in a big fancy house and their daughter's a TV star. So what? They're still just people. They're no different from anybody else. Everything's going to be all right. Harriet's tail thumps against her arm. It has to be.

"OK, this is it," the driver says a little more loudly than he did the first two times. "I can't get the cab no closer than this. She don't do stairs."

Oona will have to get out.

"Thanks." She thrusts a few crumpled bills over the seat.

"Keep it." He pushes the money away. "It's all been taken care of."

Jack Silk thinks of everything.

"Thanks," she says again, and opens the door. On the plain below, it smells like a traffic jam; up here, it smells like an expensive perfume counter.

Harriet jumps from the car, and Oona follows. But with less enthusiasm.

"You have a nice day, miss!" calls the cabbie.

"You, too." She stands with her back to the house, watching the cab disappear. What has she done? Not for the first time since she called Jack Silk (and not for the last time, either), Oona wishes that she hadn't. She should have stayed in the cab and returned home. Contract or no contract, what could they do to her? Sue her? And get what? A three-year-old cell phone and a rescue dog?

But Oona, as we know, is a practical person. She did call Jack Silk, and she didn't stay in the cab.

"Come on, Harriet." Oona climbs the steps and rings the bell.

The door is opened by a short, dark-haired woman with a dish towel in her hand and the smile of someone waiting to be attacked. She glances from Oona to Harriet to the empty drive behind them. "Yes?"

"I'm Oona," says Oona. "Oona Ginness. Jack Silk sent me."

"Of course. Of course." Maria knows about Jack Silk's scheme—or as much as he felt it was necessary to tell her. If she'd been asked her opinion—which, of course, she wasn't—she would have said that it, like so much about the Minnicks and the way they live, is ridiculous. Seeing Oona doesn't make her change her mind. She eyes Harriet dubiously. "And that is your little dog?"

"Her name's Harriet," says Oona. "Jack Silk said I could bring her. He said the Minnicks love animals."

The only animals the Minnicks love are ones you eat.

Maria shrugs. "If Mister Jack says bring her, then of course you bring her." Now it's Oona's backpack that's receiving the dubious look. "Is that all you have?"

"Uh-huh. Jack Silk said not to bring any clothes or anything." All she packed was underwear, a few old photographs, a comb, a brush, her cat slippers, a toothbrush, and a sock doll her mother made for her when she was a baby. "You know, so I can get into being Paloma."

Maria, who knows what lies in store for Oona in the teen star's bedroom, might think Jack Silk should have told her to bring a shovel, but all she says is, "Of course. Of course. Come in, come in." She flutters backward. "Leave your bag here. Mrs. Minnick waits for you."

Mrs. Minnick waits for Oona in the breakfast nook. Sunlight floods through a wall of windows, making everything shine and the woman at the round table with her jewelry and her tan and her dark blond hair look as though she's dusted in gold. A trade paper, an empty coffee cup, and a cell phone (gold) are laid out in front of her. Although she's sitting perfectly still, her eyes on an article about musicals, she gives the impression that she's chain-smoking cigarettes and tapping her fingers in a restless, impatient way. Oona stops dead in the doorway. She has an urge to run, or at least to walk backward quickly. Leone Minnick often has this effect on people, but in Oona's case it's because it never occurred to her that Paloma's mother might be the woman who was in Ferlinghetti's with Jack Silk. Lady Make-Sure-the-Cup's-Clean. The snob with less charm than snot. Apparently Jack Silk doesn't think of everything, after all. He certainly forgot to mention this.

"You must be Oola!" Leone cries as if she's never seen Oona before. "I'm Leone Minnick!" As if she might be someone else. "I was so afraid I was going to miss you. I don't have too much time. Wouldn't you know that today, of all days, I have a very important lunch?"

Moving like a robot in need of oil, Oona manages to follow Maria into the room. "Actually, it's Oona."

Leone's smile deepens, so that it could almost be described as shallow. "Actually, it's Paloma."

"Yeah, right, Paloma," says Oona. "And we did kind of meet."

But listening isn't one of Leone's greatest skills. Especially not when she's playing a part, and right now she's playing the part of a mother driven to despair with worry and concern for her only child, and she's playing it for all she's worth.

"I can't tell you how grateful we are for your help." She waves Oona to a seat. "Sit down. Sit down. Maria, maybe our guest would like a drink. Tea? Coffee? Something cold?"

Oona stays standing. "Thank you, but I —"

"You're a lifesaver," Leone gushes. "Really. A complete lifesaver. What would we have done if you hadn't agreed to help us out?" A worried mother, and a grateful one, as well. "Naturally, poor, dear Paloma wanted nothing more than to be here to thank you in person, but that just wasn't possible." She puts on a brave smile. "I'm sure Jack must have told you how they persecute my little girl."

Not in exactly those words. What Jack Silk said was that Paloma's hounded by the press.

"Yes, he —"

"Well, of course he did; that's why you're here, isn't

it?" If Leone's smile gets any braver it'll win a medal. "So the poor child can have a few precious weeks of quiet and peace. A little normality. It's always been bad, but this last year has been truly horrible." Tiny points of light glint off Leone's earrings as she sadly shakes her head. "Truly, truly horrible." And Leone starts to list the horribleness. The hacked phone. The outrageous lies in the press. The Internet pictures of Paloma crashing into fences and throwing up on sidewalks and posing in her underwear. "Her underwear!" Leone gasps with indignation. "Can you imagine? God knows where the camera was. Attached to some low-flying bird." Leone holds up her empty cup to catch Maria's eye.

"I heard all about it," says Oona. Including the incidents Leone hasn't mentioned — the YouTube video of Paloma throwing a glass of water at the famous talk-show host and the T-shirt in a teacup: 989,447,821 and 653,253,010 hits respectively, and still counting. "Jack —"

"But I'm sure no matter how sympathetic you are — and, obviously, you are sympathetic . . ."

Oona couldn't care less.

"You can't really imagine how she's suffered through it all," insists Leone. "It's one of those things that you have to experience yourself."

And it looks like I'm going to have my chance, thinks Oona.

Satisfied that Maria knows she needs a refill, Leone sets her cup back in its saucer. "It's no exaggeration to say that my poor baby knows what it's like to be crucified. Not with nails, of course," she explains, mistaking the look on Oona's face for dimness. "They crucify her with words. If the child so much as jaywalks they carry on like she robbed a bank. If she trips they say that she's staggering drunk." Leone sighs as the earth would sigh if only it could. "Trust me, it's not all glitter and gold up here, sweetie, no matter what people in your world think. There's a very heavy price to pay for celebrity."

"'Uneasy lies the head that wears a crown,'" murmurs Oona.

"Tell me about it," says Leone. "You don't know the half of it. If they get one tiny whiff of this — this arrangement, they'll be on her like a mob of vultures on a fresh corpse, and they won't leave so much as a bone or a tuft of hair behind."

"I know." Maria bustles past Oona with the coffee pot. "Jack ex—"

"What is that?" Leone's eyes have finally noticed something close to the ground. "Is that a dog?"

"Her name's Harriet," says Oona.

Leone's smile could only be more watery if she were a lake. "But what is she doing here?"

Oona sighs. *She's collecting for the ASPCA, what do you think she's doing?*

"She's going to live here," says Oona. "With me."

Leone sighs. "I don't remember anyone mentioning a dog."

Careful not to spill a drop, Maria finishes filling Leone's cup. Maria has always felt sorry for Paloma, but not as sorry as she's feeling for Oona at the moment. "Mister Jack said it is all right," says Maria. "She is part of the deal."

"Did he?" This is less a question than an accusation. "Well, then I guess we have a dog," Leone says, much as someone might say, *Well, I guess we have to hang off that bridge for an hour or two.* Leone picks up her cup. "Maria will get you settled today, and then tomorrow we'll get to work on you. Maria will take you to see to the basics right after breakfast. Hair . . . eyes . . . nails . . . height —"

"I know. Jack —"

"I'd do it myself, naturally, but I think it's important that you and I aren't seen together until you're complete."

Oona keeps her expression impassive. *And how will we know?* she wonders. *Will a bell ring?*

"We don't want to rouse any suspicions," Leone glides

on. "Believe me, honey, the only people who can keep a secret in this town are dead. And I wouldn't even trust them."

Jack Silk put it slightly differently. Jack Silk said you're safer in the jungle with a herd of lame and bleeding baby goats than in Hollywood with a secret.

"I know," says Oona. "Jack—"

"Of course, I'm sure dear Jack has explained everything to you. He's very thorough. It's what makes him such a good agent." That and his moral flexibility. "But we have a lot more to do than just cosmetics." She pulls her bottom lip in, really looking at Oona for the first time, giving the impression that she can see through clothes if not actual walls. "We're going to have our hands full here."

Oona wraps her arms around herself for protection from the X-ray eyes. "I know. The voice and—"

"Oh, much more than that. Look at the way you stand. Like someone who's always been in the audience. And then there's the way you walk. It's all wrong. Paloma is very graceful and poised. You have to move like you're on a catwalk, not like you're trampling frogs in a field."

"Right, Mrs. —"

"Mother," Leone corrects her. "Right, Mother."

Oona pries a smile onto her face. "I know I have to call you that when we're in public, but I don't see why I have to call you Mother when we're alone."

"Then call me Mom," says Leone. "Either will do."

"But I don't see what difference it makes if there's nobody around." She wants to call Leone Mother as seldom as possible. "It doesn't make any sense."

"Practice, darling," coos Leone. "If you don't do it all the time you might forget when it really counts." Her smile could freeze lead. "This project of ours is as tricky as defusing a bomb. We can't afford any mistakes. Can we?"

"Of course not, *Mother,*" says Oona. "And I'll try not to walk like I'm squashing amphibians."

"That's better." Leone glances at her watch. "God give me strength, will you look at the time?" She picks up her phone and pushes back her chair. "I'm going to have to shake a couple of legs." She gets to her feet. "You make yourself at home." The foyer of Paradise Lodge is nearly as big as their whole apartment at El Paraíso. If Oona's going to make herself at home, she probably should have stayed on the stoop. "And, Maria, make sure Oo — make sure Paloma has everything she needs."

"Of course, Mrs. Minnick."

"And you, Paloma darling, you make sure you rest

up today, because you'll need all your strength from now on." With which advice she leaves the room like a robber leaving a bank.

Oona and Maria both watch her walk sharply down the drive, her car keys in one hand and her gold phone in the other.

"Is she always like that?" asks Oona.

"*Más o menos,*" says Maria.

Oona sighs. "That's what I thought."

In elementary school, Oona's class went to a museum that was once the home of a railroad baron. The railroad baron had had a very large family—twelve children, several unmarried sisters, an assortment of parents, grandparents, uncles, and aunts belonging to him and his wife—and more than a dozen live-in servants. Besides that, like many fantastically wealthy men, he liked to show off the fact that he had so much money he could have flushed half of it down the toilet and still had far more than most people earn in a lifetime. The railroad baron's home was enormous. There was nothing you could ever think of doing that didn't have its own room. Even some of the rooms had rooms. Which makes Paradise Lodge the second-biggest house Oona has ever been in, and it isn't a museum—it's home to a family of three and their housekeeper. They didn't even have a dog until now. She may never be able to find her way around without a map.

Oona and Harriet follow Maria from room to room, all of which look like the pictures in the interior-decorating magazines Oona used to flick through in the hospital when she was waiting for her mother — everything color coordinated and the furniture all in the same style. Most of the rooms look like they are seldom, if ever, used.

At last they come to Paloma's room — to Oona's.

"Does everything match in here, too?" asks Oona.

"In a way," says Maria, and she opens the door.

Unlike Oona's room at El Paraíso, which is behind the kitchen and overlooks a patch of rubble and a major road, Paloma's is on the second floor, at the back of the house, and overlooks the garden and the pool. Also unlike Oona's room, which has just enough space for her bed, her desk, a folding chair, and a wastebasket, Paloma's is larger than the average living room and has its own balcony and bathroom.

Another dissimilarity between Oona's room and Paloma's is that Oona's is kept extremely neat, and Paloma's defines the concept of chaos in a way that no words ever could. There are things everywhere. Not just clothes, but magazines, bags, shoes, bottles, jars, stuffed animals, empty boxes and wrappers, used plates and glasses, half-eaten food, and a store's worth of gadgets. There isn't a clear square inch of space anywhere on the floor.

"This is the way Miss Paloma likes it," says Maria. Maria hasn't touched this room since Paloma accused her of stealing a pair of sapphire earrings, which were eventually found under half a donut and a bra. "I would have cleaned for you, but Mr. Jack said to leave it so you understand more Miss Paloma."

There are limits to how far Oona is willing to go to understand Paloma, and not being able to see the carpet is one of them. Even working together, it is early evening before the bedroom is finally in order. Jack Silk has called several times to see how things are going. Neither Mrs. nor Mr. Minnick is back yet. Maria goes to the kitchen to start fixing supper while Oona takes Harriet for a walk around their new neighborhood. "Watch out for coyotes," warns Maria. "They like to eat little dogs."

Oona talks to her father while they walk. She tells him about the house and Paloma's room and Maria and Mrs. Minnick's gold phone ("like whoever she calls is going to know it's not plastic like everybody else's"), but doesn't mention coyotes. He's worried that the house may be too cold. Too much air-conditioning isn't good for you. And what about the food? Are they feeding her enough?

And the Minnicks? What are they like? Oona says she hasn't met Mr. Minnick yet.

"So you're settling in OK there," says Abbot.

Oona says she's fine. "And how about you, Dad? You all right?"

Abbot says that he's fine, too.

They're both lying.

When the Minnicks still haven't returned by eight, Oona, Maria, and Harriet eat supper on the terrace.

"This is all pretty weird, isn't it?" asks Oona as the night slowly gathers around them. "You know, me pretending to be Paloma Rose."

Maria has survived so long with the Minnicks because she sees nothing, hears nothing, thinks nothing, and says nothing. But now she nods. "Yes," she agrees. "It is very weird."

"I don't think I'll ever get used to having somebody else's name," says Oona.

"You will," says Maria. *She* did. "I don't think that's your biggest problem."

"You think I'm not going to be able to do it, right? You think I'll break my neck trying to walk in heels or something."

This, in fact, is not what Maria thinks. It's her opinion that Oona's biggest problem is called Leone Minnick.

"No, it's not that." She shrugs noncommittally. "I think there are things here that are more difficult than shoes."

They clean up the dishes and then watch the first of what will be far too many episodes of *Angel in the House*, Maria explaining who everyone in the cast is but not mentioning how they all dislike Paloma and how she dislikes them. At eleven, it having been a long day for everyone, Harriet takes a last run in the backyard, and then Oona helps Maria lock up the house for the night. The Minnicks have not yet returned.

We all know how hard it can be to fall asleep in a strange place. You toss and turn, turn and toss. The pillows aren't right, the mattress isn't right, the night sounds are all wrong. This is especially true, of course, if you're taking over someone else's life. Or you're homesick. Or you think you've made an atomic-bomb kind of mistake. Or you're worried about your father. Or because every time you close your eyes you see your dead mother's face. *Mom . . . Mom . . . Mom . . .* Because as much as Oona misses her father tonight — the sight of him anchored in front of the TV, fearful and unhappy, the one certain thing in an uncertain world — she misses her mother more. Oona can see her so clearly she can smell her, feel her hair against her cheek as she tucks her into bed. She was nothing like Leone Minnick.

To keep away the anxiety monsters that come out in the night, Oona sits in the dark, watching another episode of *Angel in the House* on Paloma's iPad with the headset on, Harriet snoring gently beside her. She is so completely absorbed — not in the show but in watching Paloma and trying to commit her to memory — that it isn't until the credits start to roll that she looks up from the screen. A face is pressed against the window that leads onto the balcony.

Oona screams and jumps up, brandishing the iPad like a weapon. Her sudden movement wakes Harriet, who sees the face immediately and, barking as ferociously as a German shepherd, launches herself at the window. The intruder is so surprised that he throws himself off the balcony. Oona's scream also summons Maria, who comes charging down from the top floor, a revolver in one hand.

Harriet is still barking and Oona is standing by the foot of the bed, holding the iPad shield-like against her. "There was someone there," says Oona, pointing. "I think he jumped."

Perhaps because this kind of thing has happened before, Maria marches calmly over to the window and peers out.

"Stay here," she orders. "I'll be right back."

She's gone only a few minutes — just long enough to

turn off the alarm system—and when she returns she snaps on the track of spotlights that spans the ceiling, goes back to the window, and opens it wide. "He didn't jump," she says as she reaches out and starts heaving a body over the sill. "He passed out."

Oona and Harriet stand beside Maria, looking down at the man on the floor. He looks as if he once was handsome, before he put on a little too much weight and lost a little too much hair and drank a little too much gin. His once-white suit is stained with quite a variety of things, his chartreuse silk tie is tied around his head, and he isn't wearing shoes.

"Should we call the cops?" asks Oona.

"No, no. No police. He must have lost his keys again."

Oona looks at her, almost afraid to ask the next question. "You know who that is?"

"*Sí.*" Maria nods. "That is Mr. Minnick."

Daddy.

Meanwhile, far from the glitz and glamour of Hollywood, Paloma Rose also considers the possibility that she has made a mistake

It was Jack Silk's idea that Paloma travel incognito.

"In what?" asked Paloma. "Is that some kind of plane?"

"No, no, sweetheart." Barely touching her, he gave her a quick hug. And explained that incognito meant in disguise. So no one would be able to trace where she went. So she can have the stress-free, press-free vacation she so deserves. "It's bad enough they seem to be camped outside your door right now. We don't want those newspaper vultures finding you, do we?" Jack laughed. "Frighten the horses."

Leone dyed Paloma's hair back to its natural color—a shade of brown usually associated with small rodents. Jack took away the contacts that make her eyes that remarkable shade of blue, so that they are now a color associated with the sky over a large city. Normally, of course, Paloma would dress up to get the mail out of the box at the bottom of the driveway (should some unforeseen catastrophe happen to force her to do that), but Jack persuaded her to wear ordinary jeans, an ordinary T-shirt, ordinary sandals, drugstore sunglasses, a generic handbag, and an imitation Panama hat (all of them, like her new luggage, bought by him in a popular chain store) so that she looks like every other ordinary kid in the country. He swapped her phone for a lesser, pay-as-you-go model, so that if it falls into the wrong hands no one will know that it's hers. He booked her an economy-fare ticket under her real name, Susan Minnick. He had her ride in the trunk until they were safely past the photographers and reporters waiting outside the driveway like a pack of hunting wolves waiting for a stray sheep to wander into view.

It isn't until she is checking in that Paloma realizes she somehow left her iPad behind. "You can buy a new one when you get there," says Jack. "I told you, they'll have everything you could possibly want or need."

And so it is that Paloma, looking like an extremely ordinary teenager going on vacation, sits toward the rear of the plane, sandwiched between a middle-aged woman with dry skin and the dress sense of a leopard and a sweaty young man with terminal dandruff and large pores. Paloma has never flown anything but first class before, and within five minutes knows that she never plans to travel anything but first class again. Why would anyone choose not to? The seats in economy are so cramped and narrow it's like sitting in a box. Except that, if she were sitting in a box, she wouldn't touch her fellow travelers every time she breathes or feel the person in front of her pressed against her knees.

Space is not the only problem. Paloma has always enjoyed the meals in first class, but in economy you not only have to pay but the food is so awful that she hands back her tray untouched with the information that she'd rather starve. Even the cabin crew, whom Paloma has always found to be so charming and solicitous, is surly and snappy the closer you get to the tail of the aircraft. They wouldn't help you if you collapsed in the aisle; they'd just kick you out of the way. Not only have they stopped answering Paloma's calls, whizzing by her like robots on wheels, but when Paloma ventures into the first-class cabin just to see if anyone else there is going to the dude ranch, the flight attendant whose roots need touching up shoos Paloma back behind the curtain as if she's a stray dog with fleas. The only good thing about the flight is that it doesn't take twenty-four hours. Even if it feels as if it does.

Paloma isn't used to having time to think. Her days

are usually as scheduled as a railroad, from the moment she gets up to the moment she goes to bed. If Leone isn't telling her what to do, it's her voice coach, or tutor, or trainer, or a producer, or the director, or the sponsor. Rehearse, practice, work, sleep . . . rehearse, practice, work, sleep . . . day after day, year after year. And, as we know, when Paloma does have some free time, she doesn't spend it trying to disprove Einstein's theory of relativity.

Which means that now, packed into her seat like toothpaste in a tube, might be the perfect opportunity for her to do some serious thinking. She could ponder the rather remarkable coincidence of her nearly getting arrested and the shooting of the new season of *Angel in the House* being postponed. She might consider why there's been nothing on the news or the Internet about Audrey Hepplewhite's tragic accident. She might wonder why she's being sent to a dude ranch when the only horse she's ever been on was part of a merry-go-round.

But Paloma doesn't think about any of these things. Instead, she uses her new credit card again to buy a headset and watches a mediocre movie whose name and plot she forgets even before it's over, and thinks about how happy she'll be when she finally gets to her hotel. First, because her skin feels funny from rubbing against the fake silk of her neighbor's blouse and she's worried that some dandruff has fallen on her, she'll take a shower. Once she's done that, since she'll be starving by then, she'll order something to eat from room service. Something Leone would never let her have. After that she'll go down to the spa for a massage. Then she'll go out to the pool—there's bound to be a lot of people hanging around the pool. Paloma's deciding what she'll have for supper (Lobster? Steak? Sushi?) when the seat-belt sign goes on and the captain announces that they're starting to descend.

Paloma doesn't run anywhere unless it's in the script, but she's so happy to get off the plane, and so eager to start her temporary new life, that she walks extremely quickly to the baggage area. Her luggage—two large wheeled cases in what would be a zebra print, if zebras were pink and white and made in a laboratory, and a large makeup case—is last to come out on the belt. Of course. God isn't doing her any favors today. At least she has her iPod, or they might find her body hours from now, going around and around on the carousel; death by boredom.

Pushing a baggage cart, Paloma finally comes into the arrival hall. She's mentally composing the tweet she'll be sending the world about the hardships of economy travel (*mail yourself instead!!!*). She comes to a stop, smiling her magazine-cover smile and looking around. Paloma's expecting to see a group of celebrity teens gathered around someone who is holding a sign that says DUDE RANCH and worrying about what happened to her. Because Paloma was once a special guest on a cruise where many of the staff wore mouse ears, she assumes that this someone will be wearing a cowboy hat and a bolo tie. But there is no sign saying DUDE RANCH, no one wearing a cowboy hat and a bolo tie, and no one worried that it's taken her nearly an hour to disembark. There isn't even a driver holding up a rectangle of cardboard with SUSAN written on it. Paloma, still looking around expectantly, crosses to the doors, hoping to see a minibus emblazoned with the words DUDE RANCH waiting at the curb.

It's so hot outside that everything looks slightly blurred. There are several cars and cabs picking up people, but there is nothing that looks like it comes from a celebrity retreat. Paloma is still squinting into the mirage-like distance when an aged pickup suddenly shudders to a stop almost in front of her. Paloma considers any vehicle more than two years old a piece of ancient history, and doesn't actually see the truck. The passenger door swings open and someone starts calling, "Susie! Susie!"

In Paloma's world, everyone else is part of the crowd scene, and she is the only one center stage. Which means that she isn't aware of the truck or the open door, and she doesn't hear anyone shouting because she is listening to one of her favorite songs and half singing along. And then someone suddenly grabs the handle of one of her cases. Paloma isn't a girl overburdened with ideals or principles. If the age-old fight against tyranny and oppression depended on people like Paloma, we'd all still be serfs and slaves. But the streets of Miami will be under six feet of snow before she lets anyone steal her clothes and matching accessories. She automatically swings back her arm to wallop the thief with her handbag, which weighs as much as a loaded AK-47. She misses.

"Whoa there, Susie! What are you doing?"

Because one of her earbuds has fallen out, this time she does hear him. Paloma blinks in surprise. In front of her is a middle-aged man, bearded and gray haired, dressed in filthy jeans and an equally dirty T-shirt. His eyebrows need shaping. No cowboy hat, but he is wearing a bandanna. Which is also covered with the dust of centuries. "What?"

"You're Susan Minnick, aren't you?" It takes Paloma a second or two to remember that she is Susan Minnick and nod. "I'm Ethan. Ethan Lovejoy. From Old Ways."

Paloma's never been told the name of her destination, but he can't mean the celebrity dude ranch, can he?

Wouldn't the driver for a celebrity dude ranch be wearing a uniform, or at least a blazer with the company logo on it? And Ray-Bans? And be clean?

"What?"

"Old Ways." His voice is soft and shapeless but comforting and warm. A purring cat of a voice. As if he spends a lot of time speaking to very young children. "I'm really sorry I'm so late picking you up, Susie, but we had a couple of cows escape, and there wasn't anyone else around to bring them back."

Paloma finally sees the pickup at the curb behind him. Written across the door, in fading letters, is OLD WAYS RANCH.

"Oh, right. Old Ways." Being an actor means pretending to use words and have feelings that aren't yours. Paloma smiles as if she's glad to see him. "Hi." She takes the dry and callused hand he's holding out to her, the nails of which have been cut with a saw, and he pumps hers as if he's expecting to get water from it. A person slightly less self-absorbed and unaccustomed to disappointment than Paloma might now start wondering what's going on. But Paloma, of course, isn't that person. She tells herself that the cows and the pickup and Ethan Lovejoy himself are probably just props; for atmosphere.

Like when the director of *Angel in the House* had that ancient-Egypt party and there was a mummy case in the middle of the garden. There wasn't anybody in the case—it wasn't even made in ancient Egypt; it was made in China—it was just to get everyone in the mood. "Nice to meet you."

"What say we get your things into the truck, and we can be on our way." Ethan gives her a lopsided smile and a wink. "That is, if I'm allowed to touch your case now."

Paloma laughs. "Oh, yeah, of course . . . I just, you know . . . You surprised me."

Which won't be the last time.

She watches him pull one of her bags over to the pickup and throw it into the back as if it's a piece of junk from a discount store, causing a small cloud of dust to rise into the air.

Paloma stands there, waiting for him to come back for the rest of her luggage, which is what drivers are supposed to do, but instead he turns and waves her toward him. "Shake a leg there, Susie. Grab those bags. We want to get a move on. There's a lot to do to get you settled in before supper."

Maybe he's not the real driver. Maybe the real driver, who knows what his job is and how to do it, was trampled by a runaway cow, and Ethan's just taking his place for the day. Probably he's the janitor. Or the guy who takes care of the livestock.

"Right," says Paloma, and she yanks her bags from the cart. Just walking the few feet to the curb in this heat makes her tired. "I'm really pretty wiped out," she says as he dumps the rest of her luggage into the flatbed. "I mean, I had this really gruesome flight. It was so cramped my feet went numb and the food was disgusting and the man next to me smelled and—" She breaks off when she realizes that there's no one there and she's talking to the back of the truck.

"Climb on in!" calls Ethan from inside the pickup. "Let's get this show on the road. It's a little bit of a drive."

The drive takes over an hour and a half. Ethan Lovejoy's idea of air-conditioning is to keep the windows open, which means that though the air is still hot it's moving, and dust and insects fill the cab. For the first thirty minutes or so they ride on a paved road, and he yammers on in his monotonous but soothing voice about how the cows got out and why it was up to him to get them back and about campouts and meteor showers and the county fair, but since, as topics of conversation go, these are as interesting to Paloma as instructions on how to wire a lamp, she isn't really listening. She's watching the buildings become fewer and fewer, and the number of cars they pass become fewer and fewer, and noticing how enormous and endless the sky suddenly seems. But she still isn't worried that this may not be the vacation she expected. That's why she's come, isn't it? So no reporters or photographers or fans could ever find her. The FBI would have a hard time finding her out here.

And then they leave the road for a dirt trail. The truck rattles like a can full of bones tied to the back of a bucking horse, and her luggage bounces up and down in the flatbed, and the dust drifts through the windows in clouds. Ethan Lovejoy stops talking, partly because he is concentrating on navigating the treacherous holes and stones that have replaced the asphalt, and partly because the racket of the pickup makes conversation a challenge. This silence is the one part of the drive that Paloma doesn't mind; she's never really liked making small talk with the help.

Paloma loses herself in her own thoughts, which, though not as gloomy as they will become, are not as pleasant as they could be. This is because of the episode of *Angel in the House* in which Faith Cross is sent to a wagon train crossing the Great Plains during the gold rush. The episode was shot on location in Wyoming or Kansas or South Dakota — some place where a gas station and a general store are considered a town. The cast all had air-conditioned trailers, of course, and no one expected Paloma to ride thousands of miles in a covered wagon, but a certain amount of wagon riding was involved, and the pickup is reminding her just how unpleasant that was. Paloma is used to expensive cars with comfortable seats and good suspension, neither of which the pickup has. A certain amount of walking, poisonous snakes, wolves, buzzards, coyotes, lizards, outlaws, and American Indians were also involved in the story, as it was in the lives of the real settlers—all of which made Paloma extremely grateful that she was born way too late to have the misfortune of being a pioneer. She'd rather live in a cardboard box under an overpass. Because Paloma has had a lot of trouble with her own car, which must be at least twenty years younger than the truck, she starts wondering what will happen if they break down. It seems there is a distinct possibility of encountering things like outlaws, wolves, poisonous snakes, and miles of walking under a cancerous sun.

It's as she's discovering that her phone has no signal (and that if the truck breaks down they'll probably die out here and be eaten by wolves like the parents of the orphans in the *Angel in the House* story) that Ethan shouts to be heard above the racket of the truck, "You've never been out to these parts before, have you, Susie? What do you think of God's country?"

What Paloma thinks is that God can have it, but what she yells back, her smile bright as the relentless sun, is, "Oh, it's really beautiful. Like a postcard." Professional even in times of distress. She could win an Emmy.

"Wait'll you spend a night out under the stars," hollers Ethan. "It's a truly religious experience."

Since he can't possibly mean sleeping on the ground out here in the exact middle of nowhere surrounded by wild animals, he must mean that the rooms have skylights or terraces furnished with beds, like that hotel Paloma and Leone stayed at in the Caribbean. Paloma continues to beam. "Wow, that sounds severely awesome."

Ethan Lovejoy nods enthusiastically, but his ardent words are lost as they hit some kind of crater and the hood pops up.

Long past the point where if the FBI teamed up with Army Intelligence, the CIA, Interpol, MI5, and Sherlock Holmes they still wouldn't be able to find Paloma, she finally sees something in the distance that God didn't put there: a high, barbed-wire fence and a sign over the entrance saying OLD WAYS RANCH. And way behind it, hunkered down among the trees and hills like sentries, a dark sprawl of buildings.

Paloma was starting to nod off, but now she sits up, thinking of showers and swimming pools and cold drinks and a dance club.

Ethan looks over at her as they come to a stop. "You wanna do the honors, Susie?"

"Honors?"

He points a finger rough as bark. "Open the gate."

Paloma is not, of course, the kind of girl who opens gates—the gate at home opens by remote—but she is so relieved to have finally arrived somewhere that she jumps out of the truck without a word of protest.

"No, no," he shouts as she starts to run after him. "You have to shut it again. I don't want to lose any more cows today."

People have a tendency to see what they want to see, even when what they're looking at is the complete opposite of whatever that is. As an example of this phenomenon, although Paloma is looking at the wooden houses and barns of a working ranch in the distance, what she sees is more along the lines of the summer palace of Kublai Khan.

Even when they're so close that it would be obvious to a fish that Old Ways has more in common with a tugboat than with a luxury liner, it isn't until Ethan Lovejoy says, "I'll show you where you're bunking so you can unpack what you need and have a shower if you want," that Paloma finally starts to sense that something is very wrong.

"Bunking?" she repeats.

He swerves the truck around a pool of chickens and laughs. "That's just what we call it. It's not really a bunkhouse. Two to a room and a bath you share with the girls on the other side."

She opens her mouth to explain that she doesn't share anything with anyone, but is so overwhelmed by the enormity of what he seems to be saying that she shuts it again.

"Then you can come on over to the office, and I'll explain how everything works," he goes on. "Get you properly oriented before everybody comes back."

Paloma, unused to having anything explained to her by the hired help, says, "You? Isn't there a . . . you know, like a manager?"

His laugh, as anodyne as his speaking voice, is already getting on her nerves. "Well, that'd be me." Ethan Lovejoy, of course, is not a janitor but the president and chief psychologist of Old Ways. "Dr. Ethan Lovejoy. Founder, owner, and chief honcho. But folks just call me Ethan."

"I don't understand." Paloma has been known to throw a five-alarm tantrum because someone sat in her seat or brought her a latte instead of a cappuccino, but now that something really bad is happening she is eerily calm. "What is this place?"

"We're a working ranch and what's called a wilderness center." Paloma isn't sure what a wilderness center is, but it doesn't sound like it's likely to have a health spa or luxury shops. A stagnant pond, maybe. Maybe a dimly lit store heated by a potbellied stove. A store that only sells beef jerky and bird feed. "Which is just another way of saying we're a good place to stay and chill and take stock of things."

From somewhere very, very far away, Paloma says, "But I was told that this is, like, a ten-star hotel."

"*Ten stars*? Pshaw! Ten stars is nothing!" Ethan Lovejoy doesn't really have a voice, she decides; what he has is a whispery gurgle. The whispery gurgle of some warty creature that lives under a rock. "We have ten million stars out here, Susie. Wait'll you see them. You're going to be really glad you're not in some fancy hotel."

This, of course, is so astoundingly impossible that the only reasonable response would be to laugh out loud.

But Paloma doesn't feel like laughing right now. There's an old saying that she has never heard, and this is it: The scales fell from her eyes. Meaning that she's realized the truth at last.

Or at least some of it.

Paloma doesn't stop to unpack or shower but goes straight to Ethan Lovejoy's office, which is a small room with a large window that looks out on infinity—assuming that infinity is made of sky and sand. There are two chairs, a desk, and a bookshelf. The walls are blue and decorated not with prints or pictures like most walls, but with quotations: *The shame is not in failing but in failing to try. Goals are the fuel in the furnace of achievement. What matters is playing the game, not winning the prize. Today is the first day of the rest of your life. Your worst enemy is the one inside you. The only day you can be sure you have is the one you're in.* It looks more like a room you'd find in the basement of a church than the main building of a working ranch, though Paloma doesn't find either thought comforting.

"Sit down, sit down." Ethan takes the seat behind the desk and waves her to the one across from it. "Take a load off your feet."

Paloma doesn't sit down. "That's OK." She's not planning to be here that long. "I'm afraid a really bad mistake's been made, Ethan. Because I'm not supposed to be here. Like I said, I'm supposed to be at this ten-star hotel."

Mistakes like this do happen. Something very similar occurred in an early episode of *Angel in the House* when two babies are accidentally switched in a hospital because the lights go out for a few minutes. Paloma doesn't think that the lights went out and caused confusion at Paradise Lodge, but she does think that Jack and Leone thought they'd booked her into an exclusive dude ranch, only some underling—probably Jack's loser secretary with the big nose and the chronic split ends—went to the wrong website and signed her up for Old Ways instead. "So if somebody could just give me a ride back to the airport . . ."

Ethan Lovejoy leans back in his chair. "Oh, there hasn't been any mistake, Susie. This is sure as shootin' where you're supposed to be." Old Ways, he explains, is a residential rehabilitation center for problem teenagers. Which seems to be what they think Paloma is, though nobody told *her* that. Its motto is Old Morals, New Change. It promises results, and it gives them.

"But I'm not a problem teenager," protests Paloma. "I'm a TV star."

Ethan Lovejoy's smile glides across his face like a hunting owl glides across the sky. "I think there may be a difference of opinion on that question."

And whose different opinion would that be? Paloma

doesn't need more than one guess to answer that. She should have known. Like Leone would ever send Paloma away by herself to someplace wonderful. If this really were a celebrity dude ranch, Leone would have been in the seat next to her on the plane. And they definitely would have been in first class.

"This is all my mother's doing." Audrey Hepplewhite's accident must have been as big a blow to Leone as it was to Audrey. Instead of being freed from having to keep an eye on Paloma by the long days of shooting the new season, she was stuck with her for a few more weeks. Which would interfere with Leone's lunches and dinners and I-am-so-great networking. As if Leone actually does anything besides spend Paloma's money.

"I talked to both your parents, Susie." This, as it happens, isn't strictly true. Ethan Lovejoy thinks he did, but in reality he talked to Leone (very briefly) and Jack Silk taking the role of Arthur Minnick (quite a lot). No one likes to burden Arthur with too much information. "We had a very long conversation about you and about Old Ways. It was a decision made by both of them, with my agreement. In the end, they decided that sending you here was the best thing they could do."

This? This was the best they could do? What, were all the high-security prisons in the world filled up?

"Maybe you all should've asked me what *I* thought," says Paloma in the flat, tight way that Ethan Lovejoy will soon recognize as the calm before the really bad tornado.

"Let me just ask you something, Susie." Ethan's voice is as comforting as a fire on a snowy night. "If your folks had been one hundred percent honest with you, would you have come?"

Does she look stupid?

"But it's *my* life! They don't know what's best for me. And neither do you. I do!"

"Not necessarily." Ethan Lovejoy points to a quotation on the wall to his right: *O would some power the gift give us to see ourselves as others see us.*

Paloma's lips squeeze together very tightly, as if she's about to spit out a dart. "And?"

"It means that we're not always the best judges of what's good for us and what isn't."

"That doesn't mean somebody else is. You don't know my mother. She may've been all sweet and concerned when you talked to her, but she'd do anything to make me unhappy."

"I think you're very wrong about that, Susie." Ethan shakes his head. The world, his shaking head says, is a world of sorrow and misunderstanding, and the misunderstanding makes everything worse. "Your parents would do anything in their power to make you happy. What they've had to do this time is called tough love. And believe you me, it's a hard thing to have to do, even if it's the only way. They wrestled with their hearts and asked for guidance before they made this decision. And I give you my word that it saddened them greatly not to level with you, but it would make them so much sadder if you wasted this precious life that's been given to you and didn't grow into the wonderful woman they know you can and want you to be." He has been holding his palms together, but now he opens them as though letting out a secret. "You can't make an omelet if you don't break some eggs."

"I don't want to make an omelet," says Paloma.

"But you do want to have a wonderful life, don't you? And that's what your parents want. Only a wonderful life doesn't come without some sacrifices."

It doesn't escape Paloma's notice that she's the one making the sacrifices.

"Old Ways isn't a place of hardship," says Ethan. "It's a place of genuine opportunity and genuine change." He points to another sign on the wall behind him, the one about today being the first day of the rest of your life. "Though, naturally, we do have some ground rules." And he goes on to explain the basic system that governs life at Old Ways Ranch. If you could call it life. If you could call them rules and not weapons of torture. No phones. No personal computers. No iPods. No communication with the outside world, though parents, of course, are kept informed of their child's progress.

"What?" interrupts Paloma. "No communication?" Apparently outer space isn't the only place where no one can hear you scream. "Isn't that illegal?"

Ignoring questions of legality, Ethan Lovejoy says, "We find it makes the transition easier." Though he doesn't say for whom. "However, we do encourage families to write weekly postcards. To reassure you that they're thinking of you."

Not as much as she'll be thinking of them.

The list of delights at the ranch continues. Up at six a.m., in your room by nine-thirty, lights go out automatically at eleven. Besides classes and therapy sessions and special activities (both individual and group), everyone is expected to take part in the everyday workings of the ranch—caring for the horses and cattle, cooking, cleaning communal spaces, that kind of thing. Not that life here is all about work. They have fun, too. Hikes. Horseback rides. There are board games, cards, dominoes, Ping-Pong, a pool table, and a fifty-five-inch wide-screen

TV in the common room. They have a library. They have campfire nights when they all sing songs and tell stories — camping up in the hills and sleeping under the bejeweled night sky, more beautiful than anything made by Tiffany. Team games. Dances. They even have an annual rodeo — but no bucking broncos or steer wrestling, of course.

Well, now, isn't that good news! Paloma was a little worried she might be expected to ride a bull.

It takes a few seconds for the state of shock brought on by all the images of trekking up mountains and sleeping on the ground with coyotes slobbering over her to pass, but pass it does. "Are you serious?" Paloma's laugh comes out more as a screech. "You think *I'm* going to do any of that crap? What do I look like? A Boy Scout?" Now there is no sign of the wonderful woman the Minnicks know Paloma can be. "You have got to be kidding. I mean, you really have got to be kidding." How can anyone be expected to live without the Internet? Without her phone? How can *she* be expected to cook? Cook what? And what the hell is she supposed to do with a horse?

In his already-too-familiar talking-to-celestial-beings voice, Ethan says, "I wouldn't joke about something as important as your life, Susie. Life is the most precious thing we have. I'm totally serious."

"But this is supposed to be my vacation!" wails Paloma. "I'm supposed to be having the time of my life!"

"And that's exactly what you shall have," Ethan Lovejoy promises her. He's so calm and unruffled you wouldn't think Paloma was red with rage and screaming loudly enough to be heard back at the airport. "The time of your life. You'll never be the same again."

"No, I mean time of my life like in fun. F-U-N. You better think again if you think I'm staying here. On a freakin' farm!" Paloma looks around for something to throw, but Ethan Lovejoy's office is as unadorned and neat as an operating room. There isn't anything on the desk—no lamp, no paperweight, no pictures of his family, not so much as a Post-it note. Paloma isn't the first teenager who has stood in this office and wanted to throw something. "Because I'd rather have leprosy than stay here for more than five minutes. I'm going home!"

"I'm afraid that's impossible, Susie. You'll be here for at least three months. Possibly longer. Six months. Nine. It all depends on you and your personal growth." His smile is intended to be encouraging, but that isn't, of course, how Paloma takes it. To her it is the smile of a sadist enjoying someone else's pain.

"You have to be mental!" Having nothing to throw, she waves her hands in the air. "Completely, totally, and two-hundred-percent out of your microscopically tiny mind!"

"I think it's time for you to calm down," says Ethan Lovejoy. "Nothing's achieved by tantrums."

Which can be considered a point of disagreement between them.

"*You* calm down!" screams Paloma, though if Ethan Lovejoy calms down any more he'll be mistaken for dead. "If I want to have a tantrum, I'll have a tantrum. You're not my boss. And you can't make me stay here. I know my rights. That's kidnapping. And that's a crime!"

Ethan Lovejoy leans back in his chair. "I think you'll find, Susie, that I can make you stay. You are a minor, and I have a signed consent form and agreement from your parents."

"But I can't stay here three months!" Paloma kicks the desk. "Don't you know who I am?"

"Of course I know who you are. You're Susan Minnick." Which is all he does know. The only mentions of TV and star that Ethan Lovejoy has heard have been in connection with Susan's habit of making up stories about herself, otherwise known as telling lies. Living in a fantasy. Refusing to accept reality. The world of espionage lost a lot when Jack Silk decided to become a Hollywood agent.

"No, I'm Paloma Rose! I'm famous. I'm really, really famous. I'm the star of one of the most popular shows in the history of television."

"I'm sure you believe that, Susie," soothes Ethan Lovejoy, "but that kind of thing doesn't matter to us here. We care about inner worth, not material success."

"Of course I believe it!" shouts Paloma. "It's true! And if you don't drive me back to the airport right now, when I get out of this dump I'm going to tell everybody what you do here. How you kidnap young girls. And hold them prisoner. And molest them. And make them work as slaves." As Paloma kicks and sobs, the words tumble out, inspired by fury and an episode of last season's *Angel in the House*. "And don't think I won't, because I will. I'm on Facebook and Twitter, you know. I have a website. I have a publicist. And I—" Paloma stops abruptly, not because she has run out of either words or accusations but because she finally realizes that she's all alone.

Miracles happen every day

Jack Silk said that the first week was going to be the hardest—so much to learn, so much to get used to, so much to remember—which Oona will later realize is one of the rare times he told her the unadulterated truth.

Both the Minnicks are still in bed when Oona comes down for breakfast the next morning.

Leone, however, has left an itinerary of what she and Maria are supposed to do today to turn the rather ordinary, brown-eyed, dark-haired, five-foot-five-and-a-fraction-or-two Oona into a head-turning, five-foot-six-inch blond with startling blue eyes.

"We go in my car," says Maria. "Mrs. Minnick says it is less conspicuous."

This isn't really true. Maria's car may be less conspicuous than an elephant would be navigating the traffic of Los Angeles, but it is not less conspicuous than the Minnicks' Cadillac, Camaro, or Mercedes. In general, however, Hollywood stars do not ride around in ancient, battle-scarred Volkswagens with a plastic image of the Virgin of Guadalupe hanging from the rearview mirror on a chain of plastic beads, and Paloma Rose has never been an exception to that rule. What Leone means by "less conspicuous" is that even if Oona is spotted in Maria's car no one will believe she is Paloma. Not even the vultures strutting and stretching their wings outside Paradise Lodge's gate are likely to give the Beetle a second look.

The first thing on Leone's itinerary is to go shopping: clothes, shoes, and accessories.

Oona reads off the list of stores. She's heard of one or two, but most are so exclusive they might as well be secret societies. "You know these places?" she asks as the little car struggles up a hill.

"Not personally," says Maria, "but I can find them."

Leone, however, is on intimate terms with all of these stores and has phoned ahead to say that her niece is visiting from Arkansas and will be coming in to "pick up a few things." Maria has been told to park out of sight.

Oona buys her clothes in discount chains or thrift stores. Neither she nor Maria has ever been in a designer's shop or high-end boutique before, and for a few minutes, while they hover outside the first one on Leone's list, it looks as though they never will. And then the door opens and a woman who looks like a movie star playing a diplomat's wife opens the door and says, "Ms. Ginness? Maria? Please come right in."

Oona has never had another person pay so much attention to her body and what she puts on it before. Heads shake, lips purse, and eyes narrow. She is scrutinized, measured, and advised. Does she want something for morning, afternoon, or evening? Does she want something elegant or casual; for work or for leisure; to socialize with associates or to socialize with friends? It seems that these aren't clothes that she's trying on but personal statements. "What is it you want to say?" the salespeople ask her. "What do you want to project?"

By the time they move on to shoes, Oona feels as if she hasn't been shopping but interviewing for an important scholarship that she's guaranteed not to get.

"It is much easier to be poor," says Maria.

Buying shoes that Paloma would wear, but in the slightly smaller size that fits Oona, is only marginally less stressful and demanding.

The shoe shops are more like first-class airport lounges—places Oona has only seen in movies—than the stores where Oona buys her shoes. No aisles of shelves arranged by size. No tables of bargains. No tissue paper or box lids scattered over the floors like autumn leaves on a country lane.

She has also never worn heels before. Aware of the need to balance herself for the first time since she learned to walk, Oona, steady as a giraffe on a pitching ship, staggers across the tasteful carpets (no linoleum here, either). Maria is ready to catch her.

Oona was right to worry about walking in high heels. She only manages not to fall or crash into a wall by taking small steps slowly enough to make it feel as if time has stopped. "What happens if you need to run away from somebody who's trying to mug you?" she whispers to Maria.

"You take them off," Maria whispers back. "Then you can run."

The prices, however, could make a goldfish run on stilts. "Five hundred dollars? Five hundred dollars for a pair of shoes?"

"Wait'll you see what the bags cost," says Maria.

The next stop is the optician's, to pick up the lenses tinted the same color as Paloma's: a clear and delicate blue not unlike the waters of the Gulf of Mexico eight or so hundred years ago. Wearing contacts is another new experience. They make Oona cry.

"I think my eyes may be permanently damaged," she says as she dabs at the tears with Maria's handkerchief.

"You'll get used to them," comforts Maria. "Most people do."

Oona sighs. "Only because you can get used to anything."

Which she can only hope includes the Minnicks.

Their last port of call is the hairdresser's — another first for Oona. Her mom always cut her hair, and when illness put a stop to that Oona started cutting it herself. Paloma, needless to say, has her hair done in an exclusive salon by a sought-after stylist who charges two hundred dollars for a trim. But going anywhere like that is, of course, out of the question. It was left to Maria to choose somewhere not part of the Hollywood scene, a task at which she's definitely succeeded.

Unlike everywhere else they've been, this hairdresser is the kind of place that no celebrity would put so much as a toe in unless her car broke down in a hurricane and it was the only building for fifty miles that hadn't nailed its doors shut. The women who work here wear pink smocks and (for reasons that will never be explained) bedroom slippers, and aren't stylists but hairdressers. It's called, appropriately enough, Angel's Hair, and is decorated with Day of the Dead images. *Rancheras* play in the background, and an enormous black cat sleeps beside an elaborately sequined if faded black sombrero in the window. At least they like animals. Angel is the proprietor, Angelina Velas, a large and vivid woman as quick as machine-gun fire. "I feel like an explorer who's discovered a new continent," she says, assessing Oona with a professional eye. "Lucky for you I love a challenge." She shows Oona to a chair.

Oona has her hair washed. She has it cut. She has the color taken out of it like bark being stripped from a tree. She has a different color put in. She has the strands twisted into gentle waves. It's like some kind of medieval torture. She's sure her scalp must be bleeding.

"I know they are very good," Maria assures her. "My nephew's girlfriend and her sister come here all the time."

When she's done, Angelina stands behind Oona's chair as she stares at her new self in the mirror. "What do you think?"

"I look so different." She looks like Paloma Rose. It's kind of frightening. "I wouldn't recognize myself if I didn't know it was me."

Angelina steps around her for a closer look. "You know who you remind me of?" she says. "That girl on the TV. Justina, doesn't she remind you of that girl on the TV?"

Justina waves a pair of scissors in the air. Thoughtfully. "Which one?"

"You know," encourages Angelina, "the one who's an angel."

"You think?" Maria appears beside Angelina, looking at Oona as if she's never seen her before. "I don't know . . ." She shakes her head. "I think that girl's much taller."

Oona isn't the only one having a day of firsts. Leone is actually waiting for them when they return. She appears at the front door even before Oona—wearing one of her new outfits and a new pair of shoes with lifts, her hair blond and her eyes blue—gets out of the car. Leone stands at the top of the steps, arms folded and eyes narrowed like a general inspecting her troops. "Close," says Leone. "Very, very close." She takes a step back and shakes her head. "Now all we have to do is work on the little details."

But doesn't add that the Devil, as the saying goes, is in those little details.

It isn't long before Oona establishes a routine of sorts. She gets up early to take Harriet for her long morning walk. It's too early for there to be anyone lingering by the main entrance, but, just to be sure, they go out the back way and take a circuitous route, coming out to one side of someone else's property on a dead-end street several roads below the Minnicks'. Oona always calls her father as soon as they're out of the house. Last thing at night she and Harriet take another long walk, and she talks to her father again. These are the best times of the day for her. Peaceful. Pleasant. They haven't met any coyotes yet, but they've met quite a few dogs and their owners, as well as cats and cat owners and a man who has an iguana in his backyard. It's a surprisingly friendly neighborhood, but this, of course, may be because everyone loves Harriet. People say hello or stop to talk. By day three Oona knows several names. Ben and Bill the beagle. Lara and Pixie the Great Dane. Jason and Lilly the dachshund. Moira and Orwell the German shepherd. Mr. Jeffers and Comandante the iguana. Mrs. Mackinpaw and her cat Sunshine. Oona has twice gotten Sunshine out of a tree. In between these highlights, Oona spends all her time mastering the details of being Paloma Rose. Which is neither pleasant nor peaceful.

"Nonono!" It's been a long afternoon in what is turning out to be a preternaturally long week. If patience were gas, Leone would be lucky to make it around the block right now. "Go back to the door and try it again, sweetie." She smiles like a doll. "We're aiming to imitate poetry in motion, not a bulldozer."

Oona sits down suddenly. If you ask her, she might

as well be in boot camp. Do this. Do that. Don't do that. Don't do this. When she closes her eyes at night, she hears Leone's sweet-as-saccharin voice repeating *Nonono* and sees her winter-in-the-Arctic smile. She's never known anyone so easily dissatisfied. Leone never lets up. No wonder Paloma threw an egg at her; what's amazing is that she didn't throw the plate, too. Even when Oona does something right, Leone wants it done better. Oona can't wait till she has everything down and Master Sergeant Minnick finally leaves her alone; Maria said not to get her hopes up. Leone never leaves Paloma alone; why should she leave Oona alone?

When she's about to be totally contrary, Oona sucks in her bottom lip and pulls her eyebrows together. She's doing that now. "I'm taking a break." This is an announcement, not a request.

Snow and icy winds fall over the North Pole. "You had a break twenty-eight minutes ago."

"Well, now I'm having another one."

Leone crosses her arms in front of her. "You're not trying hard enough, sweetie. How are you going to be ready in time if you don't try?"

"I am trying." Oona crosses her legs. "But what you don't seem to understand is that you're working against the law of diminishing returns here."

Leone taps her foot. A different kind of animal would be pawing the ground. "The law of what?"

"Diminishing returns," says Oona. "We've gone way past the point where me doing it again and again is going to make it any better. It's just going to keep getting worse." Oona's been walking from the front door to the middle of the living room for nearly two hours. So now she has a good idea what it's like to live in a cage.

"It'll get better if you want it to get better." Leone is not only a woman who possesses the single-mindedness and determination of the fanatic, she is also unrealistically stubborn. "Let's try it again. And this time concentrate on being poetry in motion, not a clodhopper in muddy boots, OK?"

Oona's brow is still furrowed, but she stands up. "I'm not a ballet dancer, you know. I just want to get from one place to another. That's what walking is, Mrs. Min—"

"Mom." Just because someone smiles at you doesn't mean she likes you, a fact both Leone and Oona are very well aware of by now. "Please try to remember that, darling. It is important."

"That's what walking is, *Mom*. Getting from one place to another. Not shoving poems around the room."

Leone sighs. "But one can walk gracefully, *darling*." Paloma's main weapons are shouting, screaming, and throwing the tantrum of a three-year-old—though usually without the lying-on-the-floor, kicking-her-feet part. Oona's weapon of choice, however, is debate. You can't tell her anything that she doesn't question or want a fuller explanation of. She's not very good at taking orders. Everything is, *Why?* Or, *How come?* Or, *But that doesn't make sense.* If you gave her instructions on how to cross to the other side of the street, she'd either ask for a second opinion or try to convince you that she should stay where she is. Jack told Leone that Oona wants to be some kind of doctor and has a scientific, inquiring mind—not a charge you can lay on Paloma—but Leone thinks she's a natural troublemaker. You can tell. She sounds sarcastic just saying hello. And she is certainly a lot of trouble to Leone. "Think gazelle, not moose."

"Right. Gazelle, not moose." But Oona isn't thinking gazelle or moose. She's thinking charging rhino.

Oona recently read *The Metamorphosis* by Franz Kafka, in which a man turns into a giant insect. Mr. Kafka made becoming someone—or something—else seem relatively uncomplicated. In his story the metamorphosis happens overnight. Gregor Samsa goes to sleep a salesman and wakes up a bug. But changing from Oona Ginness to Paloma Rose is about much more than changing the way Oona looks. As Leone said, gazing at a photo of dear Paloma with a tenderness her only child wouldn't recognize, "Looking like dear Paloma's one thing. *Being* her is something else."

It'd be easier to be a bug.

Besides the hands-on life coaching from Leone, Oona spends what feels like the equivalent of at least twenty years in solitary watching DVDs and home videos of Paloma. She learns not just the timbres and inflections of her voice — from the little-girl wheedling tone, to the sweet and helpless one, to the contemptuous drawl, to the sour snarl in which she usually speaks to her mother — but the gestures and expressions that go with them. The face Paloma makes when she's being praised; the one she makes when she wants something; the way she looks when she's about to throw a fried egg. Her habits of fiddling with her earring when she's nervous, pulling at her hair when she's thinking, tapping her fingertips together when she's in a really bad mood, lighting matches when she's bored.

Maria and Jack Silk act as special advisers.

"Paloma can't fix herself a bowl of cereal," says Maria. She's never used the washing machine, cleared her or anyone else's dishes from the table, picked up after herself, or made herself a sandwich. She might recognize an iron, but she wouldn't know how to use it. Very often she doesn't wear things more than once. Oona thinks she means that Paloma wears things once and then puts them in the wash. Maria means that Paloma wears things once and never wears them again. Which may explain why her only real hobby is shopping. The only person she listens to is Mr. Silk.

"Paloma's not a bad kid," says Jack Silk. "It's just that she hasn't been formally introduced to reality yet." She's a C student at best, and that's when she's making an effort. Which makes it a rarity. She uses her phone to add anything more complicated than 2+2 and hasn't finished a book since she was three and had to have *Goodnight Moon* read to her every bedtime. She could give master classes in tantrums, sulks, and mood swings. "She can be sweeter than tupelo honey, of course," says Jack, "but not on a normal day."

Oona spends another twenty-year stretch practicing Paloma's voice with a CD Jack made. She repeats each sentence into a recorder and then plays it back, as if she's learning a foreign language. Leaving the restaurants and cafés of Hollywood lonely, Leone spends more time at home than she has in the last year—hanging over Oona's shoulder, eyes half-closed in concentration, handing out judgments like a kangaroo court. *Too fast. Too slow. Too loud. Too nasal. For the love of Hosanna, darling, think of your words as glass balls that you're gently setting down on the ground, not bullets you're using to shoot cans off a fence.*

"I feel like I'm being brainwashed," Oona grumbles. "I bet when I'm sleeping I'm still saying over and over in that silly simper, 'Oh, but miracles happen every day.'" "Miracles happen every day" is Faith Cross's catchphrase and, of course, is said sweetly and angelically—as well as very often.

"I sincerely hope so," says Leone. "That is the object of the exercise, you know. To make it all automatic."

And here she was thinking that Leone's purpose is merely to kill her will to live.

"And it's not a silly simper. It's inspirational."

Oona rolls her eyes at the floor. As inspirational as a greeting card.

"Maybe what you really need is an android," suggests Oona. "Then you could program it to be exactly how you want."

If only . . . As far as Leone's concerned, an android would solve every problem she has. The surly, rebellious, never-know-what-she's-going-to-do-next Paloma problem; and the contrary, arguing-about-how-long-a-piece-of-string-is Oona problem. And her dog. Who at this very minute is gazing at Leone the way it does, as if it's waiting for her to die so it can eat her and gnaw on her bones.

"An android wouldn't be all that terrific," says Leone. "Because then I'd have to worry about its battery running out in the middle of a shoot."

But although the walking and talking present difficulties, it's when it comes to thinking like Paloma that the real trouble starts. Except for the remarkable physical resemblance, Oona and Paloma have nothing in common. They don't like the same clothes, the same food, the same music, the same movies, the same colors, the same actors, the same flowers—the same anything. If they had a choice they probably wouldn't breathe the same air. It seems to Leone that Oona couldn't show less enthusiasm for her new life if she were a princess forced to live in a run-down trailer park, and not a lowlife given the incredible chance to live like a princess. She sits through Leone's lessons on applying makeup and styling her hair as if she's being taught how to butcher a cow. She turned all the stuffed animals in Paloma's room to face the wall because she can't stand them staring at her. She has to be forced into a decent pair of shoes or an attractive dress. She doesn't know who half the people Leone talks about are, and when she does recognize a name it's the way Leone might recognize a term she learned in biology in high school—*Amoeba, oh yeah, that sounds familiar.* She has fallen asleep watching *Angel in the House* at least half a dozen times.

How is Leone supposed to relate to her? She hasn't been raised by Leone, and so she is a total mystery—an alien being. The fact that she looks so much like Paloma doesn't make it any better. It's like having a wax likeness of her daughter that can walk and talk. Leone isn't a squeamish woman, but if she were, it would give her the creeps.

"Chocolate or vanilla?" demands Leone.

"Chocolate," says Oona. Hopefully she'll never have to eat any. Chocolate makes her break out.

"Dress or pants?"

"Dress." The last time she voluntarily wore a dress was to her mother's funeral.

"If you had to choose between going to Hawaii and going to France?"

"Hawaii."

Leone marches back and forth like a drill sergeant. One wearing a linen sundress and open-toed shoes. "Why?"

"Because they speak English." Which, says Leone, is more than can be said for a lot of California. "And I love the ukulele." She wouldn't know a ukulele unless it came labeled.

"Favorite color?"

"Pink. Because it's feminine and warm." It makes her think of bubble gum stuck under a desk.

"Movie?"

"*The Wizard of Oz*. Because it's a classic and full of positivism and love." It gives her a headache. Oona's favorite movie is *Blade Runner*.

"Food?"

"My mom's fried chicken and mashed potatoes. Because it always makes me feel better, even if I'm really blue." She has yet to see Leone so much as open a can or microwave a muffin.

"Book?"

"*Little Women*. Because it's a classic and says so much about family values." She hasn't seen a book since she got here.

Leone comes to a stop, swiveling on her heels to face Oona. Here comes the million-dollar question. "And if you're asked what you owe your success to?"

"You mean besides my loving parents, hard work, and faith in myself?" Oona ad-libs. Not without a touch of malice.

"Those things go without saying, sweetie." Leone's

mouth looks as if it's been pulled through a very small hole. "Just stick to the script."

"I owe everything to my fans," Oona parrots, sweeter than a tanker full of kittens and sounding sincere enough to fool the pope.

"That's very good, darling. You're really improving." A satisfied smile falls across Leone's face like a stray ray of sunshine on a muddy pool.

Oona's return smile is not as cheerful. *Big deal.*

Compared to all of this, learning Faith Cross's lines is less difficult than remembering who ordered the BLT without mayo and who ordered it without tomato during a busy lunch hour. Maria helps her rehearse in the evenings when Leone goes out to recuperate from a day spent doing more than eating lunch. If only being Paloma were as easy. "It isn't easy for her, either," says Maria.

And then, just when Oona's starting to feel that death isn't the only thing that's endless, Leone declares her ready for her first public appearance. Jack Silk is taking them to lunch at Paloma's favorite restaurant.

Which puts Leone into übernag mode. She hovers around Oona like an especially stubborn wasp all morning. *Are you wearing that? Why don't you wear this? You want me to do your makeup? You want me to do your hair? You want me to pick out your jewelry? You want me to go over the menu with you? You want to go over what you've been doing with your summer again? Remember, you're not Bill Clinton. Nobody's expecting you to give any big speeches. Just smile and nod and answer in monosyllables.*

"Now, you remember what I taught you about what cutlery to use?" Leone is saying as they walk to the front door together, graceful as a pair of gazelles.

"I remember." Three different knives. Five different forks. Three different spoons. Up until now, Oona has never used more than a fork and a knife — and when they lived in the truck they didn't even have that; they ate everything with their hands out of Styrofoam boxes. She can only hope that she does remember.

"And the glasses." Leone opens the door.

These people don't use just one of anything for some reason.

"And the glasses. And the plates, too," says Oona. God forbid your bread or your salad doesn't have a dish of its own.

"And you remember the difference between the server and the maître d'?"

Jack Silk is waiting in the driveway in his ivory Jaguar. He waves.

Oona waves back. "Yes." One makes more money and is better dressed.

"And don't slouch. Or put your elbows on the table. Or drink like a camel. Or pick your nose."

As if Oona slouches through the house, spitting like a grumpy camel, picking her nose, and banging her elbows down on every table in the place.

The passenger door opens, causing not so much as a nanosecond's pause in Leone's list of disasters to be avoided. "And for God's sake"—Leone's heels sound like the blows of tiny hammers against the concrete drive—"if someone stops to talk to us, don't say anything about riding on the Metro or knowing what a food stamp looks like."

"So I guess I shouldn't mention about living in the truck, then," says Oona.

Leone's smile looks as if it might snap. "I'm going to assume that's a joke."

Jack leans across the seat. "Leone," says Jack, "why don't you sit in the back?"

Leone sits in the back, silent and still as a photograph of a woman who's had days in her life when she was much happier, while in the front seat Jack talks to Oona about dogs. Although this is news to Leone, Jack Silk apparently loves dogs.

Leone, whose interest in dogs is approximately minus one hundred on a scale of one to ten, isn't listening, but thinking of all the things that could go wrong. She hasn't been this nervous since Paloma's audition for *Angel in the House*. Oona, who, of course, is very interested in dogs, isn't listening either. She's nervous, too. Not as nervous as she was the last time her mom said she had something to tell her, but nervous nonetheless. Every night Oona falls asleep imagining her and her dad in a little house with a pickup in the driveway; in a new life. It won't be the same as their old life, but that doesn't mean it won't be good. Oona really wants that money. She's worked too hard to blow it now.

Jack finally interrupts his monologue on Australian cattle dogs to say, "Well, here we are," and he turns right.

"It looks like a warehouse," says Oona.

"The only warehouse in LA that charges ten bucks for a bread roll," says Jack.

In fact, Paloma's favorite restaurant is on the first floor not of a warehouse but of what was once a shirt factory. But the building wasn't pink or its windows tinted sea green back then—and the people who sat inside couldn't afford ten dollars for a bread roll, either.

The parking attendant is delighted to see them. "Afternoon, Mr. Silk." He opens the back door for Leone. "Afternoon, Mrs. Minnick." He runs around the car to open the door for Oona. "Miss Rose."

Somehow, Oona must have slept through Leone's lesson on interacting with parking attendants—a group of people she has never had to deal with before since they don't usually park flatbeds. Should she say good afternoon in a familiar, pally way, as Jack does? Should she nod silently but regally, as Leone does? She smiles. It is a warm and friendly smile, the smile that Faith Cross wears at the beginning and end of every episode of *Angel in the House,* which she's practiced so much it seems to be automatic. And so warm and friendly that the attendant hits himself with the door.

"Don't overdo it, darling," Leone hisses in her ear. "He's unskilled labor, not a pop star in disguise."

The maître d' is also delighted to see them. "Mr. Silk, Mrs. Minnick, Miss Rose," the maître d's voice oozes around them like quicksand. "What a pleasure to see you all. You've been missed." Jack calls him Bernard, Leone murmurs that it's been far too long—and Oona smiles. The maître d' wonders if Miss Rose has done something to her hair; she looks a little different. Leone says yes. Oona says she's been out in the sun. He comments on how well she's looking. Oona thanks him. She also thanks him for showing them to their seats and for pulling out her chair.

Leone kicks her under the table. "These people are

servants," she says through her teeth. "You only have to be polite."

Their waiter is glad to see them, too. "Mrs. Minnick . . . Mr. Silk . . . Miss Rose . . ."

Mrs. Minnick smiles. Mr. Silk says, "Agosto. And what do you recommend today?" Oona, who can't seem to stop smiling no matter how hard she tries, thanks him for giving her a menu.

"They're going to think you've been medicated," whispers Leone from behind her own menu. Paloma Rose has never been known to overuse the "magic" words.

But Oona doesn't hear her. She's thanking the busboy for pouring their water and bringing them the bread basket.

Jack unfurls his napkin. "So far so good."

Leone starts to name all the people they know, bestowing nods and slivers of smiles around the room.

Oona stares down at the offerings of the day. Needless to say, she's never been in a restaurant like this before. Nothing on the menu looks familiar. Which is to say that there is nothing that even remotely resembles a hamburger or pizza.

She orders what Leone orders.

She waits for Jack to pick up a knife to butter his bread before she picks up hers.

She waits for Leone to pick up her soup spoon before she picks up hers.

Oona's never had cold soup before. It's all she can do not to spit it out.

Her main course has eyes.

There appears to be grass in her salad, as well as something that looks a lot like the poop of very small rabbits.

Leone kicks her again when she starts to eat the garnish on her plate, and she knocks over her water.

All of which turns out to be for the best, because these small disasters distract her so much that when the friends and acquaintances of Jack and Leone slither up to their table as they pass, Oona is already so traumatized that she nods and smiles with a preoccupation that seems like calm.

Jack and Leone are pleased. Leone sits in the front going home, and they spend the entire drive congratulating themselves on what a good job they've done. What a clever idea Jack had. What a good teacher Leone is. How hard she worked. How much time she's given.

But when they get back to Paradise Lodge the talk turns to how there's still plenty of room for improvement in Oona.

"She ate like she never used a knife and fork before,"

says Leone as they all collapse in the living room like soldiers after a hair-raising mission.

"I think she may have smiled too much," says Jack. "I'm not saying it didn't get a good response, but if they think about it they'll realize it's a little unusual."

"The smiling's OK," says Leone. "They'll think she's on meds or has a good shrink. But she has to talk more. She was very quiet. I'm sure Ethelda Sansom was giving her funny looks."

"Ethelda gives everybody funny looks," says Jack. "I was a little more concerned that Barnstle wanted to know if she'd lost weight."

"Her napkin kept falling off her lap," says Leone.

"She was a little too polite," says Jack.

"She didn't tip the attendant in the ladies' room," says Leone.

"I think you're right about the talking," says Jack. "I'm a little worried about what happens when she goes into a real combat situation."

"I'll take her shopping at Paloma's usual stores tomorrow and to Enzo's for a proper cut," says Leone. "See if anybody notices the difference."

"That's a good idea," says Jack. "Maybe you could stop by the office after that. See if Bryan or Lillith notices anything."

Oona has been listening to this exchange, delivered as if she isn't in the room, in silence, her head switching back and forth between Jack and Leone as if they're playing Ping-Pong and not having a conversation.

But it's been a long and stressful afternoon. Not only was Oona rigid with nerves and effort through the entire meal, she had to listen to the two of them blather on about people and things she doesn't know and doesn't care about until she thought the tedium would kill her if the food didn't. Now she's tired and she's hungry. She's hardly had any time to miss her father since she's been here, but she suddenly misses him now. She wants to lean her head against him and feel his arms around her. She wants to hear him call her Pumpkin the way he did when she was little. *Don't worry, Pumpkin,* he used to say, *everything'll be OK.* Only it wasn't, of course. Nothing was OK. And it's definitely not OK now.

Loneliness tears fill Oona's eyes.

Neither Leone nor Jack Silk notices that Oona's crying until she starts shouting.

"Excuse me!" she yells. "But I am here, you know. And I do speak English. I understand what you're saying!"

They turn to look at her in some surprise.

"And for your information," screams Oona, "I worked

hard, too. You two didn't do this all by yourselves! All you do is criticize me. I smile too much. I walk too fast. I hold my fork all wrong. What about all the things I did right? What about that?"

Oona is still shouting and crying when Arthur Minnick comes through the front door. Normally, Arthur Minnick is either not home, drunk, doing something important on his laptop, or any combination of the three. But now he is home, apparently sober, and his computer hangs over his shoulder in its case.

"You back already, Paloma?" Arthur says to Oona. "I thought you were going away for a few months."

Jack smiles.

It's a wrap.

Though, of course, this is only scene one.

Scene two is the day that filming for the new season begins. Both Leone and Oona are dreading it, which means they finally have something in common. Appearing on set is a much bigger test than using the right knife to butter a roll. If Oona blows it, they will both be humiliated in the most public way possible — especially Leone. Oona will have put herself through this ordeal for nothing, but at least she can go back to her life; Leone will never eat lunch in LA again.

"Open your mouth as little as possible," Leone advises as they drive to the studio. "These people are not Paloma's buddies, they're just her coworkers. You don't fraternize. All you have to do is nod and maybe smile, and then go straight to your trailer. No one's expecting you to give an oral report on what you did on your summer vacation. The only time you have to talk is when you're on camera." She takes her eyes off the road for a second. "You think you can do that?"

Oona, whose stomach feels as if it's been packed in ice but whose palms are sweating, says, "Yes."

"Good," says Leone. "Then we shouldn't have any problems."

As they enter the studio the director calls out, "My God, did I miss a flock of flying pigs this morning? Look who's here! Our leading lady, and she's actually on time!"

Cast and crew all clap. This is the first time it's ever occurred to Oona that applause can be sarcastic.

Leone did say that she can smile. Oona smiles.

"How was your hiatus?" asks the director. "All ready to get back to work?"

Leone did say that she can nod. Oona nods.

"We'll go straight to makeup," says Leone, and propels her forward.

Even if Oona weren't so terrified of doing something wrong that she's almost afraid to breathe, not fraternizing is far from a challenge. No one comes near her. When they're not wanted or there's a break, the others hang out in clusters, schmoozing and laughing, but no one schmoozes or laughs with Paloma. The most she gets is a small and wary smile. The few people who do speak to her—makeup, wardrobe, the woman checking the sound—need only answers of one or two words, and one or two words are all they get, usually from Leone.

Oona isn't needed on set until the afternoon, which means that she has little to do all morning except worry and wait. She watches the shoot for a while, just to get a feel for how it works and who everybody is, but Leone eventually drags her away. Paloma doesn't stand around watching; Paloma stands apart. Which leaves Oona fidgeting in her trailer, Leone on guard by the door, her phone on her lap instead of a gun. What if she forgets her lines? What if she simply freezes in front of the camera? What if she forgets to speak like Paloma and speaks like herself? What if someone does ask her something that requires an answer of several words? What then? By lunchtime Oona's so nervous she can't eat.

"You have to try to relax a little," says Leone. "If you were made of glass you'd've shattered by now."

"It might help if you didn't follow me around like we're chained together."

Leone sighs. "I wish I felt I could leave you alone for an hour. I could really use a drink."

At last Paloma is called on set. The set is of a large, corporate office — the office of an executive. There's an oversize desk in front of a bank of windows with a view of a crowd of skyscrapers. There is a leather office chair behind the desk and several less-comfortable-looking chairs in front of it. To one side are a sofa and coffee table, to the other a low bookcase and cabinet. Stiff as starch, Oona walks across the patch of carpet.

"No, not there," says the director. "Stand closer to the desk. You're looking for something in that pile of books and papers."

Oona stands closer to the desk.

"What about her phone?" asks the director's assistant. "She has to look as if she's talking on the phone if someone comes in." Faith, of course, is actually talking to God, who doesn't use electronic gadgets.

Oona takes Faith's phone from her pocket and holds it to her ear.

"Perfect," says the director. "OK, can you make the lighting a little more celestial? That's it! Paloma, take it from 'What does it look like?'"

There is a period of two, maybe three, seconds after the cameras start to roll in which Oona just stands there, holding the phone and looking at the desk. And then she says, "What does it look like?" And smiles the Faith Cross smile that could convince a man on the gallows that everything's going to be all right.

She does the scene without a stumble or a mistake, playing Faith so effortlessly that even the rest of the cast almost forgets that she's acting.

At the end of the first take the director says, "Well, ladies and gentlemen, I believe that's a wrap."

Leone only just manages not to clap.

As far as Paloma's concerned, she might as well be a bug

You wouldn't think that Dr. Ethan Lovejoy, psychologist, rancher, and homespun philosopher, and Paloma Rose, TV star, prima donna, and rebellious teenager, have anything in common besides the bizarre fact that they are in the same place at the same time, but there is one thing: Dr. Lovejoy has his own way of doing things, and so does Paloma Rose. Unfortunately, since these ways of doing things are the exact opposite of one another, this is not what you might call a happy coincidence.

Most people act out of guilt or fear, or from a sense of duty or love, or from rage. Dr. Ethan Lovejoy doesn't act out of any of those things. Which means that, unlike your average person, he doesn't cajole or bargain, threaten or negotiate. Nor does he give in. He disengages; he walks away. Just as he walked away and left Paloma ranting in his office.

Paloma Rose, on the other side of this particular stage, acts largely out of fury born of frustration. By the time she was one year old she had established a pattern for getting attention, if not what she wanted, and that hasn't changed in the last sixteen years. She screams, she cries, she slams doors, and she throws things. This has always worked for her.

But it doesn't work with Dr. Ethan Lovejoy. If Susie Minnick wants to shriek hysterically and kick the furniture, that's her business. Ethan Lovejoy has more important things to do than watch her or beg her to stop.

And so does everyone else at Old Ways, it turns out.

After she recovers from the surprise of doing a major dramatic scene with no audience, Paloma stomps out of the office, slamming the door so hard that several people in the building think there's been an earth tremor. She continues to stomp down the hall, slams the outside door even harder than the one in the office, and marches across the dirt yard, her jaw set like the prow of a battleship, her eyes shining with tears. Most of the other residents are still out having one of the Old Ways wildly good times described by Ethan Lovejoy — clawing their way up rock faces with hundred-pound packs on their backs and being attacked by wild dogs, something like that — but there are still a few people around. She sees them out of the corner of her eye; hears footsteps and doors opening and closing and what she takes to be the jingling of spurs (but is actually the art teacher hanging up a wind chime made of old spoons, knives, and forks).

Assuming that these people are watching her, Paloma stops suddenly to lean against what she takes to be a broken fence (but is actually a hitching post), bury her face in her hands, and sob like a girl in a disaster movie. Normally, such a display of heartbreak and suffering would attract at least one solicitous soul, if not several. Paloma stands there for a few minutes, her body heaving while the sun tries to bore through it, waiting for a hand to gently touch her shoulder or a kind voice to ask if she's all right. But the only touch is the tail of a passing dog slapping against her leg, and the only voices belong to chickens and cows. When she can't tell the tears from the sweat anymore, she peeks through her fingers to see if there's anyone worrying about her. There isn't. Not even the dog is in the yard anymore, and there isn't a face at a single window. Paloma stops crying. She wipes the tears and the sweat on her sleeve and starts walking again. After the screaming and crying and slamming and throwing, Paloma always locks herself in her room.

There's a problem with this part of Paloma's pattern, as well. Two problems, to be exact.

The first is that she can't find her room. She wasn't really paying attention when she dumped her bags and followed Ethan Lovejoy's truck as it wound its way through poultry, cats, dogs, and a rather ill-tempered-looking goat to the main buildings where his office is, but now she wishes that she had. The bunkhouses all look alike: dull brown wood, two dull brown wooden doors, two windows with green-and-brown-checked curtains, a narrow, bare porch. She walks back and forth among four of the bunkhouses for a few minutes, trying to recognize something, and finally convinces herself that the building on the right, with the broken step, looks familiar. She tries the door and it opens. For at least half a nanosecond Paloma thinks this must be good news—it isn't locked, so it must be her room—but she's wrong. The shabby stuffed rabbit on one of the beds and the absence of her luggage make that clear. She tries the next door and finds that unlocked, too. Indeed, by the time she does find her room—her suitcases are right where she left them, on the tiny porch—she knows that the second problem with locking herself in is that none of the doors have locks.

As well as being the same on the outside, all the rooms are the same on the inside: two single beds with a small table between them, two small desks, two chairs, one dresser, one closet, and an overhead light with a fan attached to it. No one would ever confuse it with a Hilton. Paloma drags her bags inside, slams the door (making the walls shake), and throws herself onto the bed that doesn't have a nightshirt decorated with cats neatly folded at its foot.

Three months! Ethan Lovejoy said they expect her to stay here — here on the Devil's dude ranch — for three months! That's never going to happen — it can't possibly take Audrey that long to recover from her accident — but even so, the few weeks she'd been expecting would be way too long. Paloma's too wound up to figure out how many hours that would be, but even if you subtract time spent sleeping, eating, and watching TV, it's a lot. And a lot of those hours are going to be spent doing things Paloma Rose was never supposed to do. Pitching tents. Brushing horses. Milking cows. She'd rather be almost anywhere than here: in traction (season 4, episode 8), or stranded on the roof of a house in a flood (season 5, episodes 6 and 7), or lost in the outback (season 3, episode 9). Thinking about this — and the image of Leone knocking back a martini and saying, "Can't you just picture Paloma's face when she realizes the only stars this cesspit has are in the sky?" with that migraine-inducing laugh of hers — starts Paloma crying again.

There's a knock on the door.

Paloma cries louder.

"Susan?" The door creaks open. Obviously everyone here is too busy chasing cattle to do anything practical like oil hinges. The door creaks shut again. *Just come right in! Don't wait to be invited,* thinks Paloma. *We're in the country now!* "Susan, I'm your counselor, Kara McGraw? Your personal counselor, not for group sessions."

Paloma doesn't look up. Kara McGraw's voice has a lilt that makes her sound as if she's about to burst into song. Paloma can tell from that voice that Kara McGraw thinks ballet pumps are the height of fashion and wears sweaters with snowmen and trees that light up at Christmas—probably with matching musical earrings.

"You and I are going to be seeing a lot of each other in the weeks to come," croons Kara McGraw, "so I thought I'd introduce myself right away. I know how scary new places can be. I don't want you to think that you're all alone here."

Who is this woman? Paloma doesn't point out that she *is* all alone—all alone and miles from home with not so much as a cell phone or a laptop to contact the outside world. Another weapon in Paloma's arsenal is the Big Silence. You can't talk to someone who won't talk back. She didn't speak to Leone for two weeks after Seth

Drachman dumped her and left the show because she knew why: Leone threatened him and had him fired. She only started speaking to Leone again so she could yell at her. Paloma closes her eyes and says nothing.

"Because you're not alone," Kara McGraw jingles on. "You have everyone here — we like to think of ourselves as one big family. And a pretty happy one, at that. But especially you have me. I like to think of you and me as a team."

Don't do that, Paloma silently begs. *Think of us as strangers.*

"I know you're upset, Susan." Obviously she's a counselor because she has so much insight and perception. "Ethan explained that coming here has been something of a surprise for you." Insight, perception, and a gift for understatement. "I understand that might be confusing to you. And makes you angry. But it really is true that sometimes you have to be cruel to be kind."

And sometimes people are just cruel to be cruel. People like Leone Minnick.

"But you know what they say, Susan," she continues. "It's a really bad wind that doesn't blow some good somewhere."

Paloma had no idea that everyone went around saying something so achingly stupid; if she had, she would have told them to stop.

"Well, anyway, I just thought I'd come see if you need anything," sings Kara McGraw. "A drink, maybe? Or something to eat? You must be hungry after your trip. I could get you a snack from the kitchen. The food here is really swell."

What Paloma needs is a ride to the airport.

"And if you want to talk . . . That's what I'm here for. . . . Talking. No matter what time of the day or night, my door is always open."

So shut it!

"You know, it's really important to talk, Susan," says Kara McGraw. "That's a lot of what we do here. Just talk. It really makes a difference. Most of you kids who come here, one of the problems is you've never really had anyone to talk to. And take it from me, because I know from my own experience, it'll make you feel a whole lot better."

The only thing Paloma plans to say to anyone at Rancho Ridiculous is "good-bye"—which, of course, is also the only thing that could possibly make her feel better.

"It helps put you in touch with your feelings."

Paloma's already in touch with her feelings. The sobbing goes up a notch.

But Kara McGraw is not at Old Ways because she gives up easily.

"Hey, I have a super idea, Susan! Why don't we take a little walk?"

The only walking Paloma plans to do is out of here.

"Exercise is a wonderful mood enhancer, you know. Get those endorphins bopping around like a jive dancer. And it would do you good to get some fresh air. I could give you the grand tour. . . ."

The grand tour up a pile of rocks and over a field of cow patties. Maybe we could get gored by a bull (season 2, episode 7).

"And what about supper?" asks the indefatigable Kara McGraw, still chirpy as a sparrow on a warm spring day. "We're having fried chicken tonight. Believe you me, it's the best this side of the Mississippi. You don't want to miss that."

Oh, yes, she does.

"I'll tell you what. If you don't feel up to coming to the dining room, I'll make sure the cook puts some chicken away for you for tomorrow. How does that sound?"

Like I might as well die right now since there's nothing more to look forward to.

"So . . . maybe I'll see you later, Susan."

This time, Kara McGraw does get an answer. Paloma snores.

It's quite a while later when the sounds of voices and

running water wake her up. The water is inside the building and hitting a metal shower stall; the voices are talking and laughing—someone shouts for the shampoo. In season 5, episode 2 of *Angel in the House,* Faith Cross spends a week in a college dorm. Obviously, Paloma herself didn't really live in the dorm—it was just a set. But it was a very convincing set, and it gave her—an only child with a bedroom larger than most people's homes and a bathroom much larger than most people's bedrooms—a fairly good idea of what sharing a room and living on top of a lot of other people is like. Totally gross. Everybody borrowing your stuff all the time. Sleeping in the same room so someone you don't even like much can see you with bed head and no makeup and drool coming out of your mouth. Somebody watching you shave under your arms or pick your nose. Knowing every time you farted or had your period. Going through your things when you're not in the room. If you wanted to have even three minutes of privacy, you'd have to lock yourself in a bathroom stall. It was as close to communal living as Paloma ever wanted to get. Now, however, she seems to be a lot closer. She is living in a dorm—a minidorm occupied by only four people, but a dorm. They're taking showers together in the bathroom and sharing shampoo. Any minute some girl's going to come in wrapped in a towel. And here she was thinking her life couldn't get any worse. Paloma starts to cry again.

She's crying too much to hear the door to the bathroom open or shut, but she hears a voice say, "Hey! Are you OK?" Very loudly.

At least the voice isn't lilting like Kara McGraw's, or a sinisterly calm and gentle monotone like Ethan Lovejoy's. Which is several points in its favor. Paloma doesn't look up to see if the body attached to the voice is wrapped in a towel or not, but she does decide to answer. "Leave me alone."

"You're Susan, right? I'm your roomie. Tallulah. Me and Pilar and Meg are going over to supper in like ten minutes, are you coming?"

"Leave me alone!"

"You want me to bring you back something to eat?"

"Leave me freakin' alone!"

"Nice to meet you, too."

"Leave me alone!"

"OK, so I'll leave you alone. I was only trying to help."

Paloma listens to the pulling out and pushing in of drawers. Something is zipped. Hair is dried with a towel. Springs creak. And the whole time Paloma listens, she waits for the girl to hand her some tissues or get her a glass of water or gently try to calm her down. This may not seem to make sense, given how many times Paloma told her to leave her alone, but human behavior rarely has much to do with logic—and those are the kinds of things Maria does when Paloma is splayed across the sofa and crying enough to wash her heart out to sea, no matter how many times Paloma tells her to go away. This girl, however, is clearly nothing like Maria.

Paloma is trying to get a look at her roommate without revealing that that's what she's doing when there's a knock on the door and it immediately opens. The girl who doesn't have her own shampoo says, "Isn't she coming?" Tallulah says, "No, she's processing." Someone else says, "Been there, done that." They all laugh, and then the door shuts behind them.

Paloma waits a few seconds, then gets up and peeks through the side of the curtains. Three girls are walking away from the room. The two who could do with one of Leone's not-one-gram-of-fat-or-carbohydrate-touches-your-lips crash diets wear baggy shorts and tank tops and baseball caps; the one with the stringy body and the stringy ponytail and the shapeless straw hat is in a faded sundress that makes her look like a used party toothpick. They all walk as if their feet are very large and heavy. Several others—girls and boys—are headed in the same direction. None of them look half as interesting as a cockroach. Paloma goes back to bed.

It's the overhead light being turned on that wakes her next. She sits up, blinking. It's dark outside, and for one glorious second she doesn't know where she is. But then she remembers. Rancho Nowhere. Hell with horses thrown in. Standing at the foot of the bed is the stringy girl with the stringy ponytail. She doesn't look any more attractive from the front than from the back. She has a narrow, pointy face, as though God started out to make something else—a bird or a ferret, say, but then changed His mind—and eyes the color of a mocha latte (without the whipped cream and powdered chocolate).

"I know you're having a hard landing and everything, but so does everybody," says Tallulah. "Only you're here, and we have to live together, so I'd appreciate it if you got your bags out of the way. I can't keep walking around them."

Paloma blinks some more. "What time is it?"

"Time for you to move your bags." Tallulah may look like something you'd use to spear a shrimp, but she sounds like the director of *Angel in the House*. Dictatorial.

"You're supposed to unpack them and then take them over to storage. Didn't anybody tell you that? There's no room for them in here."

Paloma flops back down. "I'm not staying, so I'm not unpacking."

"If you don't move them, I will." And she has the attitude of the show's director as well.

"Suit yourself," says Paloma.

The next sounds she hears are the door opening and her bags being thrown outside.

It's just as well that Paloma isn't planning to stay at Old Ways since her roommate seems to think that her purpose in life is to wake her up. In the morning she wakes her by standing beside her bed, shaking her a lot less gently than Maria does when Paloma oversleeps.

"What are you, drugged?" demands Tallulah. "The alarm's gotten most of the county up by now. It's, like, after six. You have to get up." If she has any sympathy for poor Paloma she hides it well. "This isn't your fancy house." She has obviously been through Paloma's things and seen the labels on her clothes. "We have chores to do before breakfast here."

Paloma doesn't open her eyes. "They can take their chores and stuff them up their cows," she mutters, and turns over. Paloma has enough attitude of her own to bring down the entire Ottoman Empire.

"So I'll tell Ethan you're not coming out again today, is that it?"

"I told you, I'm not staying here. So you can tell that sadistic creep I'm not leaving the room unless it's to get into the car taking me back to the airport."

"Suit yourself." The door slams behind her, and the sign on the wall that says BE ALL YOU CAN BE falls to the floor.

When Tallulah comes back at noon, Paloma is exactly where she was when Tallulah left.

"You still here?" she says. "I thought you were going home."

Paloma scowls back at her. "Not yet. It's going to take a little longer than I thought."

What Kara McGraw, who has stopped by three times today, actually said when Paloma asked when she was being driven to the airport was that she'd be taken to the airport when she successfully completed the program and not one second before. She said this, of course, with a smile on her lips and a song in her voice, if not in her heart.

"Damn straight, not yet." Tallulah stands at the foot of Paloma's bed. "You remember my name? I'm Tallulah. And the girls in the next room, they're Pilar and Meg. You're Susan, right?"

"No, that isn't right. My name's Paloma. Paloma Rose."

Some people look prettier when they smile, but some don't. "Why did she get up?" asks Tallulah.

Paloma just stares at her.

"That was a joke," Tallulah explains. "You know. You said, 'Paloma rose,' so I said, 'Why did she get up?'"

It may have been a joke, but it definitely wasn't funny to everyone in the room.

Paloma's scowl darkens. "Are you saying you never heard of me?"

"I already told you I heard of you. You're Susan. Everybody's talking about you."

"Of course they're talking about me. I'm famous. I'm a big TV star."

Tallulah laughs; a sound as annoying as the buzzing of a fly that's trapped in your room. "Yeah, sure you are."

"No, I am. I really am." Paloma says this very loudly and distinctly. In case, besides everything else that's wrong with Tallulah — her clothes, her hair, her face — she's chronically hard of hearing. "I'm in one of the most popular shows ever."

"I don't know nothing about that." Tallulah wipes a stray tear from her eyes; she is still laughing. "And anyway, if you want to know, that's not why everybody's talking about you. It's because you thought you were coming to some fancy hotel." Apparently the doors aren't the only things without locks at Old Ways. "Man, everybody thinks that's like hyper-awesome. They never heard anything so funny."

"Is that so?" Paloma sounds the way a freezer feels. "Well, I'm glad you all find this so funny, because this is so totally unfair that the first thing I'm going to do when I get out of here is go to the human rights thing at the UN. I am not supposed to be here. I haven't done anything."

Tallulah makes a face that even a visitor from a far-distant galaxy would recognize as total disbelief. "Give me a break, will you, Sue? None of us are here because we didn't do nothing."

"Well, I am."

"Yeah, sure you are."

"But I am. My mother did this. She wanted to get rid of me for a while."

"Why? Because you're so good?"

Paloma looks at her feet. Her pedi already needs to be redone. "OK, so maybe I stayed out all night a couple of times and drank and some stuff like that. But it's not like I burned the house down or anything." Some might say that was merely luck. "It was no major deal." She looks over at Tallulah. "What'd you do?"

In the case of Tallulah Schimmerhorn a more appropriate question might be "What didn't you do?" She is, among other things, a felon. Interestingly enough, however, it isn't the shoplifting, petty thievery, joyriding, or even the drugs and the drinking that have brought her to the ranch.

Tallulah shrugs. "I tried to kill my father."

For the first time since yesterday, Paloma smiles—though from disbelief, of course, and not happiness. "You what?"

"I didn't exactly mean for him to die," says Tallulah. "I just wanted to scare him so he'd leave me alone."

"And did it work?"

"It must've scared somebody, 'cause here I am." Tallulah shrugs again. "Anyway, I came by to see if you wanted to go to lunch."

"No. I'm not leaving this room."

"You have to leave sometime. You're gonna get pretty hungry."

"It doesn't matter. I'd rather starve."

"OK," says Tallulah. "I'll bring you something back."

Luckily for Paloma, Tallulah knows what it's like to be difficult, stubborn, angry, contrary, and argumentative—and exactly how far it's likely to get you at Old Ways. And, although it's true that Tallulah did try to run over her father, she does have a kind nature and a big heart. James Schimmerhorn is the only person she's ever wanted to see suffer. She brings back food for Paloma. She listens to Paloma's grumbles and her rants. She even buys Paloma soda and candy from the vending machines in the common room.

If Paloma were to make a list of every person in the world and rank them according to how much she wanted to be his or her friend, Tallulah Schimmerhorn would be way at the bottom. Under normal circumstances, even if they were stuck in an elevator for fourteen hours, the only words Paloma would be likely to address to Tallulah would be "Get out of my way." Indeed, it's no exaggeration to say that, under normal circumstances, Paloma would rather defuse a bomb with her teeth than have anything to do with a girl like Tallulah, the homicidal hick. And yet, by dint of her stolen meals and patience and treats, Tallulah is the closest Paloma has ever come to having a real friend.

Tallulah is kept out and busy during most of each day, but when she is in the room Paloma talks to her nonstop. She tells Tallulah how mean Leone is in exhaustive detail, cataloging every offense, criticism, and crime committed by her mother—and some that weren't.

"She said she was sending me to a celebrity dude

ranch to relax because I have to work so hard!" wails Paloma. "That's what she said."

"All parents lie," says Tallulah.

Paloma boasts about being a big star and making tons of money and living in Beverly Hills. Tallulah doesn't believe her. Tallulah has told all her friends what her new roommate claims, and they don't believe her, either. She's a fantasist. That's the correct term for it in this group. Fantasist, not liar.

"The only people I know who aren't famous are servants," claims Paloma.

"Not anymore," says Tallulah.

Paloma may only be an average actor, but she's always excelled at complaining. No matter how good things are, no matter how truly terrible things aren't, Paloma can find something to gripe about. If Paloma went to heaven, she'd complain about the clouds. It's no surprise, then, that Old Ways provides her with an endless source of grievance. There is nothing about it — from the quality of the sheets to the power of the shower to the country that surrounds it — that meets with Paloma's approval.

"I wouldn't feed this to a mangy old mutt," she says, scowling at the plate of spaghetti Tallulah brought her from the dining hall.

"So fine. Don't eat it. I'm not going to lose any sleep because you missed a meal."

Paloma pulls the plate out of the way of Tallulah's reaching hand. "I didn't say I wasn't going to eat it. I have to have something or I'll die. I just meant it's disgusting."

"Everybody else likes it," says Tallulah.

Paloma gives her a look that perfectly balances pity and contempt. *As if that means anything.*

"You keep pushing me, and I will let you starve," says Tallulah.

Although Paloma's room at Old Ways can hardly be compared to solitary confinement in a colonial penal colony, spending all day in a room with no TV, no phone, no music, and no computer does nothing to improve Paloma's outlook or mood. She feels like she's in jail. Prisoners often occupy their time doing push-ups, or making origami animals, or taming wild birds. Mostly what Paloma does is sleep or weep. Which may be just as well, since she's finding it difficult to sleep at night. Coming from a major, 24/7 city, she was unaware of all the sounds the night makes when there isn't any civilization to hide them (and the little civilization there is gets switched off at eleven). Rustlings, thumpings, snorts, and cries. Lonely, hopeless calls of longing. Wild, deranged creatures baying for blood. Then, just as she finally starts to drift off, the rooster will decide that it's day-break—whether or not it is. Tallulah sleeps through it all. "I prefer wolves and owls to police sirens and breaking glass," says Tallulah.

Paloma thinks she may be losing her mind from boredom.

Tallulah may also be losing her mind, but not from boredom. She used to look forward to the end of the day when, after watching a movie or playing a game in the common room, she went back to the privacy of her bunk. The ranch has its own library full of books and magazines, so after her shower Tallulah would get into bed and read for a while, finally falling asleep to the calls and cries and silence of the night—feeling part of the world instead of afraid of it. For her, Old Ways really is a luxury hotel; safe and friendly with no danger that someone is suddenly going to punch you in the head or slam you against a wall.

But she doesn't look forward to coming back to her room anymore. Now she dreads coming back. Gone is the peace and gone is the quiet, replaced by a moaning lump on the other bed. Tallulah has been tolerant; she has been helpful; she's followed the advice about showing kindness tacked to the wall at the entrance to the serving area in the dining room. But still Paloma just lies there whining and acting like she's the only person on the planet who's ever had a bad day.

And so it is that tonight, when Tallulah comes out of the bathroom with a towel on her head and sees Paloma hunched up on her bed exactly as she was when Tallulah went in to take her shower (and when she left this morning, and when she returned during the day and after supper), all of the things she's learned about managing her feelings and letting things go vanish faster than a falling star. The old feeling of wanting to hit something makes her bang the door behind her.

Which does at least make Paloma look over.

"So how long are you planning to keep this up? Isn't it about time you got out of that bed?" asks Tallulah. "You've been here more than two weeks, you know. Your tan's faded. Pretty soon you're going to look like you've lived in a cave all your life."

"I don't care."

"Well, you should care. You can't keep this up forever, Minnick."

Paloma closes her eyes. "I can keep it up till Dr. Death sends me home."

"You don't get it, do you?" Tallulah was once a girl who, finding a damp towel in her hand, would drop it on the floor, but now she drapes it neatly over the back of a chair. "You'll be an old lady wobblin' around with a walker before that happens. Ethan doesn't give up so easy. Nobody ships out of here until they shape up." Even Zigi Slowly, who did everything he could think of to get kicked out, including setting fire to the barn, was defeated in the end and now works at Old Ways as a ranch hand.

"Well, that's not going to happen. Not to me." Paloma's eyes open again. She props herself on one elbow. "Because anybody who thinks I'm shoveling up horse poop and herding cows is seriously wrong. I'm an actress, not the hired help. I don't do crap like that."

"There are worse things," says Tallulah.

"Yeah," sneers Paloma. "Eating in a cafeteria."

"It's not a cafeteria, it's a dining hall."

"Cleaning toilets and boiling beans."

Tallulah gets into bed. "You know, life here isn't that bad."

"Maybe it's not for *you*." Although Paloma is wrong about quite a few things, she is, of course, right about this. Old Ways isn't that bad for Tallulah, not anymore. At first Tallulah would rather have been in solitary, but now this is the best Tallulah's ever felt without alcohol or drugs. She has friends. She has a lot to do. She isn't under threat every minute of the day and night. She's proved that she can do more than get into trouble. A lot more. And where she used to shriek and scream and hit things all the time, now she rarely raises her voice. Though that, of course, isn't what Paloma means. What Paloma means is that Tallulah is a nobody. "You probably live in a trailer."

Tallulah harrumphs. *I'd rather live in a trailer without you than in the White House with you.* But she knows she shouldn't take everything personally; she isn't the problem, Paloma is. "Nobody said you have to like it here. You just have to look like you're trying."

"I want to look like I'm lying beside an infinity pool reading the *Hollywood Reporter,* that's what I want to look like."

Tallulah reaches for the switch on the lamp beside her bed. "I thought you wanted to go home."

"Of course I want to go home." If Paloma's voice were an insect, it would be a mosquito. "This may be *your* idea of a vacation, but it isn't mine."

In contrast, Tallulah's voice is sweeter than corn syrup. "Well, then, you better get in the same story as everybody else, Princess La-Di-Dah. Because the longer it takes you to do that, the longer you'll be here. That's the way it works."

"They can't just keep me here," argues Paloma. "Not against my will. This is America. I have rights."

Tallulah raises her eyebrows. "And who's going to get you out?"

There is a truth in this simple statement that Paloma has avoided facing until now. She hasn't been kidnapped; she's been sent here deliberately. By the very same people who are the only ones who can be expected to rescue her. They can only keep her here till Audrey Hepplewhite recovers from her injuries, then they'll have to bring her home. For the show. But she could still be here for a while longer. A week. Even two. Maybe three. And her tan *has* faded. If she doesn't get some sunlight soon everyone really will think she's been in jail. Paloma isn't familiar with the term *sensory deprivation* or its uses in torture and mind control, but she may be starting to feel its effects. Making friends with a cow may not be too high a price to pay for getting out of this room and having something to do, even if it is beneath her.

"I am not sitting with a bunch of losers talking about my problems," says Paloma. "That is absolutely something I am not going to do. There's no way." That and hiking up some mountain with them singing campfire songs like a bunch of Boy Scouts. "How am I supposed to do all this stupid stuff? It's not who I am."

"You keep saying you're this hot actress. So act." Tallulah turns off the light.

Out of the mouths of babes, as the saying goes. Or, in this case, out of the mouth of a difficult teenager.

Paloma spends a restless night doing what she doesn't always do best: thinking. Weighing her options. Considering the possibility of acting not out of mood, whim, or rage, but logic and reason. Maybe it's time not just to react to things she doesn't like, but to make a plan to overcome them.

When she finally falls asleep, she dreams that she is sitting beside Ethan Lovejoy in the old pickup, being bounced and shaken back to the airport. They aren't talking because of the racket of the truck, but she's so excited there are tears in her eyes. The first thing she's going to do when she gets home is go to the spa. Then she's going shopping. Then she's going to her favorite restaurant and ordering that chicken they do with the truffles and kumquats and wild rice. When they get to the airport, Ethan lets her off in front of the departures terminal. "You did real good, Susan," he tells her. "You have yourself a nice life." She's so happy she says that she will. She picks up her bag and practically runs to the entrance. And that's when she sees herself reflected in the doors and windows.

She's an old lady with gray hair and wrinkled skin, and it isn't a suitcase on wheels that she's holding but a walker. She turns around to shout at Ethan, to ask him how this could have happened to her, but Ethan Lovejoy is gone.

The next morning, when dawn is barely a crack in the darkness of the enormous sky, Paloma is up and showered before Tallulah's alarm goes off. She dresses in the jeans and T-shirt everyone else here wears—haute couture at Old Ways Ranch. It's a miracle they don't make them all dress in buckskin. She puts on the boots that have been provided for her. (Work boots, of course. If you wore them on Hollywood Boulevard everyone would think you'd been cleaning the sewers.) She is waiting with a pleasant smile on her face when Tallulah comes out of the bathroom. Tallulah raises her eyebrows but makes no comment.

They walk to the stables together. Paloma is introduced to her horse, whose name is Sweetie (a deceptive name for an animal who immediately tries to bite her). She is shown the basic, prebreakfast routine. She is introduced to the cows, and her name is put on the cattle chore sheet for later in the week. Through all of this she is polite and interested, gingerly patting Sweetie out of range of Sweetie's very large teeth and beaming on the cows as though their noses aren't larger than her fist. When those chores are done, she follows Tallulah to breakfast and sits beside her in the dining hall, showing all the politeness and interest to Tallulah's friends that she showed to the livestock.

Ethan Lovejoy waylays her as she's getting ready to leave.

"Well, Susan, what a pleasant surprise." He touches his hands together; his prayers have been answered. "You starting to feel a little more settled?"

"You know, I think I really am." She graces him with one of Faith Cross's sincere and thoughtful smiles. "Wait'll I tell you what happened this morning."

And she launches into a delightful anecdote about her and her horse that she remembers from a movie she once saw.

Acting her heart out.

Living the dream

Oona may be living the dream according to Jack Silk, but she doesn't seem to be sleeping it. Most nights, she turns and tosses and wakes every hour or two. Last night, after another fourteen-hour day—one largely dominated by the phrase *Nonono!*—she was so tired when she finally got to bed that she couldn't fall asleep at all. When she did drift off she was soon awoken by the rare event of Leone and Arthur being in the house at the same time, which led to the kind of fight that in another neighborhood would have brought the cops.

It's after that, that Oona has a nightmare.

Oona dreams that Paloma Rose never returns to LA. Oona doesn't know where Paloma is—some exclusive resort—but Paloma is having such a great time that she decides to let Oona keep on being her. Sitting under a palm tree on a beach of white sand that glitters like diamonds,

Paloma rips her return ticket into tiny pieces and shrieks, "No more stress, no more mess, vacation's best!" Even asleep, Oona knows what that means: She is trapped being Paloma forever. No more peace and quiet. No future full of domestic animals that need her help. No chance of seeing her father get back to being the man who made up songs to old rock tunes and loved playing practical jokes. All of that is gone, and in its place is Leone Minnick, telling her how to breathe and how to smile and how to brush her teeth, and a shadow of paparazzi following everywhere she goes. The dream finally ends with Oona and Harriet standing on top of a mountain, trying to see over the edge. Leone is right behind her, telling her how she should stand, when suddenly a man with a camera jumps out from behind a tree. "Teen Angel Thinks She Can Fly!" he shouts. "Smile, sweetheart!"

Oona falls out of bed.

She picks herself up off the floor, glancing at the clock on the bedside table. Even Maria won't be up yet, but there's no point trying to get back to sleep. "Time for our walk, Harriet," says Oona, and turns off the alarm.

Oona still takes Harriet for a long walk every morning before she leaves for the studio and every night after she gets home—no matter what. These walks are Oona's favorite hours of the day—almost the only times when she feels like herself.

They tiptoe downstairs, so as not to disturb Maria, and into the kitchen. Oona gives Harriet a handful of kibble and puts on coffee so she can take a cup with her, thinking about Paloma's life while she watches the pot slowly fill.

Once she got the hang of it, playing Faith Cross turned out to be easy enough. You read the script, you think about the story, you learn your lines, you listen to the director. Acting in front of a camera is about as hard as eating ice cream compared to being someone you're not in real life.

It's all the other things about being Paloma Rose that make up the stress and mess Paloma was shrieking about in Oona's dream. Her life is more regimented than a soldier's, every minute of every hour supervised and accounted for. Fourteen hours in the studio—which includes fittings and makeup, and just sitting around waiting between takes, as well as the run-throughs and actual tapings—isn't unusual. When Oona isn't in the studio, there are lines to memorize; hours with her physical trainer; hours with her voice and drama coaches; and personal appearances and photo shoots—not to mention the constant mental and physical exercise of dodging fans and that insatiable pack of paparazzi.

And then, of course, there's Leone. Since it is much more difficult to control a person by remote than it is to control a television, Leone has always been a regular visitor on the set of *Angel in the House* — especially after Paloma's ridiculous infatuation with that full-of-himself scriptwriter — but now she is there all day, every day. She has become Oona's own personal spook — the spy kind, not the dead kind. She is also Oona's greatest critic. Half of her sentences start with the words "Darling, you can't . . ." The other half start with "Sweetie, don't . . ." Almost all of them end with "Have I made myself clear?" As long as they're in public, Leone rarely leaves Oona's side. She goes with her to makeup and to costume changes, and joins in on her visits to hospitals and homeless shelters. She sits there, barely breathing, during takes and interviews. She won't let Oona go into a store for a soda by herself. They eat lunch together in the dressing room; they take their breaks together in the dressing room; they wait together in the dressing room. Even when the director takes Oona aside for a chat, Leone is right beside her, her smile like the light on a sound booth: RECORDING IN PROGRESS. The only time she lets Oona out of her sight is when one of them goes to the bathroom.

Oona fills her travel mug with coffee, then puts on the hat Maria uses when she gardens and a pair of sunglasses. She and Harriet go out the back way as usual.

It's a beautiful morning—still so early that the breaking light is fine and the air misty, but the day is already warm and promising pleasant. Birds sing; colors shine; the air hums. Despite the early hour, the streets are far from empty.

The first friends they run into are Moira and Orwell. Moira's sipping coffee from an insulated cup; Orwell's carrying a stick. Moira offers Oona half a muffin, and Orwell drops his stick so he can bend very far down to greet Harriet.

Moira, like everyone else on the dog-walking route, knows Oona as Paloma Rose, but they don't care about that. No one ever discusses anything but their pets. Today, for instance, Moira, who is a high-powered lawyer, doesn't mention the landmark case she just won, but talks about the time Orwell lost his favorite toy (a rubber duck) and was so depressed that she took him to a dog psychiatrist.

"And he got better?" asks Oona.

"Not until I found his duck behind the couch," says Moira.

They chat with Ben and Bill the beagle, and Lara and

Pixie the Great Dane. They say hello to two Brussels griffons, a poodle, and three French bulldogs. Mr. Jeffers, without Comandante, drives by in his car, waving, on his way to work. When they get to Mrs. Mackinpaw's house, she and Sunshine are sitting on their porch having their breakfast.

Oona has her morning phone call with her father for the rest of the way home, following the flag of Harriet's tail while she walks. Since Maria took over the job of making sure Abbot at least has groceries and conversation with someone who actually talks back, he's started to crawl slowly out of his cave of despair. He has things to tell her and things to do. He makes plans and talks about the future as if he now believes he has one. He's even stopped worrying so much about Oona, now that he knows she's in such safe hands—and he doesn't, of course, mean Leone Minnick.

"Really?" Oona tries not to sound too surprised. "You're going shopping today?"

"Just for food, and a couple of things for Mrs. Figueroa." Maria had been helping Mrs. Figueroa, too, but apparently Abbot is now helping Maria. He laughs. "I told you I've been getting out a lot more lately."

Although a five-minute walk around the block would be significant compared to rarely leaving the house, it's true that Abbot has been getting out a lot more lately. Last week he took the bus to buy a bag of fresh corn tortillas. The next day he took the bus to get himself a new pair of shoes. Yesterday he took the bus to get paint to redecorate the apartment. The day before he took the bus to Venice and sat on the boardwalk for nearly two hours, wearing his old cowboy hat to protect him from the sun. Tonight he's going to a movie with Maria. He forgets to mention the movie.

"Hey, you know what?" says Abbot. "I caught your first show last night. You were pretty good."

"I just do what they tell me," says Oona. "It's not that hard."

"I guess life would be a lot easier if we all had a script," says Abbot.

It's the first joke he's made in a long time.

The smile stays on Oona's face until Paradise Lodge comes into view. She sighs. *Home again, home again, jiggity jig* . . .

Inside the house, Arthur snores and Maria packs the breakfast she's made Oona.

Outside, Leone stands under the entrance portico, tapping her toe, checking her phone every two seconds and squinting down the driveway as if she's a general waiting for last-minute reinforcements to arrive. Leone isn't humming or singing or enjoying the peace of the morning; she's buzzing like a bee trapped in a jar. At last a figure comes into view—a small, four-legged, multi-colored figure with ears that belong to a much larger dog. Harriet, the Hound from Purgatory. "It's about time!" Leone mutters, and goes click-clacking off the stoop, waving her phone like a semaphore. "Where on earth have you been?" she demands as Harriet's owner appears around the bend. Strolling along as if she thinks she's going to live forever. "I was worried sick! I thought some-thing must've happened to you!" The gold of Leone's phone glitters as she holds it out to prove how late it is. "We really should've left for the studio ten minutes ago."

"I was taking Harriet for her morning walk."

Leone seems to be unaware of this routine, even though it happens every day. "Now?" she sounds genu-inely mystified. "You had to do it now? When we're in a hurry?"

"It's her morning walk," says Oona reasonably. "So she usually has it in the morning."

"But you know we have to get to the studio early today." As if Paloma Rose was ever on time for anything that wasn't an appointment with her stylist. "I don't make the schedule."

She would if she could.

"I make a lot of sacrifices for you, you know," says Leone. Meaning that going to the studio every day cuts down on her shopping, lunching, and being-seen time, but she's far too afraid of what might happen if she leaves Oona unsupervised to stay away. It's bad enough when she *is* there. Controlling Oona has turned out to be a lot like herding cats. "I don't think it's too much to ask you to at least be on time." Leone shakes her head sadly, pained, as always, to have to be critical. "I depend on you, darling. I need to know that you're responsible."

"I am responsible, that's why I always take Harriet for her walk." Oona passes Leone. "I'll just let her inside, and I'm ready to go."

"Like *that*?"

Leone's voice stops Oona and pulls her back like a vaudeville hook dragging a bad act offstage.

Oona looks at her. Blank as a steel door. "Like what?"

"Like *that*." Leone flicks her fingers at the T-shirt and jeans. "You look like a street person."

"No, I don't. *Mom*." She looks like a regular kid. "These are Paloma's clothes. I didn't pick them, I just put them on."

"Well, they look different on you than they do on her." Her frown seems almost to cast a shadow. "And you're not wearing any makeup."

Wars have been fought over far less than the makeup argument between Leone Minnick and Oona Ginness. Leone thinks that a woman should wear makeup every waking minute of the day, even if she doesn't plan to leave the house. Who knows who might drop by? A package may be delivered. There might be an emergency that requires an ambulance or the fire department. And if you are leaving the house—no matter where you're going—you have to look as if you're about to be photographed for *Vogue*. Even if you're being arrested and carted off in handcuffs with a jacket over your head, underneath that jacket your face should be fully made up.

"But they're going to make me up when I get on set, Mother dear," reasons Oona. "What's the point of putting any on now?"

Leone neither hums nor sighs. Her foot taps, her fingers flex, her mouth gets very, very small. "The point, sweetie, is that you are Paloma Rose. Icon and idol. And, as Paloma Rose, you must always look perfect. Always." Neither fire, flood, nor alien invasion shall keep our heroine from her walk-in closet and her makeup case. "Everyone expects it."

Not everyone. "That's ridiculous," says Oona. "And anyway, there isn't really any such thing as looking perfect. It's completely culturally subjective."

Leone grips her phone so tightly she breaks a nail. *Here we go,* she thinks, *more philosophical babble. The Socrates of East LA strikes again.* She's never known anyone like Oona, and definitely didn't feel that something was missing in her life. "What?"

"You know what I mean. Different people have different ideas of what's physically perfect. It depends on who you are and where you are and when. Just look at human history. Powdered wigs, tattoos, body piercings, bustles, elongated lips, codpieces, bare breasts, togas, kilts, three-inch feet . . ."

If Leone's mouth gets any smaller, it may disappear. "This is Hollywood, not Canton, darling."

"Exactly." Oona smiles for the first time since she saw Leone lying in wait for her. The only thing that comes close to giving her as much pleasure as talking to Abbot or walking Harriet is bickering with Leone. "Let's ignore the fact that this is one of the least restrictive and formal cultures that's ever existed, with an incredible range of styles and ethnicities. The point I'm trying to make is that if there isn't any objective definition of perfection, then a person is free to decide for her—"

"Life's way too short for this." Leone takes out her keys and starts toward the car. "At least wear your shades. You can do that much. And get rid of that stupid hat."

"I could always ride in the trunk," says Oona.

Hahaha. A philosopher and a comedian, too.

"You don't have to do that, darling," purrs Leone. "Just duck before we get to the road."

Conversation as they drive to the studio isn't pleasant, but it is limited. Leone wants to know what the hell that is that Oona's eating, and Oona says it's an egg-and-bean burrito. Maria, like Lorna Ginness before her, won't let Oona start the day without breakfast, even if she has to eat it in the car.

Leone says Oona's supposed to be watching her weight.

"I never put on weight," says Oona. "And anyway, I eat what you say when there are people around. I didn't think I had to starve myself the rest of the time."

Leone tells Oona to open her window, she's making the car smell like a taqueria. "There's breath spray in the glove compartment," says Leone. "Use it."

Oona sighs. "Yes, *Mother.*"

"Damn it, there he is again," mutters Leone. They're being followed. There is one photographer with the single-mindedness of a K-9 patrol dog who has made it his business to shadow them every day, as if, on the way to the studio, Paloma Rose is suddenly going to jump out of the car and hold up a bank. Sometimes he's right at the foot of the driveway; sometimes he's tucked into a side street or parked farther down the road; today he's waited until they're several blocks from the house. "Hold tight." Leone steps on the gas.

Oona holds tight. "Maybe I should've ridden in the trunk."

"It would only ruin your hair," says Leone. And then, picking up where she left off, says, "I do hope that you're going to try to do everything right today. I don't want to have to remind you again that you're supposed to be impersonating the sphinx."

Oona watches the car behind them in the side mirror. "You want me to break my nose and be buried in sand?"

"I want you to be silent and mysterious." They take a turn a little sharply and both tilt to the left. "I don't want you offering your opinion on things that don't concern you."

"Are we talking about the slippers again?"

Yesterday Oona pointed out a continuity error. It was toward the end of the day and everyone was ready to finish up and go home when Faith Cross, instead of saying, "But hope is the fuel of life, Lucinda," said, "Weren't you wearing slippers before?" They had to start the scene all over. Making Leone late for her dinner.

A shrub that is clearly standing too close to the road brushes against the passenger window.

"They have a person whose job it is to do that, sweetie. And that isn't you. I want that to be the last time you do something like that." It wasn't the first.

"I said I was sorry. It just came out." Oona stretches her legs as if braking as they sail around another bend. "I was only trying to help."

"You're not paid to help. You're paid to act. Just stick to the script."

They drive the rest of the way in their usual uncompanionable silence.

There's already a whirlpool of young fans outside the studio entrance. If the girl beside her really were Paloma, Leone would stop the car and let them get pictures and autographs, but Oona won't just sign her name and smile as Paloma would. Oh, no, not Oona. She's a girl of the people, Oona, always starting conversations. Always asking questions that lead to long answers. All Leone wants now is to get her inside. She drives through the gates as if she's in a tank; everyone gets out of her way.

Oona tenses, takes a deep breath, and steps out of the car.

Jack Silk calls every evening to see how things are going. And every evening Leone tells him that things couldn't be better. This is true. Leone might wish that Oona would be a little less pleasant, enthusiastic, and cooperative, but even she sees that this very unsphinx-like behavior has had a beneficial effect on the show. Because Oona gets along with everyone—even Audrey Hepple-white—and treats them all with the charm Paloma Rose always reserved for network executives, the atmosphere on set has improved at least 200 percent. The filming is on schedule for a change, morale is high, energy is up, and there have been no scenes of high drama that aren't in the script—and no time lost because someone is grumpy and won't come out of her dressing room. But because Leone is living proof of that old saying "A man only sees what he wants to see," she doesn't realize that the changes in Paloma Rose have been noted and discussed. Everyone knows that something is up.

Oona does realize this. Which, of course, is what makes her as tense as a soldier going into combat every time she enters the studio. She's aware that everybody watches her as if they're looking at one of those pictures with another picture hidden in it. Comments have been made. The makeup woman wanted to know what she's been using on her skin; the head costume designer said she thought that Paloma must have shrunk; the hair stylist asked if she'd changed her salon. Comments have been overheard. Someone wondered aloud if a new charm school had opened up in Beverly Hills. The grip said he thought somebody must have hypnotized the Princess Brat. After a conversation initiated by Oona, Audrey Hepplewhite asked the actor who plays her husband for a reality check.

Because she is aware of the cast and crew's suspicions, Oona tries to keep herself aloof and uninvolved, but her efforts never last for long. She can't stop herself from being friendly. She can't stop herself from being helpful. She can't keep her mouth shut when someone isn't wearing slippers and should be. Her coworkers were wary at first (and certainly surprised), smiling back like prisoners and answering in monosyllables, but gradually they've accepted the user-friendly Paloma Rose as normal. Cracks have even been made about how Paloma has finally learned to tell time, to pronounce words of more than three syllables, and to say "please" and "thank you"—though never when they thought Leone was listening. The first time Oona herself made a joke, there was a stunned silence of several seconds, broken by someone on the crew shouting out, "Who said that?" Oona has tried not to make many jokes since.

Oona and Leone are late today, but since it's a good two hours and forty-five minutes short of the lateness record Paloma set in the winter, no one starts shouting as soon as they arrive—the way someone once might have. Several people look up. Someone calls out, "She's here!" Someone else calls out, "OK, everybody, battle stations . . ."

"There you are!" The director, known to Paloma Rose as the dictator, comes striding toward Oona.

Oona immediately forgets that she's supposed to keep her mouth shut unless she's repeating a line written by someone else and starts apologizing. "I'm really sorry," she says, her eyes on the director, "but I had to walk my dog. And we kept running into people and dogs we know. And so I guess I just lost track of the time."

Leone gives her a look that would kick her if it were a mule. "Let's also mention the traffic." Leone speaks very loudly, hoping to obliterate Oona's explanation by sheer volume. "I don't think we can be held responsible for the traffic jam otherwise known as the streets of LA."

The director doesn't so much as glance at Leone. "*You* walk your dog?" He shakes his head as if someone just bounced a ball off it. "You know, I never thought of you as a dog person."

"Or a walker," mutters his PA.

Someone nearby stifles a laugh.

"So what kind is it?" The director is also a dog person. "What's its name?"

"Her name's Harriet." It's always such a relief to be able to tell the truth that Oona can't stop herself. "She's a rescue dog. She was really badly treated, and someone found her in a garbage can. She's really smart. She's kind of a ten percenter. You know, ten percent of this . . . and ten percent of that . . ."

The director laughs. "Really." If it had ever occurred to him that Paloma Rose owned a dog, he would have guessed something small and expensive. An accessory dog, not a rescue dog. "That's very interesting." And indeed he does look interested, as does everyone else.

"Yeah. She was—"

"Come on, sweetie." Leone grabs her by the arm. "There isn't time for this now. You have to get ready." She squeezes her hard enough to cut off the blood flow and starts to propel her forward.

"Slow down a minute, there, Leone." The director puts a hand on her. "I want to say something to Paloma."

"You do?" Leone is so surprised that she lets go of Oona. "I was only thinking of the schedule."

"I'll worry about the schedule, you worry about whatever it is you worry about." He puts an arm around Oona's shoulders and turns her around so that Leone is behind them. "I just wanted to thank you. That was a good call about the slippers yesterday."

"Oh, I didn't know if—" She can feel Leone glowering at her back. "I mean—"

He lowers his voice. "And also that inaccuracy." This is something Oona mentioned to him that she happened to notice in the next episode's script. "You were completely right. He never could have sent that telegram then. The first transcontinental telegraph wasn't until 1861." He gives her a hug. "You saved us about a billion tweets about that!"

It isn't until the director takes his arm away that Oona looks up to see everyone watching them. Smiling. And suddenly realizes that they don't care who she is. Some of them may know she isn't really Paloma Rose; some of them may only suspect; some of them may just think she's found religion and become a better person. But none of them care. It doesn't matter. What matters is the show. Nobody would care if Paloma were being impersonated by a dybbuk out to take over the whole of Los Angeles and annex it to Hell, as long as *Angel in the House* isn't canceled and they don't all lose their jobs. And with that realization comes a question: did Leone and Jack Silk's scheme ever have anything to do with giving Paloma Rose a holiday, or does it have to do with something else?

"What's wrong with you?" Leone hisses as she drags Oona away at last. "A rescue dog!? Who are you, Sarah McLachlan? Paloma Rose does not rescue dogs." A door shuts behind them. "And what was all that muttering about? Since when are you two so chummy? What inaccuracy?"

Oona can't believe Leone's hearing is that good. She must have used mirrors; it goes without saying that she can probably read lips.

"It's not a big deal," says Oona. "It was just something I noticed in the next episode. Something that couldn't have happened then."

"But noticing that kind of thing is totally out of character," snaps Leone. Paloma wouldn't notice if the Victorians had power showers. "You're going to ruin everything."

Oona sighs. She almost wishes she could.

Leone takes Oona home at the end of the day but is off again in less than an hour for dinner with friends. Arthur, of course, is out, and it's Maria's night off. The absence of Maria makes the house feel as warm and inviting as a deserted airplane hangar. Oona sighs.

Armed with a large flashlight and a can of pepper spray (in case they are attacked by coyotes), she and

Harriet go for their evening walk. Most people are inside now. Mrs. Mackinpaw and Sunshine are sitting together on the sofa, watching something on TV, as they are every night at this time. Mrs. Mackinpaw looks up and waves. When they get back to Paradise Lodge, Oona microwaves a frozen pizza and calls her father. Her father doesn't answer, which is less unusual these days than it once would have been. She's too tired to eat. She takes a shower and goes to bed.

In her own life, Oona would read for a while before turning out the lights, but now she puts on a movie she's seen before, just for the sound of human voices, and watches it in the dark with Harriet stretched across her. She's asleep before the opening credits.

And so another day in the glamorous life of a Hollywood star comes to an end.

Living the dream.

Home, home
on the range

Paloma Rose would have to agree with Oona Ginness that it's a lot easier to act when you have a script than when you have to improvise.

She hasn't had any difficulty doing sweet, cheerful, helpful, and sensitive to the needs and problems of others, because those are all qualities that belong to Faith Cross, and Paloma's been playing Faith Cross long enough to be very good at them.

It's all the other things that make up life at Old Ways that have given her trouble. Indeed, it's been a learning curve as steep as the Grand Canyon, but with none of the spectacular views and no gift shop.

At the beginning of this curve was the horse. Sweetie by name, Nasty by nature. She's a lot larger than Paloma feels she should be and has extremely unattractive nostrils and whiskers and a permanently disappointed look on her face that reminds Paloma of Leone Minnick. Sweetie snorts and stamps her feet if she doesn't like the way you're brushing her, or stroking her, or putting on her saddle. (Or if, as seemed at first to be the case with Paloma, Sweetie just doesn't like *you*.)

Tallulah, who is naturally, if unexpectedly, good with animals, couldn't understand Paloma's fear. "They don't make no trouble," said Tallulah. "You know where you stand with a horse." *Yeah,* thought Paloma, *far away.* Tallulah told her to bring Sweetie apples and carrots, to make friends. But Paloma was so terrified the first time Sweetie reached for the apple with her monster mouth that she dropped it and Sweetie nearly bit her foot picking it up. Likewise, the first time Paloma tried to mount Sweetie, she was so nervous that she went up one side and straight down the other. Nobody even asked her if she was hurt. They were all laughing too much. When she did finally get on and stay there, she was so frightened she couldn't even blink. It was Tallulah who finally got her to relax. "It's not the animals on the ranch who are pains in the butt with a bad history," Tallulah pointed out. "It's us. The animals are all pretty cool." Though you probably wouldn't want to get on the wrong side of the bull. "You could ride that horse into Wyoming and pass out, and it'd bring you back home. All you have to do is hold on."

Apparently, all she had to do with the cow was hold on, too.

"I thought they have machines to do this," grumbled Paloma.

They do, but not at Old Ways. It turns out that the name of the ranch is an accurate and unpoetic description of what it is. Lost in the nineteenth century would be another way of putting it. Although they do have cars and trucks and electricity and television and even a laundry room, that's as far as it goes. They definitely don't have a milking machine.

Will, the foreman, pointed to each thing as he named it. "That's the pail, that's the teat, that's the udder, and in there's the milk. All you gotta do is get the milk from there into the pail. You just do exactly how I showed you."

"I am not touching that thing." Paloma's lovely mouth was curled up on itself like a dead slug. "I'd rather hang by my ankles for the rest of the day."

Will said he could arrange that. But not in a way that made it sound like a joke.

On her initial try, it took Paloma two hours to get half a cup of milk. Her fingers hurt so much she felt as if she'd been walking on them. The cow kicked over the pail.

"You're lucky she didn't kick *you*," said Will.

But if Paloma thought she might do better with

inanimate objects she was wrong. Even just the concept of cooking and cleaning presented her with a challenge of Mount Everest proportions. Paloma had never cleaned anything in her life before. Her cooking skills consisted of pouring herself a drink or opening a bag of chips when Maria wasn't there to do it for her.

Gerda Hellman, the housekeeper for the ranch, is in charge of giving out work assignments and making sure that they're done quickly and well.

Paloma's first job was to clean up the common room.

"I don't know what you expect me to do with that," said Paloma.

"I'll give you a clue," said Gerda. "It's a broom. But not the kind that flies."

The only time Paloma had even seen a broom was in season 4, episode 2, an imaginative reworking of *Cinderella*, but with an angel helping instead of a fairy godmother.

"You don't have a vacuum cleaner?"

"After you sweep up, I'll show you where the mop is."

By the time Paloma was put on kitchen duty, she wasn't even slightly surprised that there isn't a microwave at the ranch.

"So let me explain something about onions, Susie," said Gerda. "They're like a birthday present."

Only at the ranch at the end of the universe would anyone think an onion was a present.

"I mean wrapped up," explained Gerda. "So before you chop them, you have to take off the wrapping."

Then Gerda introduced Paloma to the double sink.

"Oh, come on." Keeping Faith Cross firmly in her mind, Paloma sounded not pleading—which she was—but teasing. "You must have a dishwasher. Everybody has a dishwasher."

"Of course we do." Gerda clapped her on the shoulder. "In fact, today we have three: Ricky, Sedona, and"—she handed Paloma a pair of rubber gloves—"you."

"But what about my skin and my nails?" protested Paloma. "I mean, even with gloves—"

"So far no one's lost any skin washing a plate," said Gerda. "And as for nails, unless you're stranded in the desert and need to dig for water, they just get in your way when you're doing manual work."

Being stranded in the desert became a distinct possibility on Paloma's first daylong hike. She had walked before, of course, but not for miles, and not over rough terrain. She'd figured that, what with the scrubbing and the carrying and the riding and the milking and the hauling out of animals that were stuck where they shouldn't be (mostly against their will), she'd discovered every secret muscle her body had, but she'd been wrong. There were more. Many more. And her feet hurt so much you'd think they'd never been in shoes before. The singing of happy trail songs didn't help.

Every night since Paloma decided to get into the same story as everybody else, she's fallen into bed with a gratitude usually reserved for major miracles, but when she finally staggered back from that first serious hike, she could hardly be bothered to get undressed.

"The first time's the worst," Tallulah assured her. "You'll get used to it."

Sure, thought Paloma. *If I don't die first.*

But, as we all know, nature has made certain that the will to live is very strong in most things—whether it's a weed or a teenage girl who was born lazy and raised to be useless—and Paloma didn't die. Instead, she has shown remarkable physical resilience for a girl who, at home in the hills of Beverly, has never walked farther than to the car.

And here she is now, baking in the sun like a cookie in an oven, but listening with obvious interest to Ethan Lovejoy describing all the ways a person can come close to death and possibly expire on a wilderness trek, despite the fact that if she were a cookie she'd have been done fifteen minutes ago.

"Well, I think that just about takes care of all the important stuff you need to know right now." Ethan Lovejoy lifts one arm into the air. Because he is sitting on a very large white stallion and the land around him is very flat and the buildings of the ranch are out of sight, it almost looks as if he is touching the sky. The stallion has a feather stuck in his harness that matches the one in Ethan Lovejoy's hatband. "All right, gang, we're almost ready for departure, but before we get going, does anybody have any questions? Anything you're not sure of?"

Facing him is his gang, also on horseback: the dozen residents going on this special weekend. Ethan calls it the Oregon Trail Weekend because—although they are nowhere near Oregon—it is a test of skill, stamina, determination, and courage, just as following the Oregon Trail was for the pioneers who used it. The Oregon Trail Weekend is one of the many rites of passage that mark a person's progress in life on the ranch. First you learn to care for the animals and master basic domestic chores; then you go on long hikes and build campfires and learn to identify animal tracks and what to do if you're bitten by a snake; and then you get to relive the pioneer experience, crossing a varied terrain of desert, grassland, and forest—though hopefully with no one shooting at you and little chance of dying of thirst or hunger and having your bones picked clean by buzzards.

Paloma raises her hand.

Ethan Lovejoy smiles like the moon. "Yes, Susie? What is it you'd like to know?"

"Well, it's not really a question." She beams back. He's had them sitting so long, listening to him go on and on about challenges and human resilience in the face of adversity, that they're all sweating and they haven't gone an inch. If they don't start moving soon they may all melt. "I just wanted to say that I packed really light, so if anybody's got too much to carry I could take some extra stuff with me." She pats Sweetie's neck. Gingerly. "It wouldn't be any trouble."

"That's very thoughtful of you, Susie."

Paloma continues to smile. But modestly. She has learned a lot during what she thinks of as her imprisonment on Old Ways Ranch. The difference between mince, dice, and chop. How to slow the flow of blood from a deep cut. How to get on a horse without being thrown right back off, milk a cow without being kicked, and fry potatoes without setting fire to the kitchen. She can identify several different animals by their excrement, as well as by their teeth marks. She knows how long it takes to walk ten miles and why hiking boots were invented. She knows all the words to "Shenandoah." But, most importantly, she knows what Ethan Lovejoy wants to hear. "I just want to help if I can," says Paloma.

"I know you do." The good doctor can be forgiven for feeling a little smug. Susan Minnick may well be one of his greatest success stories. She has made steady—some might almost say incredible—progress since the day she finally left her room, and has not only thrown herself into ranch work and therapeutic sessions like an entire family of ducks getting into a lake, but has also been charming, sweet, kind, considerate, compassionate, and unflaggingly positive and good-humored. Every morning she is among the first to have her chores done, her horse fed and pastured, and her room ready for the surprise inspections that happen throughout the week. In short, she is nothing like the girl he picked up at the airport. You wouldn't even think they were from the same species. Naturally enough, Ethan attributes this change to himself, his staff, and the mission of the ranch. He has no idea that Paloma is playing Faith Cross, who is all of those things (but with the bonus of angelic powers). "However, I am a little anxious that you may have underpacked. You don't want to find yourself up a mesa without enough water."

"Oh, no, I have everything." She pulls a piece of paper from her pocket and holds it up. "See? I made a list, just like you said."

What a star.

Once they've established that everyone made a list as they were told to, and packed sensibly and sparingly, as they were told to, Ethan Lovejoy raises himself slightly in his saddle. "Is that it? No other questions?"

No one so much as blinks. Paloma isn't the only one who would like to get going.

Ethan Lovejoy raises his arm again and starts to turn his horse. "In that case, gentlemen and ladies, westward ho!"

And off he trots. One by one, his gang peels off and follows, with Paloma and a boy named Raul Riley bringing up the rear. *Come a ti-yi-yippee-yippee-yea.* Though they aren't actually heading west.

Paloma and Raul Riley bring up the rear of the line of riders because they're the slowest. At Old Ways Raul has discovered photography—the old-fashioned, nondigital kind with film and darkroom developing—and is a lot more interested in taking pictures than in making time. Paloma is on a horse whose favorite part of any journey is stopping, which she does as often as she can. Sweetie has also been known to simply lie down when she feels that she needs a rest, a habit that has shown that Paloma is not only adaptable but also has excellent reflexes, since she always manages to roll out of the way.

But no matter how slowly you go, even if you're not the one carrying supplies and a passenger and doing all the walking, the journey is a lot more difficult than riding around LA in a Mercedes. Horses have no suspension, no air-conditioning, and no sound system. Saddles are hard, and the sun is harsh. The trail is rough and narrow, sometimes dry and flat under a makeup-melting sun; the air is moving less than a corpse; and it's sometimes hilly and so thick with trees that the sky seems to disappear, every unseen snapping twig and rustling leaf a threat.

Given all that, no one would blame you for thinking that Paloma Rose would rather be back on the plane in economy, pressed between two strangers who wouldn't recognize a Louis Vuitton if they tripped over it, than bouncing along on Sweetie under a remorseless sun and getting to know new kinds of pain. Humans, however, are less predictable than ants or even the weather, and the fact is that despite the aches, the discomfort, and the occasional bursts of song, Paloma is far from unhappy. Since that first fateful commercial when she could barely toddle, Paloma has never really been allowed to just be.

No staring at her toes or gazing at the passing clouds. No walking in the rain. No dancing in the moonlight. In both her real life in Hollywood and her pretend life on the ranch, she is always "on." But not right now. Now Sweetie is doing all the work, and Paloma is just one of the billions of things on whom the sun has shone, and all she has to do is look out for small creatures darting between the rocks or snakes streaking across the trail and let her mind wander, thinking of things she'd forgotten and didn't know she cared about—and, for the first time ever, enjoy simply being alive.

In the afternoon they are in a landscape of scrub punctuated by fantastical rock formations—towers and pinnacles, arches and spires, mesas and buttes—that rise around them like the cities of a mythical kingdom. Because the sky is so enormous and the light so intense, she remembers something that for once isn't an episode of *Angel in the House* but a documentary she saw about people who survived horrible misadventures—a plane crash in the jungle, adrift in a rubber raft, lost in the desert, falling off a cliff. The only reason she watched this particular show was because Seth Drachman, a climber himself, recommended it and she wanted to impress him, but it obviously affected her more than she thought. She can almost see the man whose Jeep broke down so far from civilization that it might as well not have existed, staggering over the arid earth, his lips cracked and his skin peeling like old paint.

And then, all of a sudden, she thinks she really does see something—to the left of the trail they're on, near the base of a broken mesa, folded into a clutch of stunted trees. She stops Sweetie and peers into the distance. It's still there. She rubs her eyes and peers some more. Paloma turns to call the others, but the only other person she sees is Raul Riley, taking a picture of a rock formation that looks like an ornate candelabra—around which, she assumes, the others have all disappeared.

"Raul!" calls Paloma. "Wait a minute! I think I see something."

Raul turns around. "What?"

"Over there!" She points to the base of the broken mesa. "Do you see it?"

Raul doesn't see it.

"It's right over there." Paloma keeps pointing. "It could be a man. See how it's all sort of crumpled?"

Raul, who has backtracked only a few yards, comes no closer. "It's probably a dead tree or something like that. Forget it. Let's catch up with the gang."

"I don't think so." Paloma shakes her head. "It looks like a person to me. And I think I see a backpack. Don't you see it? That dark thing on his left?"

"What I think is that you're seeing things," says Raul. "Ethan said that can happen. Because of the sun and everything."

"Ethan also said there are a lot of hikers and climbers around here," argues Paloma. "What if he's had an accident and he's badly hurt? He could die out here." Seth told her that if someone you were climbing with fell, you had to try to help him, no matter how dangerous it might be, if you thought there was any chance he was alive. She has a vague memory that something like that happened to Seth once—he saved someone, or someone saved him. It's definitely what Faith Cross would do.

"So we'll tell Ethan you think you saw somebody lying on the ground," says Raul, making it clear that he doesn't think that's what she sees. "He'll know what to do. It's better if him or one of the other counselors checks it out anyway."

But right at this moment it seems important to Paloma to be the kind of person who wouldn't abandon someone who needs her help.

"You go on," says Paloma. "I'm just going to see."

"You're crazy. You can't go off the trail. What if your horse steps in a gopher hole or something?"

It doesn't even occur to Paloma that she's finally found someone as nervous of nature as she is. Or was.

"I don't think they have gophers out here." Not that she's really sure what a gopher is.

"OK, but they have other things that dig holes."

"Go catch up with everybody," she orders. "I mean, it's not like it's miles away. It's not going to take me that long. Just tell them to wait for me."

"Ethan's not going to like this," says Raul. "We're not supposed to leave the group."

Paloma, however, is no beginner when it comes to wriggling out from under the burden of blame. "I think the group left *us*," she says.

Raul looks behind him, as if he wants to make sure. When he turns back, Paloma is already riding away.

The broken mesa is farther away than she thought, and riding off the trail isn't as easy as it looks in cowboy movies when the good guy is chasing the bad guy. By the time she reaches her destination she wishes she'd listened to Raul. Especially when it turns out that it isn't an injured hiker after all. It isn't a dead tree, either, which makes her feel a little better. It's the remains of a wolf. The backpack is just a large rock. Now everyone's going to laugh at her. Ethan won't yell, because he doesn't, but he's going to think she's a dope. A disobedient dope. And everything she's done in the last weeks will be undone.

Ethan is waiting for her when she gets back to the trail. The first thing he asks is if she's all right. The second is, "So what is it?"

"It's a dead wolf." Paloma gives him an embarrassed and wary smile. "Am I in trouble?"

"You should've come and gotten me. For everybody's safety. That's the rules." He smiles back. "But heck, Susie. You followed your instincts. You thought somebody might need help. It's probably what I would've done." He claps a hand on her shoulder. "Don't tell the others, but I'm kind of proud of you."

"Thank you," says Paloma.

And for some reason actually means it.

That night they cook on the campfire and sing songs and tell stories, just like in the TV shows—though not any that Paloma's been in. When she gets into her sleeping bag, since there's nothing else to look at, Paloma stares up at the sky. Which is another thing she's never done before. As she falls asleep, the thought runs through her mind that Ethan Lovejoy is wrong: there are a lot more than ten million stars.

A man may work
from sun to sun,
but a princess's work
is never done

Even nineteenth-century factory workers occasionally got a day off, but as far as Oona can tell, the iconic
TV star gets considerably less downtime. Someone else
does her Twitter posts and blog, but aside from those two
things (which, really, you could do lying on the couch
while eating a bag of tortilla chips), everything else falls
to Oona. Interviews—whether they're online, on the
phone, or over a latte in a trendy café—store openings;
mall visits; charity events; and appearances at homeless
shelters, hospitals, and nursing homes (Faith Cross is
extremely popular with people who are down on their
luck or waiting to die). It really is like being a princess,
only without the tiara and boat christenings.

The appearance days are always a strain. Last week,
after visiting a nursing home, a hospital, and a youth

shelter, Leone got on Oona's case as soon as they were on their way home.

"I don't believe you did that," she fumed. "Who told you to have an opinion about health care or education or job programs or anything else? Who are you, Angelina Jolie?"

When she was asked to say a few words at the nursing home, Oona picked the few words that concerned a better service available to everyone. Asked to say a few words at the hospital, she chose "No one should have to die because they can't afford the medical bills." Asked to say a few words at the youth shelter, she said, "Those who have, get."

"I thought that's what they wanted—my opinion," argued Oona. "That's what they asked for."

"Well, it wasn't what they wanted. All they wanted was for you to say how damn happy you were to be there." Leone said that Oona's problem is that she takes it all too seriously. "Doing this kind of thing is just part of the job," said Leone. "Garbage men collect garbage. Doctors give you pills. *You* entertain people, whether you're on TV or in a video or doing a public appearance. You go in, you smile, you have your picture taken—and that's it. You're not the ambassador from the Land of Hope. You're like Santa Claus or the Easter Bunny." Minus the sack of toys and the basket of eggs, of course. "You cheer them up for a few minutes, and then everything goes back the way it is. There's nothing you can do to change their lives."

But Oona doesn't think it's fair that some people — people like Paloma Rose — should have so much and other people so little.

"Fair, schmair," said Leone. "You're idealistic. And I guess that's a nice thing. You're a kid. You don't get how things work." No matter how many times she has tried to tell her. "But let's face it, sweetie. Fair is a skin tone or part of the weather report. It doesn't mean bupkis out in the real world." In the real world, according to Leone, some people have really good lives for whatever reason — birth or talent or luck — and most people don't. And, just as the peasants of old wanted to touch the hem of the king's robe or watch the royal procession go by because it made them feel better about their own miserable lives, ordinary people today like to shake the hand of a celebrity or watch her walk up a red carpet in five-thousand-dollar shoes. "Your job is to be beautiful and glamorous, not to lead the revolution."

"You wouldn't say that if you were most people," snapped Oona.

"But I'm not," Leone snapped back.

She's been watching Oona as if she were a suspicious package left at an airport ever since.

When they come out of St. Eugenia's Hospice Home today, a troop of staff and residents already outside to wave them good-bye, the limousine is waiting to take them to lunch.

"I really don't know why you brought that creature with you," says Leone as she climbs in last and shuts the door. "She smells like a dog."

"She is a dog." Oona sits next to the window, the offending creature on her lap. "And her name's Harriet." This is one of the things she never gets tired of saying, and Leone never tires of not knowing. "And you know why I brought her." Oona's schedule has been so hectic over the last few days that she overslept, so there was no time to give Harriet her long morning walk. "Besides, it's Maria's day off. Harriet doesn't like being alone all day."

Behind her gold-rimmed sunglasses, Leone rolls her eyes. "And when did she tell you that? When the two of you were having one of your philosophical conversations?"

"You don't have to be able to talk to communicate," says Oona. "Some people talk all the time and don't communicate at all."

Leone clicks her seat belt in place. "Maria could've taken her."

"I'd rather have her with me." Oona makes what Leone calls her knock-that-chip-off-your-shoulder face— head up, chin out, mouth like a knot. "Anyway, everybody likes her. She's an asset."

The only good thing Leone has to say about Harriet is that at least she's not one of those bug-eyed Chihuahuas, so "asset" isn't how Leone thinks of her. But she occupies herself with checking the time and says nothing, mainly because there is nothing to say. Except for her, everybody does like Harriet. This is not the first time Oona's insisted on including her in their little entourage, and Harriet is always treated like she's the star. Oona's actually taken Harriet to the studio a couple of times as well, and even Audrey Hepplewhite volunteered to take her for a walk. Never has so much of a fuss been made over an animal that looks like an experiment that went wrong. St. Eugenia's was their third stop today, and at all three everyone was all over the mutt—getting her water, sneaking her treats, begging to hold her, asking for stories about her, as if Paloma Rose is taking time from her incredibly busy schedule to talk about her dog. No one has so much as offered Leone a cup of coffee all day.

"You're supposed to be promoting Paloma Rose and the show, not animal welfare."

"That's what I'm doing. Mother." The smile Oona

gives Leone makes sugar seem sour. "Most people think you're a much nicer person if you like animals."

Leone isn't going to win this argument, and she knows it. There's been much more interest in Paloma Rose since she started showing up with Harriet—interest and goodwill. Over the past year or so, Paloma Rose managed to create just the opposite. Her public appearances had been dwindling to the point where if they were a river you could barely float a leaf in it. This was partly because Paloma was often late, absent, in a bad mood, or arguing with her mother—which tends to put people off—and partly because, when she did show up smiling, she wouldn't know where she was, or she'd get names wrong, or yawn when someone was saying how happy they all were that she'd come, thus giving the impression that she'd rather be somewhere else. But now Paloma Rose is in demand, and Harriet can take some of the credit for that. So, although, as Leone understood the deal, it didn't include making Paloma a much nicer person, she doesn't have the legs of a coin to stand on when it comes to the benefits of liking animals. Leone, however, is a very resourceful woman whose ability to criticize is apparently limitless. She finds one thing. "I believe Hitler was very fond of dogs," says Leone.

"Only if they were Aryan," says Oona.

* * *

They have lunch at a restaurant so far away from the tourists and the glitter and glamour of Hollywood that they might as well be in the Ozarks. Asked for a place where Paloma could eat in privacy and peace, the driver recommended it. It is, in fact, less a restaurant than a parking lot overlooking the ocean—crammed with tables and catered to by three vintage Airstreams selling, respectively, Mexican, Greek, and Thai food. It's packed.

"Remind me not to ask him to recommend a hotel," says Leone as they take their seats at a cheap plastic table.

Oona thinks it's cool. She grins happily. "And the best part is we don't have to leave Harriet in the car."

"It's the answer to my prayers," says Leone. This, of course, is far from true. At this particular moment, the answer to Leone's prayers would be for the day to be over, and for her to be relaxing in a real restaurant (with a real roof over it, real air-conditioning, real plates and table-cloths, real waiters, a strict dress code, and a no-dogs-except-service-dogs rule), far, far away from Oona Ginness and her mongrel. But they have one more visit this after-noon before that can happen. "Now if I could just find the fountain of youth my life would be complete."

Much to Leone's surprise, however, the food isn't bad, and, although the other diners aren't people with whom she'd want to have her picture taken, no one looks twice at them. They're all too busy eating and talking. Leone sends e-mails and texts while she picks at her lunch, and Oona takes off her sunglasses and her hat, sits back, and enjoys being able to gaze at the ocean without anyone looking or pointing at her.

It isn't until she's finished her lunch and decides to give Harriet a run along the beach before they get back in the car that Oona realizes that Harriet isn't sleeping in the shade of the table anymore. She stands up, scanning the tables, the parking lot, and the shoreline, but there isn't any sign of Harriet. Oona gets down on her knees.

Leone is so engrossed in the e-mail she's writing that she doesn't notice — or, if she notices, she doesn't bother to remind Oona how much the clothes she's wearing cost, or to tell her that only drunks and vagrants crawl on the ground, or to list the many diseases Oona is liable to catch.

If Oona ever wondered what a dog sees most of the time, the answer is legs. From her position halfway under the table, that's all Oona sees for yards and yards. Legs and more legs. It must make things pretty confusing for them; it could explain why so many dogs like to chew shoes. She peers through the legs like a fish peering through a forest of reeds. And suddenly sees that familiar furry face and floppy ears, not half a dozen tables away. "Harriet!" she calls. "Harriet! Come here!"

Harriet waggles in place but doesn't come. Oona crawls forward. Now she can see why Harriet stays where she is; she's tied to the table leg by a short rope.

There's a flash, and then another. Oona's not looking at legs anymore; she's looking into the lens of a camera.

"Thanks, sweetheart! That's great!"

And now she's looking at a face that isn't as familiar as Harriet's, but isn't unknown to her either. She's seen it on the street. Outside the studio. Looking in at her when she and Leone and Jack are out for dinner. Pressed against the window of a boutique. Sitting behind the wheel of a compact gray car that looks like thousands of others—but isn't. It's the car that follows her. And there, with the grin of a man who just won the lottery, is the man who drives that car. His name, though Oona doesn't know this yet, is Ludlow Spantini.

Oona is on her feet as quickly as he is, but he has his back to her as he squeezes his way between tables and chairs and is unaware that she's coming after him. She stops only long enough to untie poor Harriet and scoop her up into her arms.

Because there are so many tables and so many people sitting at them, and because Mr. Spantini isn't expecting to be followed by an irate teen TV star and her dog, he moves slowly, still smiling to himself and thinking about captions: *Fallen angel. So far from heaven. Paradise lost.*

But suddenly there she is, blocking his way. *Avenging angel.* He automatically puts his camera behind his back.

"Don't worry, I'm not going to touch your stupid camera." Oona has learned a lot about enunciation and projection since she moved in with the Minnicks. Her voice is loud and clear and certain. The way God might sound if He were a teenage American girl. "I just want to talk to you."

"Honey . . ." Ludlow Spantini is still smiling. "I really don't have ti—"

"Oh, yes, you do. Time is something you *do* have. You sure as sunrise have enough time to follow me around like you're some kind of spy. I see you every day. Everywhere I go."

He takes a step forward, but she moves no more than a brick wall would. "Look, honey, I think you—"

"No, you don't think. That's one of your big problems. You just go around doing what you want without any kind of thought in your head, unless it's how much money you think you're going to make."

Mr. Spantini holds up his hands as if calming a restless crowd. "If you don't mind—"

"I do mind." Oona seems to be getting taller by the second. "I mind very much. I told you I want to talk to you, and I meant it. You're so totally fascinated with me, I'd think you'd be happy to talk to me. I've seen you standing around with your camera when all I was doing was buying a bottle of water. A bottle of water! How fascinated must you be by me? Well, I'm pretty fascinated by you, too. Because I don't get you. I can't figure out what kind of life you have, tailing people who are just going about their business. Trying to catch them doing something stupid or embarrassing or—better yet—something that could ruin their lives."

Mr. Spantini now tries to move backward, but there seems to be someone blocking that way, too. "I really have to get going."

"*Now?* You attach yourself to me like you're a tick, and now, when you can actually talk to me face-to-face, you want to leave? You're hurting my feelings, Mr. —I'm sorry, what'd you say your name is?"

There's no way he can go left or right, either. "Look, honey, I—"

"Stop calling me honey."

"Look, Pa—"

"You know what I really wonder about, Mr. Lots-of-Nerve-but-Nameless? I wonder if when you were a little kid, you used to lie in your bed at night dreaming of being a sleazy star snapper when you grew up. Did you think, 'Wow, wouldn't it be cool to hound and harass people? Maybe even destroy their careers or break up their families?' And how totally phenomenally great would it be to torment and terrify an innocent little dog just to make somebody look like a fool?"

At the mention of her, Harriet, who could probably have her own film career, whimpers gently and looks very sad. The air around them almost sighs.

Ludlow Spantini is aware, in a vague but uneasy way, that no one around them is eating or talking or even bent over their phones anymore. They're all listening to Oona. This is not the way his day was supposed to go. He shifts both his eyes and his body, looking for a way out. "I didn't hurt—"

"Do you know what I did this morning?" Oona laughs. "But of course you know! You've been tracking me since I left my house. So you know that I went to a homeless shelter and a hospital and a hospice this morning. And I met some really great people. Decent people who don't just want to take from the world, but want to give, too. People who are trying to help other people because they don't just care about themselves. They work really hard, and they see a lot of suffering and unhappiness. The ones

237

who get paid don't make much, and a lot of them are volunteers. And then there are the people who've had some bad luck or made some bad choices, but they want to make their lives better. That's how I spent my morning. And what do you do? You demean the art of photography, that's what you do. And you don't do much for being human, either. You make something happen just to get a picture. You have no principles, and you have no shame."

There are a few seconds of silence when Oona finishes. And then the crowd starts to clap. If Oona were on a stage and not at an outdoor eatery, it would be a standing ovation.

Just when things are going so well . . .

People used to rely on their calendars. Calendars that would sit on the desk or hang on the wall or the back of the door to the kitchen with messages scrawled in the boxes: *Joylene's party, Shopping with Annie, Pizza night, Dentist 3:45.* Now most of us rely on our phones and computers to remind us when we have a card to send or something to do. But not, of course, at Old Ways. Because the ranch insists on living in the labor-intensive past, when the residents' phones and computers are taken from them, they're given calendars to replace them. The calendar has been specially made, each month decorated with an appropriate picture of the ranch at that time of year (next year's will feature the work of Raul Riley). The ranch in summer. The ranch in autumn. The ranch at night. Pickup trucks. Horses. Cows. The barns under fountains of fireworks. A wooden fence and chickens. A

Christmas tree in the common room. A campfire burning brightly.

Since things like the birthdays of aunts and visits to the dentist don't really impinge on ranch life, most of the residents use these calendars to keep track of their chore schedules (Tuesday, kitchen duty; Wednesday, mop hall), therapy sessions (Monday, private; Friday, group), and special occasions (Saturday, camping; Sunday, barbecue). Since Paloma thought of herself not as a resident but as an inmate at first, she also used hers to tick off the days like a prisoner scratching off the days of her sentence on the wall. Every evening when she put another X through another box, she'd think, *Another day down; not long now.*

And so the days and weeks have passed—and Paloma's sense of desperation has passed with them. The routines of the ranch have given her a new rhythm to her life. She doesn't eat by herself, or spend hours on her computer by herself, or have no one to talk to but herself anymore. Now, rather than crossing off the days, she puts stars in the boxes that are special: Pilar's birthday, the talent show, the summer dance.

Indeed, it is about the summer dance that Paloma and Tallulah are talking as they leave the dining hall after supper on this pleasant summer evening. Paloma was elected head of the dance committee, a job she is taking very seriously.

"But it isn't like it's a debutante ball," Tallulah is saying. "It's just a dance on a ranch."

"So? It's a big deal for us. We have a real DJ."

"I don't know how real Calvin Meiser is," says Tallulah. "You weren't here when the goat trapped him on the roof of the chicken coop." Life at Old Ways, though dull as swamp water, is not without incident. "It didn't enlarge anybody's opinion of him."

"The goat won't be at the dance."

"OK, so we have a DJ. But it's still not exactly the prom. We're not all wearing fancy clothes and having our hair done. We're just putting on clean jeans and T-shirts."

"That doesn't mean we can't decorate the common room and make it look special." Paloma, of course, has never so much as decorated an Easter egg (Leone always buys a dozen from a local artist and pays a designer to provide a different themed tree each Christmas). But over the seasons Faith Cross has decorated a desert dugout, a cave, an abandoned airplane hangar, a mud hut, a trailer, and a giant sequoia, so Paloma feels that she knows what to do. And she's seen enough movies and TV shows to know what a dance should look like.

"You mean balloons?"

"Yeah, balloons. And streamers and colored lights. Maybe we can make some paper flowers or something like that. Or doves." Faith Cross once decorated a Christmas tree with origami doves. "Make it look like a garden."

Tallulah laughs. "You really are too much." Unlike previous occasions when Paloma has heard these or similar words, this is not a criticism. "What were the chances?"

"Meaning?"

"Meaning look at you. All heated up about the Old Ways summer dance. If anybody had told me when you first got here that you'd change so much, I'd've laughed in their face and called them stupid."

Paloma gives her a friendly poke. "You're the one who told me to get with the program." Though no one told her that she has to look forward to the dance.

"Well, yeah, of course I did." Tallulah pokes her back. "But I didn't expect you to do it."

Paloma shrugs in the new way she has mastered since she accepted that tantrums and meltdowns no longer get her what she wants: like a duck letting water roll off its back. "Well, you know what they say about Rome."

Tallulah doesn't know.

The adage Paloma is thinking of is: *When in Rome, do as the Romans do,* but she doesn't really know it, either.

"It's, like, 'When in Rome, do something'—you know, like eat spaghetti or speak Italian. Something like that."

"Yeah, but you've done more than eat spaghetti. You even did the Oregon Trail. I mean, that is really massive." Tallulah winks. "I guess you're even a better actor than you say you are."

Paloma doesn't quite hear that last sentence. Ms. McGraw, aka the McNugget, is standing outside the office block, yakking to Ethan Lovejoy. "I'll meet you in the common room later for that Scrabble game," says Paloma. "I have to go. Ms. McGraw's waiting for me."

Next to talking to Ms. McGraw, the Oregon Trail is a walk in the park.

Kara McGraw is a serious and earnest kind of person who totally believes the words of wisdom that decorate the walls of Old Ways. She always starts the day with a positive thought, and always ends the day promising herself to do even better tomorrow—a goal she often achieves. She and Paloma talk together for forty-five minutes three times a week. They discuss everything from the food and the weather to difficulties with other residents and with livestock to the anxieties and problems that have brought Paloma to this oasis of peace and security in a turbulent world. One of Kara McGraw's many sayings is "No trouble too big or too small." And, as she never tires of telling Paloma, besides these sessions, her door is always open — morning, noon, or night — even if all Paloma wants to do is shoot the breeze.

The breeze is not what Paloma would like to shoot.

Ms. McGraw is a very nice woman — not even Paloma would argue with that — but she is also the human equivalent of a Hallmark card. A platitude for every occasion, that's the McNugget. Forty-five minutes with her is like forty-five minutes wading through corn syrup in one of those old-fashioned dresses with the full skirt and ruffles. In the McNugget's opinion, the glass is not just always half full, it's always half full of the purest, crystal-clear spring water (in which no fish, bird, or mammal has peed or pooped). There isn't a cloud that isn't lined with gold. There isn't a deluge that doesn't produce acres of flowers. The darker the night, the brighter the dawn. Another of her many sayings is "God gives us problems so we can solve them." *How considerate of Him,* thought Paloma sourly the first time she heard this, but aloud what she said was, "You know, Ms. McGraw, that's really very true."

Now, as she sits down and Ms. McGraw asks her how she is today, Paloma says, "I'm good, Ms. McGraw. I'm really, really good."

"I can't tell you how happy it makes me to hear you say that, Susie." Ms. McGraw looks happy. "I was just saying to Ethan how well you're doing. You're practically the poster girl for our philosophy and methods."

Paloma, who still thinks of herself more as the poster girl for victimhood and parental cruelty, smiles her new at-peace-with-the-world smile. "Thanks. That's really nice of you to say."

"We get what we earn," says Ms. McGraw. "And look what you got." She hands Paloma a postcard. It's a picture of the sun going down over the Hollywood sign. "It came this afternoon."

Paloma takes the card. On the back Leone has scrawled, *The sunset misses you, too. Hope you're having a great time. Everyone sends their love. Hugs and kisses from me and Dad. Love, Mom.* Paloma slips the card into her pocket.

"What would you like to talk about today?"

"Well, you know, I was working on some ideas for the dance today and, I guess this is going to sound really weird, but it made me think about my mother."

Paloma usually makes things up to tell Ms. McGraw.

Things she thinks the McNugget wants to hear. Or rather, she borrows shamelessly from TV shows and movies she's seen. Tragic accidents. Horrible deaths. An extended family so dysfunctional they make the Borgias look like paradigms of human behavior. In one memorable session that had tears in the counselor's eyes, Paloma even had herself separated from her twin at birth.

But there is one thing that Paloma has told the truth about in her talks with Ms. McGraw, and that is her relationship with her mother. It seemed pointless to make it up. Ms. McGraw says it's not at all unusual for teenage girls not to get along with their mothers. In fact, it's pretty much normal. The nagging. The arguments. The trying to control Paloma's heart and soul. The constant criticism. Ms. McGraw didn't even think that the time when Leone threw Paloma's clothes into the backyard was anything special. It seems that, all over the world, mothers are hurling their daughter's belongings out of windows every hour of the day.

"And what were you thinking about her?" Ms. McGraw always sounds as if she were born understanding everything, as if she never has a bad mood or an unkind thought.

For the first time since she was a small child, Paloma's

thoughts of Leone aren't unkind. It suddenly struck her that when Leone was a teenager she must have gotten excited about going to a dance. Paloma's smile is shy and almost wistful. She isn't really used to the idea that her mother is human. "I was thinking about what you said about trying to understand how she's scared because she's getting old. You know, how she's jealous because I have my whole life in front of me and her best years are behind her?"

"I also said I'm sure she loves you very much," says Ms. McGraw. "And that while subconsciously she sees you as a rival who's taking her place, she doesn't want to lose you so she doesn't want you to grow up."

"Yeah, right. That's what I mean." Paloma's shrug is shy and wistful, too. "And anyway, all of a sudden I, like, really missed her."

Ms. McGraw nods. Earnestly and sincerely. "I know she misses you, too."

The common room is a large space, divided in two by a folding door. On one side are the tables where games are played—board games, cards, dominoes, Ping-Pong, and pool; on the other are sofas and chairs and an enormous flat-screen TV with enough channels to keep an army of problem teenagers happy. Several people nod or wave to Paloma. Meg points Paloma to a far corner where Tallulah is deep in a fierce paddle battle.

"Five minutes!" she grunts, whopping the ball over the net.

Paloma watches for a while, but, as in many things, her interest in Ping-Pong is limited and she soon wanders off. She admires the progress on the jigsaw puzzle Albie and his bunkmate have been doing for the last three weeks. She stands for a few minutes watching Pilar playing a game of chess with all the intensity of a brain surgeon performing an especially delicate operation. Everybody's immersed in whatever game they're playing and too busy to hang out for a while and just talk.

Paloma has avoided the TV section of the common room for all these weeks because it's too painful a reminder of where she should be and what she should be doing (in Hollywood, entertaining millions, not on the back acres of hell pushing livestock around), but now, with nothing else to do but hang around like an uninvited guest, she pushes the folding door open enough to step through.

Almost every seat is occupied. In the middle of the sofa Raul sits with the remote gripped in his hands, flicking through the channels. *Blipblipblipblipblip.* Around him, the rest of the audience calls out commands that he ignores. *Blipblipblipblipblip.*

An image flashes past that catches Paloma's eye. It's a very familiar image.

"Stop!" she orders. "Go back to that girl. The blonde."

"Oh, come on, Suze," groans Raul. "Nobody wants to see that." *Blipblipblipblip.*

Paloma leans over the back of the sofa and snatches the remote from Raul so quickly that it's gone before he knows it. "Just for one minute," she promises.

It's the opening credits for *Angel in the House*—she'd recognize them in her sleep. It must be a rerun. Because they couldn't start the new season. So they must be showing old shows.

A chorus of moans erupts. "For God's sake, turn this crap off."

"Just a second," she repeats. As the show begins, Audrey Hepplewhite gets out of her car and walks toward a sign that says St. Anthony's Care Home. And there's Paloma, getting out of the passenger seat. "I just want to see something."

"No, not in a second—now!" screams someone else. "We don't want to watch this junk."

But Paloma pays no attention to the protests and rude remarks. She recognizes the scene. Faith and her mother are visiting a relative in a nursing home. Paloma frowns. But they haven't filmed that episode yet; that episode is in the new season. She stares at the screen, feeling as if cement has been poured into her blood. Very cold cement. How is it possible? How can they be showing an episode that hasn't been filmed yet? How has Audrey Hepplewhite made such a complete and miraculous recovery without anyone telling Paloma? How can Paloma be walking down the hallway in the nursing-home set in LA when she's been living at Old Ways all this time?

The answers to these questions, of course, are: it isn't, they can't, she couldn't, and she isn't. Up until this moment, Paloma thought her mother had simply taken advantage of the postponement in shooting the series to get rid of her for a while. How naive can she be? Now she sees that just as there was no luxury hotel, there was no car crash—and no coma, and no canceled season. And the perky blonde marching into the home may look like Paloma if you need glasses, but she isn't—even from here Paloma can see that her earlobes are all wrong, her nose is slightly larger, and she almost has an overbite. Now Paloma understands just how devious and treacherous Leone really is. The wicked stepmother in *Snow White* is practically a saint next to her. Miss Leone? That would be like missing a headache. A headache that you've had for seventeen long and agonizing years.

Someone makes a lunge for her and yanks the remote from her hand. There are cheers from the rest of the audience.

But Paloma still stares at the screen. Her hand reaches for the postcard in her pocket. *The sunset misses you, too. Hope you're having a great time. Everyone sends their love. Hugs and kisses from me and Dad. Love, Mom.* Everything she knows about lying she learned from Leone.

Little pitchers have big ears

Leone Minnick and Jack Silk are happy. Happy? Happy doesn't begin to describe how they feel. If Leone Minnick and Jack Silk were bells and not people, they'd be making such a racket that you'd think every church on the planet were having a wedding at exactly the same time on the same day. And the reason for all this ding-donging and clanging? The reason is that things were going well, but they suddenly took a turn for the better. The much, much better. Far better than they ever could have dreamed. To quote Jack Silk's comment to Leone when he heard the news, "I was hoping she'd save our bacon, but it looks like she saved the whole damn hog and stuck an apple in its mouth."

Because she never saw Oona crawling away under the table during lunch, it wasn't until Leone realized that she could hear only one voice and not dozens — and that she knew whose voice it was—that she looked up from her phone to see what was going on. What she saw didn't exactly put a smile on her face. *Oh, my Lord,* thought Leone. *She's doing it again! Why can't this girl ever keep her big trap shut?* Paloma was always taught that you never confront an annoying photographer or reporter. You don't break cameras, throw things at them, or hit anyone with your bag. You walk away, or, possibly, run, but you don't make things worse by actually having a conversation.

Leone got to her feet, planning to step in and cut the lecture short, but then she noticed the rest of Oona's audience. They were mesmerized. Transfixed. Nodding and gesturing. Taking videos and pictures. And when Oona was finished and they started to applaud, Leone clapped, too. But even then she wasn't expecting Oona and Harriet to become an Internet sensation. The YouTube clips and the tweets went viral. The news stations picked up the story. After so many months when you couldn't pay to get Paloma Rose on a talk show, suddenly everyone wanted her on. And then, like the perfect rainbow after months of dark clouds and rain, The Call came: Lucinda Chance, the doyenne of daytime television, wants an hour interview with Paloma Rose and her dog in their own home; wants to hear Paloma's story from her own lips. The hog not only has an apple in its mouth, but also is covered with pineapple rings and cherries. Things can't get any better than this.

Though it might have occurred to at least one of them that things can get worse.

Leone's been so nice to Oona since the scene at the outdoor food court that Oona wonders if she misjudged her a little. Maybe there's more to Leone than ambition, name-dropping, expensive restaurants, and gold; maybe she has hidden depths.

Leone no longer corrects Oona constantly or hovers over her as if she's a three-year-old who's going to dump her juice all over the carpet. Her criticisms are gentle and good-humored. She's been known to pay Oona the occasional small compliment. She's been seen giving Harriet a pat on the head.

This evening, after a long and stressful day of publicity visits, they stop on the way home to get takeout since Maria has the night off to see her cousin's new baby. Leone even lets Oona pick the restaurant. They eat together on the patio, discussing the upcoming interview with Lucinda. Since the invitation came through, Leone talks about little else. She has said several dozen times that she wants Oona to be herself, since that's the girl who was given the invite. Leone worries about what they should wear. Slouching-around-the-house clothes, or a little more formal and dressed up?

"I thought you said I should be myself," says Oona.

Leone says, "Within reason, sweetie. Within reason." Maybe they should have the house redecorated or at least spruced up. Oona points out that the interview's only a week away. Spruced up, decides Leone. But what about food? Should they have refreshments for Lucinda and her staff? Will she want to have the whole family on the air? Is there any chance that Harriet could go to that place where everybody takes their dogs and have a professional shampoo, cut, and manicure?

"I thought this was supposed to be laid-back and casual," says Oona. "You know, like she was in the neighborhood and decided to drop in?"

"Darling, please. Even around here no one just drops in with a camera crew in tow."

"No," says Oona, "but they do pretend."

After supper, Oona takes Harriet for her nightly walk. When they get back to the house Leone is stretched out on the couch in the living room, making to-do lists for next Sunday. Oona goes up to Paloma's room. Her room. She and Harriet make themselves comfortable in the big armchair; Oona reads while Harriet sleeps. It's taken a while, but Oona's starting to relax. The things that used to drive her crazy about the Minnicks don't bother her as much; the things that seemed so bizarre may not seem natural but they've become normal. Possibly because she's gotten used to being Paloma Rose, or possibly because Leone is being more pleasant, it isn't as bad as she used to think. It's bearable. If her father and mother were down the hall, it would actually be good.

Oona gets so lost in her book that she loses track of time. She finally looks up to realize that two hours have passed and she's thirsty.

Knowing that Leone's likely to be asleep on the sofa by now, she tiptoes down the stairs so as not to wake her. And stops on the landing when she hears a man's voice. It could be Arthur, of course—there is, after all, such a thing as a blue moon—but it isn't. She wouldn't recognize Arthur's voice, but she does recognize Jack Silk's. She strains to hear what they're saying, not making a sound herself. Jack doesn't come to the house that often, but it isn't as unusual as snow in Los Angeles in July, either. It happens. Sometimes. Now and then. When there's some particular reason why he and Leone can't meet in town, or he's already in the neighborhood. But Jack Silk is Paloma's agent, not Leone's friend. They don't do social calls. Not at this time of night.

There's an old saying that adults used to use to warn

one another when they were discussing something private and a child moved into their vicinity: "Little pitchers have big ears." It's a saying that neither Jack nor Leone has heard in decades, but they might do well to remember it now.

Oona sits on the stairs to listen. This is where things start to get worse.

Leone was about to turn in for the night when Jack Silk called. He sounded stiff and far away, as if he were up some mountain calling from a pay phone in a bar filled with drunken nomadic warriors who were looking for trouble. His words were cryptic. "I'm coming over," he said. "Make sure you're alone. I should be there in half an hour." Leone said she couldn't wait.

"Sorry to be so *Spy Who Came in from the Cold*," says Jack as he follows her into the living room. "But I couldn't risk discussing this on the phone. Those damn reporters. You never know who's hacking or listening in these days."

"What about a drink?" says Leone. "Would you like a drink?"

"I'll have a beer if you have one. But you might want something stronger for yourself."

She gives him a look. "Cut it out, Jack. You're starting to get me worried."

"At least that makes me feel less alone," says Jack.

Leone comes back with a beer for Jack and a martini for herself, and sets the drinks on the coffee table. She sits back on the sofa, waving Jack, who's still standing, toward one of the armchairs. "So what's all this cloak-and-dagger stuff? You hear something about the renewal? They can't possibly be canceling. Not now."

Jack doesn't sit down. "Where's Arthur? Is he lurking somewhere in the house or is he out?"

"He's out," says Leone. "And Maria's visiting some screaming child she's related to. She won't be home till the morning."

"Maybe you better tell her not to come back for a day or two. We don't need her here to complicate things. Tell her you think she needs a break. I can drop off whatever she needs."

Leone's smile flickers. "Jack, the interview with Lucinda's only a week away. I need Maria here. You can't be serious. There are a million things to do."

"I'm as serious as God or the Devil. Where's the kid?"

"Sound asleep by now, I'd think. We had a busy day."

Jack rocks back and forth on his heels. "You're not the only ones."

In the world of image that is Hollywood, breaking a toe or buying a new handbag can be turned into a major drama—one with the potential for both tragedy and a miniseries—so Jack's sudden visit hasn't caused Leone any real alarm. Until now. Now she has one of those oh-no moments that we all get from time to time—the moment you realize you're going to fall off the ladder, or you're going to drop that priceless vase, or you're about to hear some really bad news. "This isn't about the renewal, is it? Nothing's gone wrong?"

"Not with that. Everything's fine. We should have the contract by the end of the week. It's something else." Jack pauses, looking as if he's selecting his words one by one. "Thing is, Leone, she's gone."

"Gone?" repeats Leone. "Who's gone? I told you, she's—"

"Not her. The other one." Jack breathes as if he's been holding his breath. "Against every conceivable odd in the universe, it's Paloma. Paloma's gone."

"Gone?" Leone laughs. Not because she finds this news especially funny, of course, but because she's very much hoping that it isn't true. Really, where could Paloma possibly go? "She can't be gone. You said this place is miles from nowhere. In the middle of the desert. How could she leave? Paloma'd take a cab to cross Hollywood Boulevard if she could."

"She's a magician," says Jack. "Or she sold her soul to

the Devil, and he got her out. I don't know how she did it; all I know is she's gone from the ranch. Vamoosed. Vanished like the dinosaurs. Only without leaving any fossils behind."

"But that's impossible." Leone couldn't sound more certain if Paloma were sitting beside her. Psychologists call this denial. Leone wants so much for this not to be happening that she convinces herself that it isn't. "Paloma waits for someone to open the door for her. She wouldn't just *go* by herself. Is there somebody else involved? Some boy? Some man?"

"Not as far as anyone knows. Lovejoy seems pretty sure that she did this all on her lonesome. He's questioned them all, and no one knows anything about it."

Leone is still refusing to believe him. "But she couldn't. I mean, I know she's always skipping out of here, but we're not in the middle of nowhere, we're in Beverly Hills; she can take a cab. She —"

"Watch my lips, Leone." He points to his lips. "Paloma is gone. We don't know how — maybe she's eaten some desert cactus and made herself invisible." Jack finally sits down. "But she's definitely not there. Lovejoy called me about an hour ago. Said he couldn't believe it. Nothing like this has ever happened before."

At last, a situation for which the good doctor doesn't have a wall sign.

"But I thought he said she was adjusting well. Really well. You said his reports were glowing. I thought he said she'd settled in like a prairie dog in its burrow."

That is, in fact, exactly what Jack reported Ethan Lovejoy as saying. Jack was quoting directly.

"Then there must've been a flash flood or a rattle-snake or something in that burrow, because she's left it."

"Are they sure? Maybe she just went for a walk or something."

"Well, if she did, she's walking pretty fast and far—either that or she's turned herself into a lizard," says Jack. "Lovejoy thinks that however she got away, she couldn't have been on foot. They've been searching most of the afternoon, and they didn't find her. That's why he didn't call me sooner. Figured she'd turn up before too long." Jack smiles. "Didn't want to panic the parents needlessly. Very considerate people, these reformers."

Leone pales beneath her makeup as another vehicle in the car crash that her life has suddenly become hits her. "Have they called the cops? My God, it'll be—"

"No, and he isn't going to. Not yet, at any rate. They want to have another look in the morning." Jack Silk and

Leone aren't the only ones who don't want any publicity. "And anyway, I convinced him we can handle it more discreetly. Told him we have connections. And that if this goes public it'll make your average hurricane look like a spring shower. Said the last thing we want is to bring any disrepute to the ranch." He smiles again. "Just so he knows we're very considerate people, too."

"And he bought that?"

"Of course he bought it. He has the reputation of the ranch to consider. Lovejoy's not going to want to bring any negative publicity to Old Ways. Not with what they charge. Besides, I said I know our girl. She's not going to be sleeping under bridges, is she?" Paloma's idea of sleeping rough would be staying in a hotel without room service. "She'll be coming home. Just like a pigeon."

"And then what?" Leone isn't thinking of pigeons, but of chickens coming home to roost. "You think she's going to be glad to see us, Jack? You think she's not going to tell the world and its cousins what happened? What we did?"

Jack flicks a piece of lint from his sleeve. "She's not going to tell anybody anything. Which is why I want Maria out of the picture for a couple of days. We don't need her finding out the truth and going into *Dios-mío* mode. I need time alone with Paloma to reason with her.

Explain that she'd be cutting off her head to spite your face. If she brings us down, she goes down with us. I'll make very sure of that."

"But you know how irrational she can be," says Leone.

"And you know how persuasive I can be." Jack's is a victor's smile. "Besides, we have the mama of all insurance policies, don't we?"

Leone's fingers tap on the arm of her chair. "Do we?"

"Yes, we do. We have Ms. Chance. Once that interview's been aired, Paloma won't dare open her mouth. Not if she wants to stay on this planet."

"OK. I'll give you that," concedes Leone. "That'll keep her mouth shut. But what if she doesn't come home? What if something happens to her?"

Jack is still smiling as if he can never lose. "And what could happen to her?"

"What could happen to her? Are you serious?" Leone isn't overburdened with either imagination or empathy, but suddenly she can see very clearly all the things that could happen to Paloma. "I know it's my fault because I spoil her, but Paloma can barely make herself a piece of toast. How's she going to survive for more than an hour all by herself out in the big cruel world?"

"She'll be fine," says Jack. "She'll be back home tomorrow. A couple of days, tops. Besides, the minute she uses her credit card we'll know where she is. I already have a man on the job. One of the best in the business. There's nothing to worry about."

But where there's guilt, worry is rarely far behind.

"What if there is? What if she isn't fine?" Leone suddenly feels the way people who watch everything they own burn to the ground or get washed out to sea feel: totally alone on the day hope died. "Anything could happen to her!" Rape. Murder. Kidnapping. Imprisonment. Disfigurement. An accident that leaves her paralyzed for the rest of her life. "Absolutely anything! I've tried so hard to protect her. What haven't I done for her?" And if any of those things happen, it will lead to questions. And answers. "My God, everything we've worked for—"

"Leone," says Jack. "Why don't you stop channeling Edgar Allan Poe and get yourself another drink?"

"You don't seem to be taking this very seriously," snaps Leone. "This could change everything. If they find out what we've done—"

"Nobody's going to find out anything."

"Really? And how can you be so sure? What if someone finds her wandering in the desert, hallucinating, dehydrated, and half-starved? Don't you think people might want to know how she got there?"

"Leone, you're getting carried away. She's not in the Sahara, for God's sake. I'm sure there must be a road."

"But—"

"But nothing," Jack assures her. "We just have to keep our heads. We've invested way too much in her to let this go belly-up now. That was the whole idea, wasn't it? To protect our investment?"

"I know, but—"

"Don't worry. I'll handle everything."

"And if she doesn't come back?" Leone's voice cracks. "How are you going to handle that?"

"Leone, she's going to show up eventually." If not of her own volition, then with the help of the ex-LAPD detective he's hired. "It may take a little while," admits Jack, "but this guy could find a grain of sand on the ocean floor."

"You mean dead or alive, don't you?" asks Leone.

"God forbid. But if some terrible tragedy did befall Paloma, it wouldn't be our fault. We did it for her own good, Leone. We were trying to help her." No one has ever accused Jack Silk of being either impractical or senti-mental—and with good reason. "Given the way she was headed, the odds are that, if we hadn't stepped in, sooner rather than later some terrible tragedy would've befallen her anyway." Overdose. Drowning in the bathtub. Booze.

Preventable accident. Abusive boyfriend. Plane crash. Suicide. "Everybody dies," Jack reminds her.

"You should've been a minister, you're such a comfort," snaps Leone.

Jack shrugs. "I'm only stating a fact. And besides, if the worst-case scenario happens and Paloma doesn't come back, we don't have to worry because she's already here."

"I can't believe you can be so callous." Leone's voice is not so much cracked as shattered. "We are talking about my only child here, remember."

Jack nods. *And your only meal ticket.*

Don't listen if you don't want to hear. This is not an old saying, but it probably should be. Oona thinks so. While Leone's showing Jack out, Oona goes back to her room as quickly as she can. She almost can't believe what she heard. And here she was feeling almost kindly toward Leone. And Jack Silk! She knows he's an agent — a wheeler-dealer — but, unlike Leone, he always seemed pretty OK. Not a mensch, maybe, but definitely human. She locks her door with a groan. But of course Jack Silk is human. All too human, really. Greedy, manipulative, and two-faced as a coin. And Leone, plotting against her own child like that. She certainly does have hidden depths, but these aren't the kind Oona meant.

266

She throws herself on the bed, trying to sort out what she heard and take it all in. So Paloma Rose isn't in some luxury hotel, being pampered and waited on and having a deserved holiday from all the stress and demands of her celebrity life. She's on some kind of ranch. Dead in the center of nowhere, apparently. Old Ways. That's what they said. Old Ways. Making it sound rustic, if not actually primitive. And what's a girl like Paloma doing in a place like that? Learning to start a fire by rubbing two sticks together? Baking bread with her own fair hands? Making soap? Whatever they do there, you can bet it's not your typical celebrity vacation.

Oona stares at the canopy above her, thinking of all the times Leone has talked about what a good time Paloma is having. Remembering all the phone calls, texts, and e-mails she's claimed to have received from her beloved daughter. All lies. And everything Oona's been told about poor, dear Paloma and how concerned everyone is about her has been a lie, too. They don't care about her, just about how famous she is and how much money she makes.

Oona closes her eyes. *We don't have to worry because she's already here. . . . our investment . . . We don't have to worry because she's already here. . . . our investment . . .* The words play over and over in her head like a bad song that she can't shake loose. If only she'd stayed in her room. If only, having left her room, she'd either marched down the stairs banging a drum or acted like the person she used to be—a person who doesn't eavesdrop on other people's private conversations—and turned right around and gone back. Why couldn't she mind her own business? Except, of course, that this *is* her own business. She's part of it. If it weren't for her, it never could have happened. She signed the contract. She's as guilty as anyone. She might as well have done a deal with the Devil. Oona sighs. Maybe she has.

There's never a paparazzo around when you really need one

Paloma's mad at everyone. She's mad at God for having her born to the Minnicks. She's mad at her father for being so useless and probably not even knowing that she's not at home. She's mad at Jack Silk for letting Leone trick him into helping her. She's mad at Ethan Lovejoy for believing Leone's lies. She's mad at Ms. McGraw for trying to make her feel sorry for Leone. But most of all, of course, she's mad at her mother. The jealous, controlling old witch. Leone's main purpose in life has always been to ruin Paloma's, but this time she's outdone herself. If she were an actor instead of the Darth Vader of motherhood, she'd be up for an Oscar.

Last winter the littlest thing—a broken nail, the wrong lunch order—would set off Paloma into a major tantrum. If something as horrible as this had happened, Paloma Rose would have torn through her world like a swarm of tornadoes, leveling everything in its path. She would have yelled and screamed and thrown things until even the birds in the trees and the worms in the ground begged for mercy. There wouldn't have been a person who came within ten miles of her who wouldn't have known how upset she was, and each of them — in one way or another — would have been made to pay for her unhappiness.

But it isn't last winter. Paloma acts as if nothing has happened, shouting at no one. Instead, for the next two days she spends as much time as she can by herself. Thinking. Brooding. Paloma's new approach to disaster is partly down to the fact that no one at the ranch is going to dance to the tune of her bad mood, and partly because she is now a girl who can ride a horse and milk a cow and make a pretty good marinara. And when Albie Delgado set himself on fire on the Fourth of July, it was Paloma who had the presence of mind to push him into the horse trough. Last winter she wanted people to take care of her. Now she can take care of herself.

Only Tallulah seems to notice how withdrawn Paloma is. "What's up with you?" she keeps asking. Paloma says there's nothing up with her. Tallulah says, "Don't give me that garbage, Suze. You haven't mentioned the dance since Thursday. And when we're together you're like a million light-years away." Paloma says she has stuff on her mind besides the dance. "Like what?" Tallulah persists. Nothing, just stuff. "Maybe you should talk to Ethan or the McNugget if something's bothering you," says Tallulah.

"And maybe you should mind your own business," says Paloma.

So she's also mad at Tallulah for not leaving her alone.

Paloma has learned a lot more at Old Ways than how to use a broom, but the one thing she hasn't quite mastered yet is Ethan Lovejoy's philosophy of forgiveness and understanding. Paloma wants revenge. Ms. McGraw says Leone is finding aging difficult and frightening? Well, Paloma's going to make her wish she'd never been born. Better than that. She's going to fire her. Her *and* Arthur. Leone's supposed to be her personal manager, and Arthur's supposed to be her business manager, but what do they do, really? Suck Paloma dry, that's what they do. They're barnacles on the ship of her talent and fame. All they do is take, take, take. She's almost seventeen, which is almost eighteen; she can manage herself and her money. She can't wait to see Leone's face when she tells her she'll have to look for another job! She'll take a picture: The Day My Monster Mother Joined the Unemployed. She'll put it on her website and on Facebook.

Maybe she'll even make a video of Leone running out of the house in tears and put it on YouTube. She'll tell all her followers on Twitter. The whole world will laugh itself dizzy over Leone Minnick's shame and humiliation. Paloma's going to make her really glad she's old and doesn't have that long to live.

Unfortunately, in order to get even with Leone, Paloma needs to be home, not tramping around the desert scraping horse manure off her shoes. The question is, when will that be? In a week? Two weeks? A month? Six months? A year? Any time she's asked the McNugget or Ethan Lovejoy, all they've ever said is, "When you're ready." As if she's a chicken in the oven. Before the revelation in the TV room, Paloma figured she'd be at Old Ways till Audrey recovered or died and they started filming again. Which couldn't be more than a month or two. But now? She doesn't have much hope of that anymore, not with that impostor in her place. What if she's here so long that there's nothing to go back to? What if Leone never had any intention of bringing her home at all?

And then, on Sunday morning, the minister arrives. This, of course, is not an extraordinary event. The minister comes every Sunday to give an ecumenical service in the ranch chapel, and then he joins them in the dining hall for lunch. What is unusual is that he normally drives an appropriately somber-looking black minivan with an IN GOD I TRUST bumper sticker, but on this Sunday he is driving a pickup with a Cardinals decal in the window. The pickup was loaned to him by the man repairing the church roof because the minivan wouldn't start (which could be an example of one of Ethan Lovejoy's favorite sayings about God working in mysterious ways).

As soon as Paloma sees the truck, she sees her escape. The Reverend Candle, who has saved so many souls in his career, is about to save her. It's such an obvious, such a simple, and such a perfect plan that you'd think she's not only in a movie, but also writing the script herself. The flatbed of the truck is filled with an assortment of what Paloma calls junk but Mr. Sandysman, its owner, calls work stuff. All she has to do is hide away in the back, and she'll be driven off the ranch—not in style, perhaps, but with relative speed and ease. No staggering over miles and miles of burning sand. No worrying about dying of thirst or hunger or heatstroke, or about being attacked by wolves, buzzards, spiders as big as Chihuahuas, or killer snakes. No being caught by Ethan Lovejoy, leaning out of the driver's window with that we-are-all-God's-children look on his face, saying, "The Devil makes work for idle hands, Susie Minnick. We haven't been keeping you busy enough."

The minister lives in a town. It may not be a major city, but it's bound to have a police department or at least a sheriff. Paloma will go to the law and tell them who she is. She doesn't want to be taken home. She's given this a lot of thought since Thursday night, and the last thing she wants is to be back in Leone's clutches. That would be like escaping from jail only to turn right around, walk back into your cell, and lock the door yourself. No, Paloma is never setting foot in that house again unless it's with the police when they go to arrest her mother. What she wants is to call a press conference so that she can tell the world what her mother has done to her, and expose Leone Minnick for what she is: a corrupt and scheming criminal. *Her own daughter,* people will say. *She did a horrible thing like that to her only child.* Leone will be dumped by every friend she has, receive death threats and hate mail, and possibly go to prison. She'll be as popular in the business as a writers' strike. She'll have to move somewhere where no one knows her—somewhere in Wisconsin or South Dakota—and shop at Wal-Mart for the rest of her life. However, Paloma, the victim of a twisted mind, will be the darling of Hollywood. All the mistakes Paloma made in the past will be forgiven and forgotten, and she'll be asked onto every talk show in the world. Her story will sell for millions. She'll have so many offers for work that she'll have to hire a second agent just to turn them down. Jack Silk can be her guardian until she comes of age, and she'll live by herself in some supermodern apartment (with Maria to cook and clean and do all that kind of thing), and she'll never be bossed around again. She might send Leone and Arthur a Christmas card every year, just to annoy them, but then again she might not.

After the service, Paloma, looking pale and fragile, goes to Ms. McGraw and tells her she feels ill.

"I'm really, really sorry, but I'm, like, all achy and hot and cold, and I think I'm going to throw up." Paloma's voice is soft and halting with the effort of trying to speak and not be a nuisance despite how ill she obviously is.

Ms. McGraw puts a hand to her forehead. "You do feel a little warm," she says. "You go straight to bed, and I'll tell Ethan you're not well. I'll check on you after dinner."

"Oh, you don't have to do that. It's your day off. I just want to lie down," gasps Paloma. "I think if I can sleep I'll be OK. . . . Maybe if you could just make sure I'm not disturbed for a while?"

"Will do," says Ms. McGraw. "You just get some rest."

As soon as she gets to her room, Paloma closes the

curtains and stuffs some of her dirty laundry in her bed to look like a body (season 1, episode 3). Most of her things—including her phone—are locked away in the storage area, so she takes only what she needs: a change of clothes, her credit card, and the money she brought with her because she thought she was going to be shopping, not camping. Then, while everyone else at the ranch is eating fried chicken and potato salad, Paloma darts across the yard like a cartoon character and climbs into the back of the truck. It's as if all the junk in the back had been arranged just for her. She hunkers down in a nest of boxes covered with a tarp. God may be working mysteriously, but he's also working overtime today.

Paloma makes herself as comfortable as possible with a satisfied smile. She's practically already on the *Tonight Show*.

Really, it couldn't be any easier if she had written the script.

"You want a soda pop or something?" asks the sheriff.

Paloma isn't sure what happened to the show she thought she was in, but the script is no longer the one she could have written. She couldn't have written this in the darkest hour of her darkest day. She wouldn't.

"No, thank you."

Things stopped being easy approximately three minutes after she heard the door of the pickup open and shut and Ethan Lovejoy saying, "Thanks for coming, Charley, we'll see you next week. You be careful on that road." It was as they started bouncing over the series of ruts that join Old Ways to the rest of nowhere that Paloma knew she'd made a really big mistake. Riding *inside* a pickup, she's discovered, is like riding in a Cadillac next to riding in the flatbed. Especially with Mr. Sandysman's work stuff falling on you and bumping into you every few seconds. It was hot under the tarp, hotter than a sauna—though if the amount of desert that managed to get under the tarp and onto and into Paloma is anything to go by, not hot enough to melt sand. The minister couldn't have hit more bumps, holes, or debris if he'd been deliberately aiming for them—and once he almost hit some animal and braked so hard Paloma nearly flew out of the truck.

"I told you what I want. I want to call a press conference," says Paloma, using the new patience she has acquired dealing with malicious animals. "I have some important things to say."

The sheriff—who herself has accumulated vaults of patience in her years of dealing with people at their very worst—looks around with a bemused smile. "I think you may be a little confused, Miss—"

"Rose." Paloma sighs. She has already told the sheriff this, too. "Paloma Rose. The TV star?" Her smile is the patient smile of an angel.

"Only I can't call your family to verify that, am I right?"

"I told you, they're in India. With my agent. On one of those ash things."

"Ashram."

"Yeah, that's it. Ashram. It's a religious retreat. They're not allowed to communicate with the outside world. That's why I need to call a press conference."

"I don't call press conferences, Miss Rose. This isn't Hollywood."

Really? How can she tell? Because there aren't any palm trees? Or because the town's only one block long?

"It doesn't matter. If you tell them who I am, they'll come. I mean, surely you must have heard of me—"

"I've heard of Paloma Rose. And I know she's on TV. . . ."

"That's right. And I'm her."

The sheriff nods, but not in a way that suggests agreement. "I'm afraid this is where the horse leaves the trail, Miss Rose. Because, much as I hate to break this news to you, you aren't her."

Paloma's patience thins to shrill. "Then who am I?"

"Well, that's the million-dollar question, isn't it?" The

sheriff's brow is furrowed with the curiosity of a professional investigator. "Who are you?"

"I'm Paloma Rose! Really! I really am! Why would I lie about something like that?"

"I have no idea. Maybe we just live in that kind of world. People do all kinds of crazy things that don't make any sense."

"But I'm telling you—"

The sheriff leans forward, her elbows on her desk. Now more earnest than curious. "Look, you may think that Dry River is a no-account hick town where people don't know the difference between mud and chocolate. And you may think that you can tell me any cockamamy story and I'll believe you. But you're very mistaken about both those things. We do have electricity. And I happen to get very good TV reception, so I do know what Paloma Rose, the TV star, looks like. And you"—she points at Paloma, dark haired, dirty, dusty, dressed like a ranch hand, and with a bruise on her cheek from hitting the side of the truck—"you look nothing like her."

"But that's because I've been through an ordeal. I bet you'd look different if you'd been through an ordeal like I have."

"It turned your hair brown? Isn't trauma supposed to make you gray?"

"No, the hair has nothing to do with it. It's everything else."

"The calluses and scabs?" The sheriff raises an eyebrow, her gaze on Paloma's scratched hands. "I can't say I've met many TV stars right up face-to-face, but I'm willing to bet a month's salary that they don't have callused fingers or hands that look like they've been putting wet cats in a bag. What's all that from? Turning the pages of a script?"

Paloma sighs and tries again. "You have to believe me. I was kidnapped—"

"By a person or persons you can't identify."

"I'm not saying I wouldn't recognize them. Like, in a lineup, or mug shots, or something. But they were, you know, kind of not describable really. They looked like anybody." She can't tell the truth, of course—that she's run away from Old Ways Ranch; they'd be on the phone to Ethan Lovejoy before you could say, "Saddle my horse." The kidnapping is a plotline from season 2. "I was just getting into my car. In LA. And somebody grabbed me from behind and they kept me blindfolded and put me on a plane and took me here and I was lucky to escape with my life."

Although she isn't even holding a pencil, the sheriff nods as if she's taking notes. "Was this before or after they dyed your hair and changed the color of your eyes from electric blue to gray?"

"After. I—"

"But you can't remember from where you escaped. Is that right? It's just one big blur of sky and desert."

"I told you. I—"

"And you have no ID?"

"Of course not. I mean, kidnappers don't let you keep your wallet." The only identification she has is her credit card, and that's in the name of Susan Minnick. If there's one thing Paloma doesn't want, it's to get the Minnicks involved before she tells the world what they've done to her. Not only would that be the second-quickest way of getting her back at Old Ways Ranch, but her plan depends rather heavily on the element of surprise.

The sheriff holds up one hand, looking over as the deputy comes back. The deputy shakes his head. The sheriff turns back to Paloma. "Only, apparently, no one's reported you missing, Miss Rose. How do you account for that?"

The deputy perches on the edge of the sheriff's desk. "I talked to Paloma Rose's publicist. She says you're in the middle of shooting the new season. And that today you've been all over LA promoting the show."

"She must've misunderstood you. She must've thought you meant last week. Last week I—"

"Don't think so." The deputy is shaking his head again. "Your publicist definitely said today."

"Why don't you tell us what's really going on here?" asks the sheriff. "You know, before we have to arrest you for wasting police time."

Paloma can see her mistake now. She never should have said she was a TV star. She should have said she was a nobody, an orphan who'd been kidnapped and held prisoner for the last two or three years. *That* they'd believe. Then she'd get her press conference; they'd be falling over themselves to get her on the evening news. But they refuse to believe the truth—at least not the part of the truth that she's been trying to tell them.

"OK. You're right." Paloma, thinking of the time when she was six and had to miss Lula Hirschbaum's birthday party because she was shooting an ad for potato chips, sighs. It is a heartfelt, heavy sigh that brings back all the pain and disappointment of that time. Her lips tremble and her eyes fill with tears. Lula Hirschbaum never invited her to anything again. "I mean . . . the thing is . . . see, I had this fight with my boyfriend, and it was really horrible, and I was so mad, and . . ." Season 3, episode 8.

*   *   *

The sheriff might get excellent TV reception, but it's unlikely that she ever actually watched *Angel in the House*. Paloma lifted the story almost word for word, right down to the detail that the woman who gave her a ride into Dry River after she ran out on her boyfriend was wearing a blue hat and came from Indiana. The sheriff hadn't believed the truth, but she believed that. The sheriff also believed that Paloma had no idea why she concocted such a cockamamy story about being a famous TV star who had been kidnapped. "I guess I was still so mad I just said whatever came into my head." The sheriff said she guessed so and offered to let Paloma call her folks on the office telephone. Paloma said it was OK, she'd text her boyfriend to pick her up; they'd had fights like this before. The sheriff didn't seem surprised. Paloma apologized for being a nuisance and said she'd go over to the diner to wait for her boyfriend. Instead, she got on the first bus to the nearest city with a Greyhound station.

Which makes the bus she's now on the second bus Paloma has ever been on in her life. A weight presses against her a little more heavily; a head falls on her shoulder. Paloma shifts in her seat, trying to get away from the head and the weight, but she is already squashed against the window and there is nowhere to go. She sighs. It's been a long day, and it looks as if it will be a long night as well.

The head, which smells like what a field of spring flowers would smell like if it were made in a chemical lab, belongs to Mrs. Buckminster, who is traveling back home to Los Angeles. Mrs. Buckminster was visiting her son Farley and his family. Farley is a developer, his wife is a chef, and his children are small but remarkable. Mrs. Buckminster has told Paloma all about them—at great length and in great detail—and now, exhausted, has fallen asleep. Surprising as it may sound, Paloma is grateful for Mrs. Buckminster's company. The ride in the back of the pickup was unpleasant, the sheriff and her deputy were both unpleasant and scary, and traveling by yourself is terrifying if you've never done it before, which, unless you count taxi rides, Paloma hasn't. The wait in the station seemed interminable. Everybody else seemed to be traveling in couples or families, or at least had people to wave them good-bye. She ate a candy bar and thought of Sunday night at Old Ways. They always have pizza on Sunday night. They put the tables in the dining hall together to make one large one, and everybody eats together like a big family at Thanksgiving. There's always a lot of laughing and fooling around.

Paloma's stomach clenches like a fist around a straw. She's never felt so alone in her life. Being alone is something she has been demanding for some time, but, now that she is, she can see its downside. She's all by herself; all by yourself can be lonely. Which brings to mind another old saying: "Be careful what you wish for; you might just get it." When Mrs. Buckminster asked her about herself, Paloma told her she's a famous TV star. Mrs. Buckminster smiled at her the way her television mother smiles at Faith Cross when she does something that only an angel would do. "No, I meant what are you doing now. Not what you want to be." Paloma said she's been working on a ranch. "Oh, so you're a cowgirl," said Mrs. Buckminster. Paloma said yes.

It's a long and uncomfortable bus ride back to LA — a journey that makes economy air travel look like a magic-carpet ride in comparison — but Paloma didn't have enough cash for a flight and she's afraid to use her credit card. Credit cards can be traced. Besides, no one would think of looking for her on a bus; it'd be like expecting to find the president having lunch at McDonald's.

She bought a phone so that she could call Jack Silk and have him arrange a press conference for tomorrow. Paloma isn't used to thinking about how much things cost; she's always just handed over a piece of plastic. Her business manager, her father, pays the bills. Indeed, she's never even seen a bill, though she occasionally hears about them. Now, between the phone and the bus ticket, she has almost nothing left. Her hand touches the unused phone in her pocket. She can't wait to talk to Jack. Just wait till he hears what Leone's done. And when he finds out how Leone duped him . . . He'll be horrified and outraged. He'll insist on becoming Paloma's guardian. Insist? He'll *beg* her to let him take charge. Unfortunately, however, Paloma is going to have to wait to talk to Jack. Paloma doesn't know Jack Silk's private number. In fact, she doesn't know anyone's number — not even Maria's or the landline at home. She never dials numbers; she just presses buttons. She could probably get a number for Jack's office or even go there, but she doesn't want to do that; she doesn't trust his secretary. She'll have to get his number from somewhere; from someone. Paloma doesn't know about phone books, and, if she did, she wouldn't know where to find one. So it'll have to be a someone. Not Maria. She can't risk going home.

Unless you're counting her followers on Facebook and Twitter (who, really, are following a woman named Natalie who lives in Long Beach, since it is she who keeps the pages going), Paloma doesn't really have any friends. Although she did have one. Until her mother found out and broke it up. Seth. She'll have to go to him. He'll know Jack's number.

Mrs. Buckminster snuggles against Paloma, making the kind of deep, gruff snuffling sounds you'd expect from a bear, not from a grandmother. Paloma stares through the window at the night, thinking of all the other things she's missed besides Lula Hirschbaum's party. It's starting to rain.

Waiting for Paloma

Monday morning arrives dark and scowling. The city is wrapped in curtains of rain, and thunder from the mountains rolls toward it like a train. Oona's mood when she wakes isn't much better. Outside the wind moans and the trees rattle, but inside the house is tense with the silence of anticipation — as if it's waiting to be attacked. For the first time, Oona is aware of the absence of Paloma Rose. Where is she? When is she going to show up? Oona lies there for a few minutes, barely breathing and listening for Paloma to start ringing the bell and banging on the door: *Let me in!* Harriet whimpers in her sleep, and Oona gives her a gentle shake. They tiptoe down the stairs. Oona puts on coffee, and then she gets her rain parka, and she and Harriet go for their walk. Usually, of course, she calls Abbot, no matter what the weather, but today she is watching every tree and bush and car and building, half-expecting to see a face very like her own looking back at her.

Leone doesn't wake up in what could be called a good mood, either. Yesterday morning she was happy as a pig in mud, and now she's about as happy as a pig on her way to the butcher. You'd think Paloma was psychic, picking now to run away from Old Ways, when so much depends on the interview with Lucinda — an interview that could mean the difference between permanent fame and permanent obscurity — to pull a stunt like this. "I'd swear she did it on purpose just to annoy me," Leone mutters to herself as she marches into the breakfast room. Which does nothing to make her feel any better.

Oona is already there, drinking coffee and staring at the rain. She has, of course, been sitting here for a while, waiting for Leone with the patience of a fisherman. When she hears the sharp click of Leone's heels, Oona turns, her expression as warm and friendly as a closed steel door. She skips the good morning. "So what have you done with Maria?" she asks. Now that she knows what she knows, there's no need to try to get along anymore.

Leone doesn't meet her eyes. "I haven't done anything with Maria." She puts her phone, her iPad, and her notebook — the equipment of someone organizing a major event — on the table and continues on into the kitchen.

"She wanted a few days off to help her cousin with the new bundle from heaven." Leone says this last sentence with such casual sincerity that someone who doesn't know her as well as Oona wouldn't guess that she usually counts Maria's hours the way a miser counts pennies.

"She didn't say anything about that to me," says Oona.

"Well, why would she?" Leone slaps a cup down on the counter. "You're not her boss."

"It's the kind of thing she'd mention," says Oona. "You know, because we talk to each other? And anyway, I thought you needed her. I thought you have to rebuild the house before the TV crew gets here."

"Actually, darling, it's probably easier to organize everything without having to stop every minute to explain things to Maria." Leone lifts the coffee pot as though she's testing its weight. "You know what she's like."

Of course Oona knows. Maria's like the person who does everything in the house.

"You mean you're going to do all the cleaning yourself?"

Leone sighs. Are all teenagers difficult, or is it only the ones she has to deal with? "If I have to, I can hire someone to blitz the place on Friday." She comes back to the table and sits to one side of Oona, not across from her. "If that's all right with you, that is."

"What about food? Who's going to do the cooking?"

Leone's smile could wither a rose. "This is the twenty-first century, sweetie. We have caterers."

"But what about—"

"Excuse me." Leone holds up the hand that isn't gripping her cup. "I thought you wanted to be a vet, not a lawyer."

"I'm just curious," says Oona. "I came down for breakfast like usual and Maria was gone. It all seems pretty sudden if you ask me."

"I didn't ask." Leone touches her forehead. "And I think I may be getting a migraine. So, if you don't mind, I could do without the cross-examination."

Oona taps her spoon against her cup. "I didn't know you get migraines."

"It's the weather," says Leone. "All these thunderstorms. They play havoc with the electricity in your brain."

Oona gazes at her with an expression that could be mistaken for concern. "I thought migraines were caused by things like stress and hormones."

"That, too." Leone gets to her feet. "I certainly have plenty of stress dealing with you."

Oona watches her go into the kitchen for another cup. "You really shouldn't be drinking coffee, you know. Caffeine's not good for migraines."

"Thank you, Dr. Ginness. But I didn't say I had one. I said I thought I might be getting one."

Oona's still watching her with what might be concern — were Leone someone else, and she someone else, and the two of them on a different planet. "You're coming to the studio, right?"

"I can't, sweetie. I really can't." Leone waves at the tools of her trade. "We've less than a week to get ready. I have someone coming about flowers. And doing the carpets. And the caterer. And I have to get a new outfit. I'll need at least half a day at the spa. So I'll have to stay close to home." A very small smile darts across her face. "I just hope I can trust you not to mess up without me."

Oona finishes her coffee, saying nothing. She isn't the one who can't be trusted.

All the way to work, Oona stares out the window, her eyes sharp as new blades, looking for a girl standing on a corner who may be looking for her. The closer they get, the more her head flips from left to right and right to left, as if she's watching a trapeze artist swinging across the road. But, of course, the acrobat is really Oona — who will catch her if she falls? When they reach the studio, she leans forward, searching the hive of fans and tourists, but there's no one who looks as if she used to be on the other side of the security gate.

She calls Maria as soon as she's alone in her dressing room.

Maria says she should have known that Leone was up to something. She wasn't sure which surprised her more — that Leone gave her time off out of the blue like that, or that Jack Silk, who brought her the bag Leone packed, was able to find her cousin's neighborhood.

"It's incredible," says Oona. "Every single thing they told us, and probably everything they told Paloma, was a lie."

"But are you sure?" Maria likes to hope that people are better than they often seem. "You didn't misunderstand? Miss Paloma, she was very excited about this vacation. She said it was going to be just like being in Hollywood, only everybody would leave her alone." Meaning Leone. She'd never been away from her mother before. She thought it meant that at last her parents were finally paying attention to her, not treating her like a little girl anymore. "That is what she always says," says Maria. "That Mrs. Minnick won't let her grow up. I thought she was going on some kind of cruise."

"I misunderstood before," says Oona. "I thought they

were trying to help Paloma." She can't believe how gullible she's been — not so much born yesterday as born two seconds ago. "But this time I haven't misunderstood anything. They didn't send her on any big-deal vacation; they sent her to a brat camp. I looked it up online."

"A brat camp," repeats Maria. "You mean like on TV? For children who are always getting into trouble?"

"Yeah. Like that."

"Dios mío, why didn't I think . . . after last time . . ."

"Last time?" They're becoming echoes of each other.

"Sí, last time," sighs Maria. "Just before she went away. When the police brought her home . . ."

This, of course, is the first Oona's heard of Paloma Rose's relationship with the LAPD.

"It wasn't a good day," Maria says, "but Mr. Jack, he fixed it again."

So now it all starts to make a strange if unpleasant sense. Mr. Jack fixed it again. It was never about Paloma, except in the sense that she was causing them problems.

"I know she was being a little hard to handle, but . . ." Maria's voice trails off. She's never been known to criticize the Minnicks — though that doesn't mean that she couldn't. She has never expected much of them, and in this, if in nothing else in life, she has never been disappointed. Which is why, despite the tantrums worthy of a

Castilian prince, Maria has always felt sorry for Paloma. It's not her fault she's a spoiled brat and useless. You can't blame a pup for howling if it's raised by wolves. This time, however, Leone has managed to surprise even Maria. She thought before that Leone's heart is small and hard; now she doubts that Leone actually has a heart—be it small as a gnat and hard as steel. Imagine treating your own child like that. "But I still don't understand why they would lie like this. Why not just tell her? Everybody in Hollywood gets sent away somewhere at some time."

"Jack and Leone were protecting their investment," says Oona.

"Dios mío," mutters Maria. Nonetheless, Jack Silk has surprised her even more than the Minnicks. She knows how ruthless and controlling he can be when it comes to business, but he's always been so much more pleasant than Leone. Charming. She touches the MP3 player in the pocket of her apron—a gift from Jack. Thoughtful. Kind, even. She assumed that meant that he's a nicer person. As if only good people smile. "What will happen to her now?"

"They think she'll come home."

Maria doesn't agree. "And why would she do that? So they can send her back? Or to somewhere else?"

"Well, where can she go?" reasons Oona. It's not as if she has any friends.

Maria suggests the studio. "To embarrass her mother," says Maria. "She would like that. She would make a big scene."

Oona frowns. Thoughtfully. From what she knows of Paloma, embarrassing Leone is exactly what she would do. But that might not be such a good idea. Paloma can't possibly know it, of course, but things are getting better both for the show and for her. A big scene would embarrass her as much as it would Lethal Leone. The publicity would all be bad, the sponsors would go into a tailspin of unhappiness, the new energy and enthusiasm around the show would be destroyed, and the grand prize — the interview with Lucinda — would be canceled faster than you can step on an ant. What was it Jack said? *If they go down, she goes with them.* Oona believes him. Jack Silk is turning out to be the human equivalent of an iceberg; there's a lot more of him that you don't see than there is that you do — and most of it is dangerous. He's "fixed things" in the past; who's to say he couldn't "fix things" now?

"She's liable to hurt herself more than she'll hurt anyone else," says Oona.

"But she doesn't know that. And she will have to do something," says Maria. "She's not going to pretend that nothing ever happened."

"No . . ." Oona's attention has started to wander off into a new thought. "No, she's not going to do that."

The new thought that occurs to Oona is that the important thing is not to embarrass Leone and Jack Silk, but to teach them a lesson. A lesson they can't ever forget; a lesson that takes the control away from them and gives it to Oona and Paloma Rose, and makes things better for both of them. But in order to do that, Oona needs to get to Paloma before Paloma gets to anyone else.

There's nothing to do but wait.

And possibly pray.

"Calm down, Leone," says Jack when she finally stops for air. "There's nothing to worry about. Everything's A-OK."

Leone would like him to define *A-OK*. "It's been over twenty-four hours, Jack. Surely we should have heard something by now. What if Lovejoy decides to go to the police after all? He can't keep quiet forever."

"He's not going to the police," says Jack. "I told him she's back and we're keeping her here. I told him she was just homesick, and he's done a terrific job. We'll tell all our friends to send their delinquent kids to him. He's not going to say bupkis."

"That's great, Jack, but that doesn't change the fact

that she isn't home," Leone reminds him. "So where the hell can she be? What if—"

He cuts her off before she can launch into another of her macabre scenarios of what's happened to Paloma. "There is no 'what if.' I keep telling you, you're worrying over nothing. Paloma has a very highly developed survival instinct. She knows how to look after number one." As if bad things only happen to people who are too nice for their own good. "No news is good news," says Jack. This, of course, isn't necessarily true. No news is no news; the bad news may just be taking its own sweet time to get to you.

"You really think so?" Oh, how she wants to believe him. If Jack Silk were a snake-oil salesman and not a Hollywood agent, Leone would probably buy the biggest bottle he has right now.

"Absolutely. There's been no activity on the card." Which means that she hasn't hired a limo or bought a plane ticket or put herself up in some pricey hotel. "She's holed up somewhere to make everybody worry about her. It's just the kind of stunt Paloma would pull. High on drama, low on effort. She may even still be somewhere on the ranch. She'll come out when she gets tired of pretending she's in a war movie, hiding from the Gestapo."

Leone suggests that Paloma has some cash on her.

She's always helping herself to what's in Leone's wallet; she should have quite a little nest egg by now. So maybe she took a bus.

Jack laughs. "Yeah. And then she got off at the first big town and took a job cleaning motels."

Leone laughs, too, but hers lacks confidence. "OK, maybe not a bus. But what if someone gave her a ride? What if—"

"Look," says Jack, "I'm in a public place, and I can't really have this conversation now. Over the phone. Why don't you try to relax?"

"Relax?" squawks Leone. "How can I relax? Not only do I have ten million things to do, I have to stand guard. The other one'll be back from the studio soon. Can you imagine if Paloma does turn up and walks into her double? Somebody has to be ready, or God knows what'll happen." And obviously, Leone is that someone. She sighs. It's not easy being called Mom.

"Of course," says Jack. "Of course you do. But try to chill. We'll talk in the morning, if not before."

"Don't worry," Leone assures him. "If she does show, you'll be the first person I call."

Monday comes, and Monday goes. Tuesday follows it like a tail. Leone busies herself with making the arrangements for the interview, but although this is the kind of job she loves, a lot of the joy has been taken out of it by the shadow of Paloma that hangs over her. She is skittish as a deer on ice—jumping at every creak and bang, pacing the rooms like a prisoner waiting for a reprieve, even sleeping with her phone on the pillow beside her. When Oona's in the house, she watches her as if she thinks she might steal the silver, always trying to position herself so that if the landline or the doorbell rings she, not Oona, will be the one to answer. The samples of pastries and finger foods from the caterers turn to ashes in her mouth. She might be a billionaire banker hosting a gala charity event, all the while waiting for the police to come and arrest her.

Wednesday comes and starts to go. Leone has been forced from the house to have dinner with Lucinda Chance's PA to run through the agenda for Sunday. She has just parked and is undoing her seat belt when her phone rings. Perhaps because she's afraid it might be Paloma and also afraid that it might not be, instead of answering it she throws it onto the floor, and then bangs her head on the steering wheel when she goes to retrieve it. It's Jack Silk.

"We've had a breakthrough," he announces.

Leone's so surprised she almost drops the phone again. "What?"

"My man's found something." Jack laughs. "Turns out you were right. She did take a bus. Two buses. She came into LA on Monday. She was with some old lady."

Leone thanks God. At least that's one set of worries out of the way. "So where is she now?"

"Ah," says Jack. There's always some small complication. "We're not really sure about that. He's checked hotels, motels, and hostels, but there was no sign of her. He even had a word with what's-his-name, that scum-for-brains scriptwriter, but Drachman swears he hasn't heard from her."

"So she's vanished again."

"No, Leone. She's not Houdini. She's here. In the city. We just don't know where yet."

"What about this old lady you mentioned? Maybe Paloma went with her."

"He's working on it. But it looks like she bought her ticket with cash, too. So it'll take a little time."

Leone is, of course, relieved that Paloma is all right— or was as of Monday. What mother wouldn't be? But one of the problems Leone has always had with being a mother instead of being God is that a mother can't know or control everything. And right now she would like to know where Paloma is and what she's planning to do.

"It's Wednesday," she reminds Jack. "The interview's on Sunday. I'm just about to go into the restaurant to finalize everything. If Paloma—"

"Just sit tight," Jack advises. "I'll call you as soon as I hear anything."

Leone hasn't been to church since she was twelve, and isn't what you'd call a praying kind of person, but she does believe in negotiation. The second she hangs up from Jack she starts negotiating. "Please," Leone whispers as she gets out of the car. "Just keep her away until Monday. Or at least Sunday night. Don't let her ruin the interview. That's all I ask."

Poor Leone. The time may not be far away when she wishes she'd asked for something more.

Oona collapses into the back of the car with a sigh. It's been a long day. For a change, Paloma Rose isn't on her mind. It's already the middle of the week. If Paloma was going to show up at the studio, surely that already would have happened. No, tonight what Oona's thinking about is the interview with Lucinda. She's starting to feel nervous, as would anyone who's never been interviewed on network television before. And although Oona is used to dealing with people and answering questions, the people she's used to dealing with aren't one of the most influential women in the country, and the questions she's used to answering are along the lines of "Does it come with fries?" and "Do you have soy milk?" What if she makes a fool of herself? What if she stumbles and stutters and shows herself to be a fraud? If she does blow the interview, will Leone try to murder her on air, or will she wait till everyone's left?

These thoughts and others are running through her head as the car leaves the lot and pulls into the road, and is almost immediately stuck in traffic. It moves, but it moves slowly. A few feet. A yard or two. Half a block.

It'd be faster to walk, thinks Oona, and glances out the window at the people who are walking, leaving the traffic behind. Some tourists with guidebooks, searching for stars. Several men in suits, walking briskly and with purpose. A girl moving slowly, lost in her thoughts. It's not the face of the girl that makes Oona look twice; it's the way she walks. Oona has studied that walk. She has it down cold.

Without a second thought, Oona opens her door and leans out. "Hey! Hey!" she calls. "Over here!"

Paloma stops as if she's suddenly been turned to stone. Her eyes meet Oona's.

There is no surprise in Paloma's look. No confusion. *She knows*, thinks Oona. *It isn't a coincidence that she ran away. She found out somehow.*

"Come on." Oona beckons. "Come on, get in!"

Paloma doesn't think twice, either.

"How did you find out?" whispers Oona as Paloma sits beside her.

Paloma shuts the door. "I saw you on TV."

Why Paloma finally went to the studio

Paloma's favorite interviews have always been the ones where she's asked fun questions, like which ten famous people from history you'd invite to a barbecue or what your superpower would be if you could choose one. She usually picks being invisible or being able to travel through time as her superpower—things she figures would be really useful. Imagine Leone nagging at her about something, and all of a sudden Paloma just disappears or whisks off to have lunch with Marilyn Monroe.

But that was before her first (and hopefully last) overnight bus journey. What a ride. Somewhere between the air-conditioning breaking down and the man locking himself in the toilet, Paloma decided that the next time she was asked what her superpower would be she'd say, "To be able to sleep like Mrs. Buckminster." Mrs. Buckminster could snore her way through Armageddon.

Even strapped to a camel balanced on a log on a boiling sea. Nothing disturbed her. The seats were as comfortable as solid rock, but Mrs. Buckminster curled up like a kitten on a cushion. When the AC died and the temperature in the bus turned it into a moving sauna, Mrs. Buckminster smiled in her dreams. When the windows were opened to let in some air and they all nearly choked with the dust, pollution, and baked heat that swamped them, Mrs. Buckminster made the sound of a well-tuned engine. Two babies and the old woman in the plastic shower cap cried through most of the night, while someone who hadn't seen the NO ALCOHOLIC BEVERAGES sign sang "Dancing Queen" during the short intervals when the crying died down, but Mrs. Buckminster didn't hear a thing. A small child threw up in the aisle, and, sound asleep, Mrs. Buckminster patted Paloma's knee.

Mrs. Buckminster only wakes as, after what seems to Paloma like several unusually long days, they finally reach LA.

"Goodness me," says Mrs. Buckminster, straightening up in her seat and rubbing her eyes. "I must've dozed off." She peers out the window. "Will you look at that weather!"

It is raining in an unwelcoming, why-don't-you-go-back-where-you-came-from? way.

Paloma wouldn't care if it were snowing. She's so happy to get off the bus that she's ready to climb out the window and kiss the ground. But the closer they get to the bus station, the clearer it is that this isn't a part of town where you do anything with the ground except move over it very quickly. No wish-you-were-here postcards of Los Angeles have ever included this neighborhood. Run-down and dirty, the station looks as if it's waiting for a violent crime to happen. Again.

"So what are you going to do now?" asks Mrs. Buckminster as they clamber off the bus.

Paloma told Mrs. Buckminster that she's staying with a good friend in the city, but since she lost her phone and doesn't know his number and his landline's unlisted, she has to wait for him to get home from work.

Paloma shrugs. She hasn't thought that far ahead. "I guess I'll stay here till it's time to go over to my friend's place."

"Oh, no, no, no, no, no." Mrs. Buckminster shakes her head. "You can't just sit around the bus station all afternoon in this weather. I won't allow it. Do you know what kind of people hang around bus stations?"

Paloma glances around, trying not to look at anyone or anything specific. This is the kind of place where you wouldn't be surprised to see a rat run over your foot or someone peeing against a wall. "Not just people waiting for buses, right?"

"That's right," says Mrs. Buckminster. Perverts. Criminals. Crazies. Rapists. And unlucky people who have nowhere else to go.

Paloma puts on Faith Cross's nothing-daunts-me face. "You don't have to worry about me. I'll be OK." Even she doesn't sound convinced.

"I know you will be, because you're coming home with me." Mrs. Buckminster picks up her case with one hand and takes Paloma's elbow with the other. "I insist. You've been on that bus for nearly an entire day. You need someplace to relax. If you fall asleep in this dump, you'll be lucky to still have your shoes on your feet when you wake up."

They take another bus to Mrs. Buckminster's bungalow. Bus number three for Paloma. At least the air-conditioning works on this one.

Like Mrs. Buckminster (and, indeed, like Paloma Rose at the moment), the bungalow has seen better days. It could use a coat of paint, and there's a damp patch in the living room where the roof leaks, and you have to be careful of that loose board on the porch. Leone Minnick has Paradise Lodge redecorated every year or two by flocks of professionals who flap around with color charts, and fabric swatches, and laptops and iPads filled with ideas, but Mrs. Buckminster's decorating has been done by life and time in their higgledy-piggledy way. Furniture from the sixties. Wallpaper from the seventies. Curtains from the eighties. A Styrofoam Santa Claus made in 1992. Nonetheless, although small and full of the many things Mrs. Buckminster has collected or simply not thrown out over the years, the bungalow has a warm and welcoming feeling. A lot warmer and more welcoming than the greeting Paloma is likely to receive at Seth Drachman's.

Mrs. Buckminster makes lunch for the two of them — scrambled eggs with cheese, toast, and a salad of lettuce and tomatoes from the garden. Then she puts Paloma in the spare bedroom for a nap. "You just have yourself a little siesta," says Mrs. Buckminster. "If you're not up by supper time, I'll give you a shout."

Paloma is asleep as soon as her head hits the pillow. She dreams that she's home. But the home in her dream isn't Paradise Lodge. It's a small white cottage with a thatched roof and green shutters at the windows. There's a garden of wildflowers in front of the cottage, and smoke rising from the chimney. Rabbits leap through the high grass and birds chirp in the trees. Paloma is in the kitchen, baking. The table is covered with pies and cakes and fat golden biscuits. Paloma sings while she works.

I'm so happy, she says to the dragonfly that's landed on the windowsill. *I'm really, really happy.* And then thinks, *But this is just a dream. I'm so happy anyway.* And she rolls out a piece of pastry shaped like a heart.

When she wakes up, the house smells of just-out-of-the-oven chocolate-chip cookies. She looks around at the unfamiliar walls covered with unfamiliar photographs and the shelves crammed with unfamiliar books and knickknacks, and doesn't know where she is. At first Paloma thinks she's still dreaming; then she thinks she's back in the episode of *Angel in the House* with the lonely old woman and the runaway. And then, as if she has some extrasensory power that enables her to know when guests are awake, Mrs. Buckminster appears in the doorway with a glass of iced tea and a plate of cookies. She looks, to Paloma, exactly like the really sweet grandmother in season 2, episode 8. The rain pounds on the roof, and a wave of lightning bleaches the sky. A black-and-white cat Paloma hasn't met before passes Mrs. Buckminster in the doorway and jumps onto the bed, purring. Just as Mrs. Buckminster is the first old lady to bake Paloma cookies, this is one of the few animals Paloma has been near in weeks that hasn't immediately tried to bite her. She nearly bursts into tears.

Mrs. Buckminster won't let her leave yet.

"I don't know what happened to you on that ranch of yours, but you're in no state to go wandering the streets of this city looking for your friend. I'm going to cook you a nice supper, and we're going to listen to the radio and have a quiet night. You can go to him tomorrow."

Mrs. Buckminster takes Paloma with her to buy the fixings for the nice supper. They walk slowly under one large umbrella, Mrs. Buckminster pointing out all the interesting sights of the neighborhood. The street that was in a movie. The house where the woman who does Mrs. Buckminster's hair lives. The tree Mrs. Buckminster's grandson fell from last time he visited. The dog that saved its owner's life by jumping out a window and going for help. The house that always has the best decorations at Christmas. When they get to the store, Paloma can't get over how big it is — so big that you'd think it must hold at least one of every possible food in the world. Paloma has met countless celebrities, two governors, three senators, and the prime minister of a country whose name she's forgotten, but it is this store that has her speechless with amazement. She loses Mrs. Buckminster four times.

"Anybody'd think you'd never been in a supermarket before," laughs Mrs. Buckminster.

Paloma hasn't. She's been in several gourmet delis and at least one convenience store (which, of course, ended badly), but never a store the size of an airplane hangar.

On the way home, Paloma carries the bags and Mrs. Buckminster holds the umbrella.

"You want to give me a hand with supper?" asks Mrs. Buckminster, slipping an apron over her head.

Until she was exiled to Old Ways, the only time Paloma ever gave anyone a hand with anything was when she shook one. "Sure," says Paloma. "I'm a pretty good cook."

She doesn't want to sit by herself in the living room while Mrs. Buckminster makes the pasta sauce. She wants to be in the bright, crowded kitchen with the photos stuck to the fridge with magnets, and the bulletin board that takes up one wall and is covered with postcards and more photos and drawings made by Mrs. Buckminster's grandchildren, and the Little Red Riding Hood cookie jar on the counter. At Paradise Lodge, unless Paloma and her mother are fighting, the house is usually pretty quiet. If Arthur's home, he's on his laptop or his phone if he isn't passed out; if Leone's home, she's on her phone; if Paloma's home, she's plugged into something in her room. The Minnicks don't really talk to one another except to argue. Maria used to listen to some

Chicano radio station while she cooked, singing along, but Leone finds Mexican music either too loud or too sad or too Mexican, so Jack Silk bought Maria a personal MP3 player, and she listens to that without joining in. Which means that the only sounds you are likely to hear are from machines, and those will be at a distance and behind a closed door. As if they live in a waiting room. It is only now that Paloma wonders what it is they're all waiting for.

Paloma likes to listen to Mrs. Buckminster's rambling stories, to the radio playing on the counter, and to the purring cat on her chair at the table. Although she's not really aware of it, it reminds her of something that happened when she was eight or nine. Leone and Arthur had gone away somewhere and left her with a woman who frightened her because she smelled like bleach and made her eat cauliflower. Between the bleach and the cauliflower, Paloma threw up her supper and was sent to her room. She lay on her bed crying for what seemed like hours. Until she finally noticed the light that was filling the room. It was so bright she thought her mother had come home and tiptoed in to comfort her. But it wasn't her mother; it was a moon so large it seemed to be pressed against the glass of her window, watching over her. And she stopped being scared and fell asleep with the moonshine on her like a hug. Mrs. Buckminster reminds her of that moon.

Mrs. Buckminster watches Paloma chop the onions. "You really do know how to cook, don't you? I didn't think you young people went in for that kind of thing anymore."

"Some of us do," says Paloma. Modestly.

Tuesday comes, and Paloma stays. Mrs. Buckminster could use some help with her garden. And there are a few odd jobs in the house that need someone tall and strong and more agile than a seventy-five-year-old woman with a bad knee. Paloma teaches Mrs. Buckminster a card game she learned at Old Ways, and Mrs. Buckminster shows her some of the scrapbooks she's been making since her children were small. Neither of them mentions the fact that Paloma is still there.

She stays Wednesday, too. Paloma hasn't quite finished with the garden. It's early evening before she's done. As she nears the house she can hear voices in the kitchen. She's about to open the back door when she hears her name. Or one of them.

"So who do you think this Susan is?" The voice is unfamiliar to Paloma and belongs to Mrs. Laguna from next door.

"I think she must be a runaway. She never talks

about home." This voice is completely familiar, of course, because it belongs to Mrs. Buckminster. "I don't know what to do. I really don't." Mrs. Buckminster sighs. "I keep thinking how worried her poor parents must be. Can you imagine? They must be beside themselves. Not sleeping. Not eating. Jumping every time the phone rings. Remember how I was when Lilly disappeared that time?" She lost ten pounds and cried even in her sleep. "And Lilly's a cat."

"You should call the police," says Mrs. Laguna. "You pretty much know where she came from. There'll be a report. They'll know what to do."

Mrs. Buckminster says, "Ummm . . ."

"You can't keep her here," says Mrs. Laguna. "You have to go to the authorities. You don't know what trouble you could get in if you don't."

"You really think I should call the police?" Mrs. Buckminster is torn. She wants to do what's best for Susan, but she doesn't want to make things worse for her, either. And she doesn't want her to leave. She likes the company. Lilly is a wonderful companion, but she is limited. Susan's such a sweet girl, helpful and considerate, and she seems very alone. Most girls her age never lift their heads from their phones or whatever it is they carry around with them all the time, but Susan hasn't so much as sent a single text. Who knows what made her run away? "What if she has a good reason for leaving home?" she asks Mrs. Laguna. "All those stories in the paper, what horrible things people do to their children . . ."

Mrs. Laguna, however, isn't torn at all. "And all the stories about what children do to their parents, let's not forget about them. You don't know what she's planning. Maybe she wants to rob you."

"I don't have anything worth stealing," says Mrs. Buckminster.

"She could be on drugs or something," counters Mrs. Laguna. "You could wake up dead."

Mrs. Buckminster tells her not to be ridiculous.

"You can't just keep her here. What if she's committed a crime? That'd make you an accessory."

Mrs. Buckminster sighs. "She was working on a ranch, not robbing a bank."

"The police will know what to do," insists Mrs. Laguna. "That's what they're there for. You pay your taxes. You have rights."

"I don't know . . ." Mrs. Buckminster's voice is dragging its feet. "I think I should talk to Susan first. I won't do anything behind her back."

Unfortunately, this last part of the conversation is the part that Paloma doesn't wait around to hear. She's already gone in the front door, and is jamming her few things into her bag. By the time Mrs. Laguna leaves, Paloma is already long gone herself.

She takes a cab to Seth's place. Seth lives in a modern apartment house, all glass and chrome and bonsai palm trees in the foyer.

The cabbie, who has three daughters of his own, wants to wait until Paloma's inside, but Paloma sends him away. "It's OK," says Paloma. "My friend knows I'm coming. He's waiting for me."

This, of course, is so far from the truth that it's barely in the same language. She hasn't seen Seth Drachman since last winter. When he told her he didn't want to see her anymore. Unless he was on the couch and she was on the TV. He said you could call it a case of delayed maturity. She might think the secrecy and sneaking around and danger of their relationship were romantic, but he didn't. He could lose his job, his reputation—his whole future—if anyone found out. He didn't think it was worth it for either of them. She didn't believe him. Not at first. She thought Leone must have threatened him and scared him off, but she was sure that once he realized how much he loved Paloma he would stand up to her mother. Instead of standing up, he quit the show. She called and texted and called; he changed his phone.

She sent him notes and letters, she turned up at his door, she parked outside his building; he moved. She only knows his new address because she gave the janitor at his last building two hundred dollars she stole from her mother to tell her.

She presses the button next to DRACHMAN, S.

The light on the closed-circuit TV comes on. He can see her. "Yeah?" But he doesn't recognize her with her longish, straight dark hair and glasses, standing there in her jeans and T-shirt and a flannel shirt Mrs. Buckminster found in her closet. "What is it?"

"It's me," says Paloma. "Paloma."

When Paloma drove her car into a fence that time to get even with Leone for making Seth break her heart, there was one, maybe two, seconds of silence after the crash. It was the silence of a mountain after you've fallen off it. There is that silence now, and then Seth says, "Go away."

"I can't." For once she manages not to whine. He said he hated it when she whines. "I really need to talk to you."

"There's nothing to talk about. Go away."

"It's an emergency."

"Your whole life is an emergency."

"I just wan—"

"How did you find out where I live?"

"Look, I have nowhere to go. I—"

"Well, you can't stay here. I'm busy. Go away. Or I'll call security and have you removed."

In her tiny bungalow, Mrs. Buckminster and Lilly the cat sit on the couch, watching a movie. Back at Old Ways, everyone is in the common room by now, playing games or flicking through TV channels or just hanging out. Arthur will be out getting drunk somewhere, Leone will be sipping a martini on the terrace, and Maria will be listening to her radio station and knitting something for someone's baby. And upstairs Seth is about to go back to being busy with his new girlfriend. Only Paloma is all by herself.

This is when she finally bursts into tears.

And then decides to go to the studio. Someone from the show may still be there. Someone from the crew. Or even the security guard. All she needs is someone who can give her Jack Silk's phone number or tell her where his office is. If she can find his office, she can sit in a doorway across the street and grab him when he shows up in the morning (season 3, episode 6). Wiping away the tears, Paloma turns and walks away, wondering where she can get a bus.

Don't get mad, get even

The impostor's name is Oona. Because they both now know that it is wise to be wary, neither of them speaks much during the drive from the studio in case the driver is listening in, but as soon as he drops them off, she introduces herself to Paloma. "My name's Oona. Oona Ginness."

"Well, you know who I am." Paloma looks up at the house. "I don't want to go in there." She's not even sure why she got in the car. Where else would the phony Paloma be going at this time of the day? But curiosity and resentment got the better of her. That and the fact that this girl can help her; she owes Paloma that much. And it seemed better than sleeping in a doorway. "I don't want to see my mother."

"She's not home. She went out for dinner."

Paloma laughs. Sourly. At least Leone is reliable in some ways.

Harriet greets them at the door, her tail moving so furiously it looks like it's wagging her. *Of course she has a dog,* thinks Paloma. *I don't even like dogs; I like cats. How out of character can you get?* But she pets the brown head anyway. She seems OK for a dog.

The three of them go upstairs.

Angry as she is with her mother, Paloma thought that some part of her would be glad to be home. In her own house; in her own room; in her own life. But it isn't just other people who can surprise us; we can even surprise ourselves. As Oona shuts the bedroom door behind them, instead of thinking *Safe at home at last,* Paloma feels like a stranger in a very strange land. Or maybe it's just that she's really seeing the room for the first time. The furniture, the curtains, the bedspread, the canopy, and the wallpaper weren't chosen by her but by Leone and a decorator named Lucas. The stuffed animals that fill the shelves were all gifts from fans. The only things that made the room hers were the clothes she threw everywhere (most of them bought by Leone or given by designers as promotional gifts), and now they've all been put away. It's no more her room than a room in a hotel would be.

Oona has heard enough about Paloma's moods and tantrums to be expecting a scene of epic proportions as soon as they are by themselves, but Paloma merely looks around the room with a slightly dazed expression—almost as if she's never seen it before. "You OK?" Oona finally asks.

"Yeah." Paloma shrugs. "It's just really weird being back. I feel like I've been away for years. Like that guy in that story."

Harriet jumps on the bed, but Oona stays standing by the door with her hands behind her back, Paloma a few feet ahead of her, her mouth so small she seems in danger of swallowing it.

Oona sees a girl who is nothing like the one she studied so closely—whose clothes she wears, whose voice she mimics, and whose mannerisms she's memorized. She sees a girl who could be any teenager you pass on the street or sit next to on the bus.

Paloma almost feels as if she's looking at an old photograph of herself. Maybe not when she was younger, but when she was different—although until now it didn't occur to her that she'd changed at all. "I don't think you look that much like me," she says at last. Oona's earlobes are thin, her fingers are short and kind of stubby, her nose is at least one-sixteenth of an inch longer than Paloma's.

"Neither do you," says Oona. "I don't think I would've recognized you if I didn't know who you were. You look really different."

Paloma sits down beside Harriet. "I bet you look really different, too."

Oona sits in the armchair. She says she's heard a lot about Paloma, but nobody ever mentioned that she has a sense of humor.

Paloma smiles for the first time since she left Mrs. Buckminster. "I guess I picked it up over the summer." Calluses. Milking skills. Bed making. Fire building. An impressive repertoire of hiking songs. And the ability to crack a joke instead of throwing the nearest inanimate object. All in all, a vacation she'll never forget.

"So . . ." Oona shifts in her seat. "You going to tell me your part of the story? Then I'll tell you how I wound up here. And then we can figure out what to do next."

Miles away, Jack Silk sits on the deck of his house. He's smoking a cigar and giving his sister in New Jersey advice about her problems with her teenage son. At a corner table in a Hollywood restaurant, Leone picks at her salad and smiles gracefully as she learns that, besides Paloma, the only family member to be on camera during Sunday's interview will be Harriet. In this room, Harriet sleeps, snoring softly and dreaming she's playing ball with Oona. And so the world turns and time passes while the stories are told.

"I hope you know that if I'd had any idea of what was really going on —"

"Oh, don't worry." Paloma shakes her head. "I know that. I don't blame you at all. I know exactly whose idea this was."

"It's really incredible, isn't it?" Oona shakes her head. "I mean, you couldn't put this story in a movie or anything like that because nobody'd believe it."

"They'll believe it when I'm through telling everyone."

"Telling everyone?" repeats Oona.

"You bet. I'm going to make her pay. I am going to make her so sor—"

Although Oona was paying very close attention to Paloma's story, she suddenly feels as if she's missed something. "Her?"

"Yeah, *her.* My mother's going to be sorry she was ever born."

"Oh, but Leone—I mean, yeah, she went along with the scheme and everything, but I don't think this was her idea. Leone's . . ." Too stupid? Too unimaginative? Not quite ruthless enough? "Leone's no Lady Macbeth."

Paloma frowns. "Lady who?"

"It doesn't matter. What matters is that I'm sure this was Jack Silk's idea. I told you, he's the one who arranged everything. He's like the evil puppet master or Svengali or something. He's the one who always takes care of things."

Paloma shakes her head. "No, not Jack. Jack wouldn't do something like this to me. Not unless she poisoned his mind. Jack really cares about me." Unlike some people much closer in the gene pool. "I already figured it all out. After I fire my parents, Jack's going to be my guardian."

Oona leans forward as though a sudden passing formation of fighter jets is making it hard to hear Paloma. "Jack? You're going to make him your guardian? Are you kidding? The only person you have to be guarded against is *him*."

"You're wrong," says Paloma. "Maybe he was weak enough to let my mother talk him into sending me away, but—"

"But nothing. I heard him. He persuaded Leone. And it was Jack who came to me." Maybe Paloma wasn't listening closely enough to what Oona had to say. "It's Jack I have the contract with. It's Jack who's been dealing with the honcho at your ranch. I think it's Leone who got talked into it. Jack's a really smooth operator." Smooth as oiled ball bearings. "I bet you anything that if you go to him, he'll put you back at that place so fast you'll think you were never out. And if he doesn't do that, he'll make it so no one listens to you. And if they listen, they won't believe you. If you ask me, you'd be better off putting yourself up for adoption than going to him."

"But my plan . . . I have it all worked out, and I think it's a really good plan. I'm going to get Jack to call an all-media press conference so I can tell the whole world exactly what happened to me. Name and shame, that's what I'm going to do. And then my career's going to start all over. Only the way I want it to be this time, not the way Leone wants it to be."

Oona shakes her head. "I really don't think your plan can work, Paloma. He won't do it. Not in a billion years. You're wrong about Jack Silk—he's not on your side. The only side he's on is his. I told you, I heard him. I know what he said. And I know what he did."

Paloma leans back on her elbows, chewing at her bottom lip and thinking—remembering. She goes back to the night Jack and Leone called her into the living room. She thinks about Audrey Hepplewhite's car crash, and how worried Jack said he and Leone were about Paloma. About his description of the resort where she was going. She can see him waving good-bye to her at the airport. *Bon voyage, sweetheart. Have a great time!*

She sits up straight, her expression grim. "Maybe you're right," she says. "When I think about it, I—well, I guess I've been kidding myself." She stands up and starts to pace. "But if that's true, then I want them both punished. Leone *and* Jack. I don't think they should get away with treating me like this. Or you. They've been using you, too. Do you think they should get away with it? You think we should just do nothing? Just say, 'Oh well, that's OK'?"

"Of course I don't." This is something to which Oona has given quite a lot of thought. "But you know what they say: revenge is a dish best served cold. Or at least at room temperature."

"What?"

"Don't get mad, get even. You don't want to rush into this. You want to make them suffer. Let them really start to panic. Leone's already a wreck, worrying that you're going to show up at any minute. And then worrying that you aren't. She's terrified everybody's going to find out what they did."

"But see, that's what I said! I want everybody to know what they did. I should have a press conference."

"It's not going to help you, though, is it? They'll be toast, but you'll be toast, too. What you need to do is to be as calculated and methodical as Jack Silk's been. You want to take control. Real control. Not just have a public melt-down. You want to get into the driver's seat, and make sure the two of them are in the trunk."

Paloma folds her arms in front of her. "And how am I supposed to do that?"

Oona snaps her fingers. "Easy. You just slip back into your life like you've never been away. Only since you have been, you have something on Jack and your mother that you can use to your advantage."

"But you said if Jack knows I'm here he'll just send me away again."

"Not if you have witnesses," says Oona. "Not if you do it before he knows what's happened."

Paloma tilts her head to one side, as if looking at Oona from a different angle will make everything clear. "What witnesses?"

Oona grins. "How does half the country sound?"

"Half the country? What are you talking about?"

"I'm talking about a major network interview. Where you can just take over where you left off. Only because you'll be the one with the power. Jack Silk won't be able to bully anybody or buy them off. And there's nothing he can do to you."

Paloma sways in place. "Um . . . maybe nobody told you, but if you're thinking of something like the *Late Show,* I kind of messed up with them."

"Not the *Late Show,*" says Oona. "Better than that. Lucinda's *At Home With* show. It's like a whole hour interview. If you really want to tell the world your story, that's the place to do it."

"You're crazy. I'm telling you, I really messed up. They'd never book me on that."

"You're already on. Sunday. Right downstairs. Leone's been running around like she's in a marathon getting ready for it."

Paloma sits back down. "Oh, my God, but that's perfect. Lucinda! How did you ever manage that?"

"It's a long story. But Jack and your mom aren't going to want anything to go wrong. This is the miracle they've been waiting for. So that's where your finger's on the button."

"But where am I supposed to go in the meantime? I—"

"That's no problem."

"It isn't?"

"Nope." Oona opens her arms wide. "Where do you hide a tree?"

"Hide a tree?" repeats Paloma. Maybe it's not Oona's fault that she's the way she is. Maybe being her would make anybody crazy. "What are you talking about?"

"You hide a tree in the forest," explains Oona.

"We're going to hide me in the forest?"

Oona shakes her head. "We're going to hide you here."

The last place they'll ever think to look.

Show time

Sunday at last.

There has always been something slightly unreal about Paradise Lodge, but now it has been turned into a television studio. There are people everywhere, all of them as busy as blackbirds in the spring. They run cables and check the lighting. They check the sound and rearrange the furniture that Leone spent all last week arranging. They set up cameras and shout commands. They march from room to room with clipboards and phones and a lot of purpose. They sit on the stairs with laptops on their knees or talk into headsets with serious expressions.

Leone, who cannot believe that Lucinda would rather meet Harriet than meet her, has been hanging around in the hope of attracting someone's attention. Which she has finally managed to do. A youngish man who is wearing a Hawaiian shirt and is wired for sound comes up to her and thrusts a vase of tiger lilies into her hands. "This has to go," he says. "And I'm afraid you'll have to go with it. You're getting in the way."

"But—but I live here," she stammers. "I'm Leone Minnick."

She might as well be the housekeeper.

"Sorry. I don't make the rules, I just obey them." Gently but firmly he steers her toward the door. "No civilians on set."

"But I'm not a civilian," she protests. "I'm Paloma's personal manager. And it isn't a set. It's my—" The door shuts behind her. Holding the lilies in front of her like a battering ram, she stomps down the hall.

The TV crew arrived at about the time the rooster would have begun crowing if the Minnicks had a rooster, and they have spread through the ground floor of Paradise Lodge like a flood pushing everything out of its path. Including Leone, who has stormed through the house like a small tornado in high heels all week, but now has been metaphorically shoved out to sea.

"It is my house," Leone is muttering as she comes into the kitchen. "I don't see why I should be treated like a second-class citizen in my own home. After all, I have been very important to Paloma's career. No one can deny that. Where would she be without *me*?"

Maria, who has been summoned back by Leone and is being treated not like a second-class citizen but like a servant, glides past her with a fresh urn of coffee. "At least they give you a monitor so you can watch," she says as she passes.

Lucky me, thinks Leone, but in reality even she has to admit that she is lucky. They've made it to Sunday without any interference from Paloma. You can't get luckier than that. Leone has been so busy over the last few days that a family of five could have moved into one of the guest rooms and she wouldn't have noticed, so she is, of course, completely unaware that her missing daughter has actually come back home. As far as Leone's concerned, God heard her prayers, and kept Paloma away. Not only that, but Jack has sent Arthur out of town so that he doesn't stagger in on the interview unexpectedly. And—just in case Paloma decides to put in an appearance after all—there are four young men (also provided by Jack) who look like gardeners but wouldn't know a hibiscus from a hosta patrolling the property.

Leone gazes out the window of the breakfast nook. It seems like only yesterday that she was worried that the show would be canceled, or that Paloma would go so far off the rails that they'd never get her back on track, or both those things together—and possibly some other disaster thrown in for good measure. Leone smiles as Jack Silk's ivory Jaguar appears at the top of the driveway and comes to a stop behind one of the equipment vans. Jack's bought a new handmade suit. She waves. It's the wave of someone who believes that victory has been snatched from the jaws of defeat. Jack waves back.

While Jack Silk has been upgrading his wardrobe and Leone was moving the furniture around, Paloma has been re-entering her life. She watched every episode of the new season of *Angel in the House* with a lot more interest than she'd ever showed before. Even she could see that it's better than it was. "It actually looks like you guys are having fun," she said to Oona. Oona said, "Yeah, sometimes we do." Which is more than Paloma can say. She watched the YouTube video of Oona telling off the photographer at least a dozen times. "You'd like my friend Tallulah," she told Oona. "She's feisty just like you." She watched things on the computer and read a little on Oona's Kindle, and she thought about things. She wondered what the kids back at the ranch were doing. How the big dance went. If Tallulah missed her at all. If somebody else was bringing Sweetie apples from her lunch. She wished she had Mrs. Buckminster's number so she can tell her she's all right; she doesn't want her to worry. And sometimes, when she knew Leone had left the house, she wandered through the rooms, but was like a ghost visiting the past — not a place she wants to be anymore but a place she's left.

Right now, however, what Paloma is doing is getting ready for the interview. Her hair is blond again, and her eyes are blue, but she rejects the outfit Leone has chosen for Oona to wear.

"It's too goody-goody." She holds the dress in the air with two fingers as if it may be infected. "And little-girly."

"Wear whatever you want." Oona is looking not at Paloma, but at her phone, which is a few feet away on an end table and has begun to play the theme song from *Angel in the House*. "You're the boss now."

"I think I should just wear jeans and a T-shirt," says Paloma. "She's going to want to talk about you yelling at that photographer, so I figure I should look pretty down-to-earth. Not like some princess."

"It's Maria," says Oona, her head bent over the screen. "Jack's here."

Paloma drops the dress on the bed and comes to look over Oona's shoulder. "What else does she say?"

"Maria says they'll be watching the show in the breakfast room. They've put a monitor in there for Leone, to keep her out of everybody's hair."

"That's perfect!" Paloma claps her hands. "Then you can go into the kitchen from the back and surprise them. But make sure you have your phone with you. I want a picture of their faces."

A sharp knock on the door makes them both jump. "Miss Rose? Makeup's ready for you."

Paloma calls, "Just a sec" while Oona gets up and heads for the window. If Arthur can get up that way, she can get down.

"Good luck," she whispers as she climbs onto the balcony.

Paloma crosses her fingers. "You, too."

In the breakfast nook, Jack Silk and Leone sit side by side, Maria standing behind them, all three sets of eyes on the monitor on the table.

"Oh, my God," says Leone as Paloma and Harriet come into view. "Look what she's wearing." At least the mutt's wearing the new collar Leone bought her. "That's not what I picked out for her. She looks like a mall rat."

"She looks like a regular kid," says Jack. "That's what we want. The People's Star."

But Leone is nervous. "I can't help it," she says. "Practically the whole country is watching. What if she lets something slip?"

"She's not going to let anything slip." Jack pats Leone's hand. "You're worrying about nothing. She's going to have half the nation rushing out to get rescue dogs, and the other half looking online to see when the next episode of *Angel in the House* is on. I bet when she's done there won't be a dry eye in the house." He glances over his shoulder. "Don't you think so, Maria?"

Maria, who is also demonstrating a talent for acting, says, "Yes."

In the family room, Paloma sits on the small sofa with Harriet beside her, and Lucinda Chance sits in the armchair to her left. They chat a little before the cameras begin to roll. Paloma introduces Lucinda to Harriet, and Lucinda introduces the crew. And when the show begins the atmosphere is relaxed and warm, as if they are two old friends and a dog hanging out on a lazy Sunday afternoon.

Lucinda begins with the outburst at the outdoor food court. "What made you respond like that?" asks Lucinda. "After all, you've been in this business since you were no taller than this coffee table. You should be pretty used to that kind of thing by now."

Paloma says that she is used to it, but it wasn't about her. "I know part of the price you pay for fame is not being able to blow your nose without some guy taking a picture of you. But this time he targeted my dog." She lays a hand on Harriet's head. "She's totally innocent. She's not a celebrity. He had no right to touch her." Right on cue, Harriet looks at the camera and wags her tail.

In the breakfast nook, Jack says, "Atta girl," and even Leone starts to relax.

Lucinda brings up the fact that Paloma used to have a reputation as being something of a Hollywood brat.

Paloma says it's true. She talks about how, like Lucinda said, she's been in the business for even longer than she can remember. "It's not a normal way of living," says Paloma. "I'm sure you understand what I mean, but it took me a long time to figure that out. I've never really had any friends, or any interests even. All I've done is work. I'm not saying it's a hard life. I mean, gosh, that would be a stupid thing to say. But it is weird. You don't really know what's what. Or even what's real."

Jack draws his eyebrows together. "My, my," he says.

Leone leans forward slightly, squinting at the screen.

"So what brought about this change?" asks Lucinda. "How did you come to understand that?"

Paloma says that some things happened to her recently that made her see things differently. "First of all,

I got Harriet. And then I made some friends who aren't in the business, and I did a lot of things that I never did before."

Lucinda crosses her legs. "Like what?"

"You're not going to believe this," says Paloma, "but I went camping. Like, under the stars? And I sat around a campfire and sang old, hokey songs."

"Oh, my God . . ." Leone's voice is barely audible because of Lucinda's laugh of delight.

Lucinda reaches over and touches Paloma's arm. "Well, you certainly don't seem like a spoiled Hollywood brat now."

"I don't want to be that person," says Paloma. "I've really been thinking about it, and I want to be a regular teenager. I want to have friends and go to school and figure out what *I* want to do with my life."

Leone is practically on top of the monitor by now. "Oh, my God . . ."

Lucinda leans toward Paloma. "That almost sounds like you're thinking of giving up your career."

Paloma nods. "I am. At least for a while. I mean, I'll finish this season. But then I might take a break. I've never had one before. I think it's good to step away from your comfort zone now and then, don't you?"

Lucinda says she does.

Leone clutches Jack's arm. "That's Paloma. That's Paloma talking to Lucinda."

"It can't be," says Jack.

Oona comes out of the kitchen, eating a cookie. "Yes, it can," she says.

It was a great show, watched by millions. In the days when people would call the station to comment on programs, the switchboard would have been lit up like Times Square. Instead, the interview went viral. It trended on Twitter and was all over Facebook. Tens of thousands of American mothers expressed the hope that their daughters would grow up to be just like Paloma Rose. Lucinda Chance said it was one of the best she's ever done — so relaxed, so like real friends sitting around the living room talking. She kept telling Paloma how happy she was to meet her. She's sure there will be future projects that they can work on together. They hugged and promised to keep in touch.

At last the crew packed up the equipment, and they all climbed into their trucks and cars and drove away, leaving behind several rooms in disarray and piles of dirty glasses, plates, and cups.

And Jack and Leone still sitting in the breakfast nook, looking like people who have survived some natural disaster. Except that they aren't wrapped in blankets and aren't drinking coffee brought to them by rescue workers. Paloma and Oona sit down across from them. Side by side, they look like bookends.

Brave as a soldier leading the charge over the hill, Leone smiles. "So," she says, "I guess you two must be pretty proud of yourselves."

"That's more than I can say for you and Jack," says Paloma.

Leone's nails click against the top of the table. "There's no need for that attitude, darling. We did what we did for your own good." She raises her glass. "And look how well it turned out! You're a complete success!"

Neither Paloma nor Oona smiles back.

Jack puts a hand on Leone's arm. "I think what your mother means," he cuts in, "is that you should be proud of yourselves. Both of you. You've done a fantastic job. Absolutely fantastic." He turns his big-bucks smile on Paloma. "And you, sweetheart, you were incredible. Success? My guess is you can write your own ticket from now on. I mean, my God! You had Lucinda Chance eating out of your hand. Which, let me tell you, is not an everyday occurrence."

Oona makes that face Leone knows so well — the one

where she sucks in her bottom lip and pulls her eyebrows together. Leone silently sighs. *Here we go . . .*

"But Paloma's success has nothing to do with you and Leone," says Oona. "Anything either of us has done, we've done in spite of you. All you did was lie and manipulate."

Jack's smile doesn't lose so much as a penny. "But, as Leone said, it was with the best intentions, sweetheart. It was for Paloma's own good." He spreads his hands, as if holding an offering; his shrug is sad. Why is he always so misunderstood? "And it didn't exactly do you any harm, did it? You've had quite a large portion of success yourself. You're definitely a lot better off now than you were when I first saw you. You can't deny that."

"But that wasn't your *good intention,* either." Oona doesn't misunderstand Jack Silk at all. "The Devil may make you a great guitar player, but it isn't because he likes music. You didn't do any of this to help Paloma or me. The only ones you two were helping were yourselves." She leans slightly forward, her eyes on Jack. "I heard you talking about Paloma. You didn't even care if she got home safely or not."

But this is not a topic Leone and Jack want to discuss.

"This is all very fascinating, of course," says Leone,

"but I think I've had enough of the pleasantries. I think we should get down to business." She refills her glass from the shaker beside her on the table. "Just what is it you plan to do now, Paloma? Sell your story to the tabloids?"

Paloma shakes her head. "Not unless I have to. What we plan to do, me and Oona, is get back to our own lives."

Oona nods. "As long as you and Jack cooperate, we won't say a word."

Leone glances over at Jack. "Cooperate how?"

"You mean besides pay Oona every cent you promised?" A smile lights up Paloma's face the way a klieg lights up a set. "I'm firing you, Jack, and Arthur; I'm filing for legal emancipation; and I'm selling the house. I don't care where you and Dad go," she says to Leone, "just as long as it's nowhere near me. I don't want to have anything to do with any of you."

Jack straightens his tie. "And what if we won't cooperate?"

"Then we go public with the whole sordid story," says Oona. "We're pretty sure Lucinda Chance would be really interested in it."

Jack straightens the cuffs of his jacket, considering the future. Which at the moment appears as rosy as a lump of coal. "You know, girls, it's been a very long day," he says, soothing as balm. "Things may seem pretty black-and-white to you right now, but there's a lot to think about. Why don't we all get a good night's sleep and continue this discussion tomorrow? Things are bound to look different in the morning."

"There's nothing to continue," says Oona. "That's the agreement."

"I've already talked to a lawyer." Now the spotlight of Paloma's smile falls on Jack. "The deal isn't negotiable. Take it or leave it."

The four people in the breakfast nook have been so involved in their conversation that none of them are aware that Arthur has come home until he suddenly calls out, "Hey, what's the good word?" from the doorway.

They all turn, but no one speaks.

The smile is frozen on Arthur's face, but his eyes move from Paloma to Oona and back again. It takes him a few seconds to register what he's seeing. And then he says to Jack, "How are you doing that, Silk? Is it mirrors?"

"If only," says Jack.

Just because things don't always turn out as you expected doesn't mean they don't turn out well

It's a small, simple wedding held in the backyard of the newlyweds' new home, but it's a happy occasion nonetheless. Among the guests are most of Maria's family, Paloma, Mrs. Figueroa, and Mrs. Mackinpaw. Paloma and Oona have hung lights, balloons, and brightly colored paper birds from the trees. One of Maria's nephews is in charge of the music. Harriet is wearing a silver bow.

The girls stand by the buffet table, watching the party together. They don't look as if they might be sisters.

"Who would've thought your dad and Maria would wind up getting married?" says Paloma. "Don't you think it's kind of amazing?"

Oona laughs. "I don't know if I can tell anymore. My amazement readometer's broken. So much that's happened has been amazing. I mean, who'd've thought?"

Oona has a point, of course. It's been two years since Paloma and Oona first met, and in that time quite a lot has happened that could be called amazing. Or at least unexpected.

Paloma did finish the season of *Angel in the House*. When she told Mrs. Buckminster her story, Mrs. Buckminster said that if she didn't want to stay in the same house as her mother after the way she behaved, she would be happy for Paloma to stay with her. This was another instance when Paloma didn't have to be asked twice. She stayed with Mrs. Buckminster for the year she took off to finish high school, and has just moved into an apartment of her own. Now, having decided that she doesn't want to abandon her career after all, just change it, Paloma has a new agent and a new business manager, and has been offered a serious part in a film.

Abbot found an interest in living again and started doing odd jobs in addition to his work at El Paraíso. Encouraged by Maria, he eventually started up a handyman business of his own, which, though small, is proving a success. Oona has finished her first year of college and is walking very surely up the pathway of her dreams.

"I mean, will you look at my dad?" Oona gestures to the groom, dancing around the lawn like a man who doesn't think he might trip or strain his heart or be hit by something falling out of the sky. "He doesn't look like the same person."

"I guess none of us are the same people," says Paloma.

"No, I guess we aren't." Oona sighs, her eyes still on the happy bride and groom. "But I'm really going to miss them next year."

Paloma gives her a quizzical look. "You're moving out?"

"Just while I'm taking classes. This house is a hassle for getting to campus. And I'm going to need to be at the college a lot more next year."

Paloma's look is still a question. "You know," she says, "if you wanted, you could move in with me. My new apartment has two bedrooms. And it's conveniently located."

"Move in with you?"

"Why not? We're good friends, aren't we?"

There is, of course, no reason why Paloma and Oona shouldn't share an apartment. Not after all they've been through together.

"Yeah," says Oona. "We are good friends."

Who would have thought?